Mill Point Road

Road

By JK Ellem

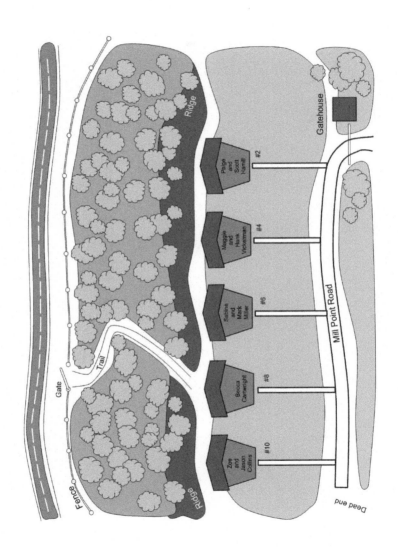

Mill Point Road

Epilogue

"Can you tell me why you killed him?"

The woman just shrugged. "Because he tried to kill me."

She thought the answer was so obvious that the question didn't need to be asked. "Inside my own home," she then added. It sounded better, more justifiable.

The woman wasn't at all fazed by the small room in which they sat, with its sickly bland walls and brown laminate table scarred with the frustration of others, or by the camera in the corner looking down at her, or by the wide rectangle of two-way glass that was behind the man who sat opposite her.

The man held up a sealed evidence bag. Inside was a handgun. "Is this your gun?"

The woman nodded.

Another irrelevant question. She had already given them the ownership papers and permit. All they had to do was match the serial number.

"Can you please verbally acknowledge that this gun is yours."

The woman gave an impatient sigh. "Yes, the gun belongs to

me. I fired it just once. Killed him. I believed I was in immediate mortal danger."

The man nodded, placed the bag back on the table and went back to the open folder in front of him and wrote something down.

Next he lifted up another sealed evidence bag. Inside was an eight inch chef's knife, layered Damascus steel, wooden handle, made in Japan. Dried blood coated the entire blade all the way back to the bolster just before where the handle started. "Do you recognize this?"

The women nodded. "It's one of my kitchen knives. Part of a set of six that sit on the kitchen counter, next to my coffee machine."

The man turned the evidence bag over in his hand, his eyes fixed on the woman opposite him. Had the blade not been coated so completely in blood, it would have glinted under the harsh overhead lighting. "How do you think this came into the possession of the deceased? You would think he would have brought his own weapon with him, given"—the man searched for the right words—"what we now know about him."

The woman held the detective's questioning gaze. Another stupid question, so she couldn't resist. "I guess you'd have to ask him," she replied. She had been through this before and it was becoming tiresome.

The detective didn't see the humor.

"Like I said, I was upstairs. I had to tend to my friend. She was upstairs in my closet, trying on a pair of shoes she wanted to borrow."

"And?" the detective asked.

"He must have gone into the kitchen while I was upstairs, taken the knife out of the block, then came looking for me."

The man seemed to consider this for a moment, while he studied the woman carefully, her responses, the direction her eyes went, any slight inflection in her voice, any signs of nervousness or agitation.

But she just held his gaze, her demeanor cool and focused.

"Did you have any idea who he really was?" The detective resumed his line of questioning.

The woman shook her head. "I had no idea about his past, what he had done. No one did."

The detective smiled. He more than understood, had built a career on it, finding out who people really were, not who they appeared to be on the outside, the persona everyone else saw in the community.

"I guess you really never know someone," the detective said, holding her gaze.

"How long have you been married, detective?" the woman asked, noticing the wedding band on the man's finger.

The question had taken him by surprise. "Almost twenty years now."

The woman responded with either a smile or a slight grimace. He couldn't tell which one it was. Either "good for you." Or "you poor bastard."

The woman leaned forward, and so easily reversed the interview.

"How well does your wife know you, detective? Like really know you?"

The detective gave a smirk and thought back to all the past comments his wife had made about his little idiosyncrasies. Like why he stays up late at night and watches Ben Shapiro videos. Or why he spends all Sunday morning polishing his Ford Mustang GT only to put it back in the garage and not drive it.

Or why he irons all his boxer shorts instead of just folding them out of the dryer.

"She knows me. But I guess there are things about me she just doesn't get or understand." The detective scrutinized the woman across from him. "I guess we never really know anyone, even those closest to us."

The woman smiled, enjoying the role reversal where she was now asking the questions, prodding, poking, putting doubt into someone else's head. "Knowing someone, detective, is not the same as understanding them. Understanding how they think, understanding why they do what they do."

"Now you are starting to sound like a detective yourself." He gave the woman a sly grin. "I see it every day. The disillusioned looks in people's faces as they try to make sense of why someone harmed another person. I've seen husbands murder their wives with simple household items. I've seen wives shoot their husbands. I had an elderly couple just last month, married for sixty years, three grown-up children of their own, and numerous grandchildren. Then one day the husband gets up and strangles his wife across the breakfast table all because she made a comment about his dead mother." The detective nodded at her. "He told us that's all that provoked him, sat right where you're sitting now in that same chair."

The woman said nothing, just sat back and folded her arms like she was waiting for him to make the next move.

The detective closed the folder. He couldn't think of anything else that he wanted to ask her. The case file notes were extensive and complete. It was a clear-cut case of self-defense. She had ticked all the boxes for the right to use deadly force in the state of Maryland.

Blind luck, if you ask him, that the man, the intruder, was

now dead. The man who she had killed was wanted by police, had been living right here in town, right under their noses and they had no idea.

Strange how things worked out.

"You're free to go," the detective rose and beckoned the woman toward the door.

"Really?"

Again the detective couldn't distinguish between surprise or sarcasm in the woman's tone and expression.

"Yes," he replied, opening the door for her.

The woman stood and walked toward the door.

"Oh, there's just one thing," the detective said.

The woman stopped in the doorway, halfway in, halfway out, and looked at him.

"Some good news," he continued. "Your friend, she's out of surgery. The doctors say she's going to make a full recovery. Her wounds were serious and she'd lost a lot of blood but luckily the blade didn't penetrate any of her vital organs. I thought you should know."

The woman smiled. "Thank you, detective. That certainly is good news." And with that the woman turned and walked out of the interview room.

Outside in the corridor the detective hung back and watched her from behind. She had a sure and confident gait, no rush but no lag. The woman pushed open the front glass doors of the police station and vanished into the bright sunshine outside.

She had left him wondering about her reaction to the news he had just shared with her.

Was that a smile of relief or one of veiled disappointment?

Chapter 1
The Devil

In the beginning it was without form, just an empty expanse of dark nothingness, a void that needed to be filled.

It smelled of earth, of rot, of damp and dead decaying things.

Even though it was a raw space, he saw it for what it was: a blank canvas he could shape into something that had purpose.

On the first day he rigged up portable lights, separating the light from the darkness. Then taking a steel crowbar, he removed the wooden boards so that natural light could flow in through the basement windows. The window glass was frosted, obscured, so curious eyes could not see clearly inside.

An electrical contractor was paid cash to install overhead fluorescent fixtures so that there was light, day and night, at the flip of a switch.

On the second day he installed moisture resistant wall sheeting over the existing walls and wood frame to keep out the damp and mold. Then he applied a moisture retardant paint to all the surfaces so that everything was dry and waterproof.

On the third day he installed a mini refrigerator and plugged it in. Next he filled the refrigerator with an assortment of food. In the door he neatly placed 16-ounce bottles of spring water. On the single glass shelf he placed fruit and dairy snacks. The freezer compartment he filled with packaged meals, quick and easy to heat in the microwave oven that he placed on top of the mini fridge.

On the fourth day the steel box was installed.

It was ten feet wide by twelve feet long and seven feet tall, with steel-plated walls reinforced with a two-inch channel frame. It had a custom-made eight-inch air vent, and he had paid extra for a portable AC unit to be installed so it would be cool and comfortable inside the steel box. The reinforced door was precision cut with heavy duty hinges, a commercial keypad lock, and a rectangular letterbox-style viewing window made from bulletproof glass. He had modified the door mechanism so it could only be opened from the outside.

The steel box could survive an EF5 tornado or hurricane, which meant that, while the house above it could be torn away, the steel box would remain in place and intact. Three thousand pounds of concrete blocks could be dropped on the steel box from a height of forty feet and they would barely scratch its surface. A mid-sized sedan could also be dropped from the same height, simulating an impact during a tornado, and the steel box would be undamaged.

The box had been installed in a day by qualified contractors, and at his request they had placed it in the corner of the basement. The contractors were then paid a generous tip when the installation was complete and the owner bid them farewell.

There was a battery-powered LED internal light but apart from this, there were few other creature comforts inside the box. So the owner then installed a single bed of tubular steel, and a folding chair for the occupant. It would be a spartan existence with only a four-inch by ten-inch glimpse of the world outside provided by the rectangular glass window.

Then when everything was complete, and the bed was made with white cotton sheets and a thin covering blanket, the man stood inside the steel box, inside his basement, inside his house and surveyed the finished product.

He was pleased with what he saw.

On the fifth day he donned white hooded coveralls, goggles, thick rubber gloves, and a disposable face mask and sprayed commercial insect killer and scattered rodent repellent granules. There would be no other living creatures in his subterranean paradise.

On the sixth day he found his Adam. For there would never be an Eve. For it was Adam who was so totally and utterly responsible for the vile filth, the senseless destruction and widespread depravity that infested the heavens and the earth since the dawn of creation.

Like Adam in the biblical sense, his Adam that he had taken was fashioned in his own image.

Adam, like the rest of mankind, could have refused the forbidden fruit when it was offered to him. But he couldn't resist, and that was mankind's biggest downfall. He had to taste, to eat, to consume, to gorge himself on everything until there was nothing left.

On the seventh day, he rested and admired his Garden of Eden as he watched his Adam through the plate glass window.

And when his rest turned into restlessness, he got up and made plans for taking his next Adam. For he needed to fill his Garden of Eden. There were four Adams to date, and endless possibilities for more.

But unlike the Book of Genesis in the Bible, he was not God. Far from it.

He was the Devil incarnate.

Chapter 2
Ravenwood

Detective Marvin Richards and his wife lived in Ravenwood, a small town located eleven miles south of Hagerstown, in Washington County, Maryland, among rolling farmlands, narrow roads and farmhouses.

The town had a population of just over 3,500 according to the last census taken in 2010 and was steeped in history, surrounded by numerous Civil War battle sites. The town itself filled an area three miles square, and sat just off State Highway 66.

During the American Civil War, the town was the location of two significant battles, and many of the wounded soldiers were housed in the town to recuperate from battlefield injuries.

The Hagerstown Police Department was housed in an old brick building that was once the Western Maryland Railway Station. It was just a short drive from home for Richards where he was one of nine detectives in the Criminal Investigation Division. The largest division of the police department was the Uniform Patrol Division, which formed the backbone of the department's over one hundred police officers. It was the patrol officers who conducted criminal investigations, however it was the Criminal Investigation Division, where Richards had worked for the last three years, that undertook more in-depth investigations and follow-ups on incidents passed to it by the Uniform Patrol Division.

Richards liked the slower pace of Ravenwood, and the housing was certainly more affordable than New York City. He was able to purchase a nice three-bedroom house and still have enough money left over from the proceeds of selling his house in New Jersey to put a good sum toward his retirement fund. And the commute was a lot easier as well. It was only a fifteen-minute ride to work, compared to New York, when there were days when it took him up to an hour in traffic to get to the precinct.

Whenever coming off shift allowed, Richards would go for long evening walks with his wife and admire the sky at dusk, an endless stretch of molten orange and indigo. But most days he stayed back at the station, when others had gone, enjoying the solitude, to finish off a report or tie up loose ends.

He planned to retire in five years when he was fifty-five. Working in New York City had aged him. It had that kind of effect on people. The crime, the noise, and the fragile divide between sanity and insanity that gradually ground you down to a coarser and more abrasive version of your former self.

Richards had no regrets. He loved the city, but had seen enough of what the worst of humanity could do to each other.

It would be an early retirement. He and his wife planned to just relax, read, and tend to their garden. He grew seeds in his basement during the winter months, where it was warm and dry, then planted the seedlings in the spring. There was something to be said about being self-sufficient, growing your own food; it tasted better too. God's food.

Ravenwood—which fell under the jurisdiction of the Hagerstown Police Department—was just a quieter, less stressful place to live, and he loved the town, the people, and the pace.

He was settled, and for the first time in a long time in his life, he felt good about himself, content. He was sleeping better too, had trimmed down in his weight, and the nightmares were less frequent.

But like ink on blotting paper, the blood spilled in the pores of the larger cities gradually spread to the smaller towns and communities. Science termed it *the capillary action,* the process whereby liquid moved and spread between the fibers, the molecules dispersing and pulling the others along. In the reality of policing and crime, evil didn't settle in neat, stationary puddles at the point of origin. Eventually the molecules adhered to anything that happened to walk by. And like a virus, it slowly but surely spread to the houses across the street. The next suburb. The next town. Until everything was stained red.

Ravenwood was the idyllic kind of town. Sleepy. Peaceful. A great place to raise a family, the only fear coming from a parking ticket or a DUI.

The town was still like that today...on the outside.

Richards used to think like that. That nothing much happened around there, around town, around the county. That was until twelve months ago.

There were two folders open on his desk. One contained the autopsy report on the latest victim. The other folder contained a single sheet of paper, what viable leads they had so far on the case for the other three victims.

Chapter 3
Zoe

The bruises on her forearms could be covered up, hidden from view. That would be easy. The months were now cooler, fall was here, winter was coming. Wearing long-sleeve blouses wouldn't draw suspicion.

She would also refrain from sitting for long periods of time, spend more time on her feet until the swelling had reduced. And if she chose to sit, she knew how to shift her weight from one butt cheek to the other, ease the tenderness she now felt, without giving the appearance of a lopsided spine requiring the services of a chiropractor.

No one would know. Only herself… and of course, Jason.

Zoe Collins had become very skilled over the years at hiding what she didn't want others to see. Most women wouldn't tolerate it, couldn't tolerate it. Couldn't understand. They had no idea what real love was. What she had with Jason was *real* love, something deeper and more meaningful. And real love involved forgiveness.

For Zoe it was something to be endured, to suffer in silence, to mask it from the prying eyes of others. It was none of anyone else's business anyway.

Other people they knew, their so-called neighbors and circle of friends, had their own selfish, self-centered lives to go on with.

Sure, Jason had his flaws, everyone did. No one was perfect.

But that was no reason not to continue to love him no matter what. Doesn't love conquer all? Zoe certainly wasn't bitter or angry at him. Well, not now, anyway. He was getting better, she was making progress with him.

Last night she was riled, angry, disappointed in him. Containing his anger was something he really needed to work on. Not to take everything so personally. So literally.

Jason had left before Zoe had woken this morning, left his car at Hagerstown and caught the early Amtrak into Union Station in D.C. Sometimes he would drive the seventy-mile journey. Other times, like today, he took the train. He'd be gone for a few days, as was normally the case. He split his time between home and the apartment they owned in D.C. rather than doing the daily commute. He was working on some important appropriations bill his firm had been engaged to lobby for on behalf of some corporate interest group. Something about the oil companies wanting to drill in Alaska. Zoe never really understood what he did other than it took him away from home for days at a time, and she was grateful for that.

Zoe stood naked in front of the full-length mirror and cast a critical eye over herself. She was petite, flat stomach, barely touching five feet five, olive skin with hazel eyes, and blessed with a metabolism that ignored whatever she ate, which wasn't much anyway. She enjoyed abstinence, being thin, controlling her caloric intake. Somehow it made her feel cleansed, whole, complete. She certainly didn't starve herself, just controlled what she ate and made sure she got all her nutrients, preferring to eat less than everyone else around her.

She rubbed scented body cream into her skin, carefully avoiding the bruised areas on her forearms, inner thighs, and buttocks. Next she opened the dresser and selected her undergarments for the day.

Inside her panties she applied a slightly heavier liner than normal with extra padding, affixing it more towards the rear, just in case the bleeding started again. But she was only spotting now and that was a good sign. One time she had bled heavily for three days, came close to being rushed to the ER. Thankfully, the bleeding had stopped before she had to resort to that. In a hospital, questions would be asked, police then involved, and she wanted to avoid that at all costs.

Voices outside floated up from the street below and Zoe went to the bedroom window. Through the part in the curtains she could clearly see the moving van parked in the driveway of Number 8.

The house had been vacant for a while, then suddenly a week ago the "For Sale" sign had been removed.

Zoe had never understood why the houses on Mill Point Road—an exclusive enclave of just five sprawling residences built high on a ridge overlooking the picturesque landscape of rural Maryland—were numbered as they were. The land had been purchased by a developer who had built the five sprawling mansions on the plots of land.

They all had uninterrupted views on both sides of the ridge with complete privacy and no possibility of anyone being able to see into the houses through the windows.

She and Jason had purchased Number 10 for half the original price just after the housing market downturn. Otherwise they certainly wouldn't have been able to afford it. Jason had a good job, had his own lobbyist firm in D.C. that was lucrative. That meant Zoe didn't need to work.

She knew Maggie and her husband, Hank, had paid full price for their house, a fact that did create a little animosity between them. But they were older and had lived on Mill Point Road for longer, been one of the first to buy into the enclave direct from the developer.

Sabine and Mark boasted that they had paid full price for theirs and didn't really care. They had "money to burn" according to Sabine, who would gleefully remind anyone and everyone who would listen. Zoe knew, however, that deep down, Sabine harbored some resentment. The woman could be amazingly gracious and generous to your face only to cut you to shreds behind your back.

As Zoe watched, two beefy men wheeled a truck dolly up and down the loading ramp of the moving van next door, her face partially hidden by the edge of the curtain. She couldn't help but feel a little curious as to who the new owner was.

Zoe could just picture Sabine calling Tracy Vanderschoot, the real estate agent in town who the property was listed with, trying to coax out of her the details of the new owner, maybe even the final price it had sold for that was never advertised on-line.

Sabine, like her husband, Mark, could be very persuasive. They were like a tag-team couple, feeding off one another's brazen drive and ambition. Mark had his own investment company and it was a cash cow, according to Sabine.

They had tried to get Zoe and Jason to invest in it. But they had their own financial advisor in Washington they were happy with.

Sabine had hit up Maggie and Hank to invest, and they had put some money with Mark to manage. Was doing really well, apparently. According to Sabine.

Zoe stepped away from the window and continued to dress. She selected a comfortable pair of faded jeans, and a loose-fitting sweater, leaving the sleeves rolled down to her wrists. A pair of white canvas sneakers completed the casual weekend look.

She checked herself in the mirror one more time.

Good, nothing showing.

Her thoughts drifted back to Jason again. He had become more withdrawn lately, more abrupt with her than his usual self. She could tell he wasn't happy. Maybe a few days in Washington buried in his work would do him good, give him some space.

No matter how hard she tried, it seemed to make no difference lately with him. It was like he didn't care about her feelings or what she wanted. She had tried to express herself, tell him what she wanted out of their relationship but it seemed to fall on deaf ears. He just didn't understand.

He would be kind and loving one moment, totally surprise her with an unexpected bunch of beautiful wildflowers or breakfast in bed, or a night at her favorite restaurant. Then the next moment he would be withdrawn, cold, brooding.

At least he'd said sorry to her this morning. In her drowsy, sleepy state she could just make out the whispered apology in her ear as he brushed back her hair and kissed her softly on her cheek before leaving.

That counted for something, didn't it? He said he was sorry. But Zoe hadn't quite forgiven him yet. He had to do a lot more than a quick peck on the cheek or a bunch of flowers to make up for how he had behaved last night. Her forgiveness had to be earned, not abused, not to trot out an apology so often that it became meaningless, hollow, and insincere.

It was a start at least, and that's all she could ask of him. He was slowly changing, improving. Things would get better, she promised herself. He would get better.

Love conquers all.

Zoe smiled at herself in the mirror. She would have to try harder as well.

Chapter 4
Sabine

"Well, well, well. What do we have here?" Sabine Miller, dressed in her yoga gear, stood in the shadows of her garage, the door up, the black shape of her Bentley convertible hunkered like a beast next to her. Her fingers absentmindedly stroked the front fender of the car, feeling the gloss of its metallic coat, her mind marveling at the heat of the hood and the huge throaty V12 engine under the skin. She had seen the moving van parked outside next door when she had driven up the street and pulled into her own garage after her morning class.

For Sabine, her car was a reflection of her. Refined and exquisite exterior, brutish and guttural underneath. Her car turned heads as she drove down the street and so did she. That's how she liked it, to turn heads. She wanted everyone to notice her. Powerful, obvious, dripping with overstated wealth.

Whether she was shopping at the mall, dining in a restaurant, or something as simple as walking down the sidewalk, Sabine Miller was always on display, a living, breathing statement of wealth and success. She wanted wives to be nervous, husbands to be envious. Envious as to why their own wives didn't dress like her, have breasts like her, fuck like her, and do all those intimate, unashamed things like all the good wives did on the porn channels.

Like Zoe Collins, she, too, was watching as the men unloaded boxes and furniture from the back of the van then wheeled a dolly up the path and straight through the front door of Number 8, Mill Point Road.

She pressed speed dial on her cell phone and brought it to her ear, all the time never taking her eyes off the two men as they diligently worked.

The call was answered after three rings, and like most of Sabine Miller's conversations, there were no pleasantries, just straight to the point, all business.

"So when were you going to tell me I had new neighbors?"

Tracy Vanderschoot winced on the other end of the line. "Sabine, I was going to give you a call but I've been too busy."

I bet you were going to give me a call, Sabine thought sarcastically. "So, who are they, the new people at Number 8?"

"You know, Sabine, I can't tell you much with privacy and the like."

Sabine tapped her foot impatiently. She had referred so many clients to Tracy over the years and that was how the bitch rewarded her? "How's that new tenant in the commercial building down in that office park?" Sabine asked pointedly.

The line went surprisingly quiet.

"Surely you haven't forgotten, Tracy, the tenant that Mark referred to you? I heard they signed a ten-year lease on the place. I'm sure you would have gotten decent coms on that transaction." What Sabine really wanted in return was information from Tracy. Quid pro quo. Something for something and Sabine Miller, the queen of information, traded information like wheat futures, and always kept a mental tally, a diary of who owed what to her. To her, information was a tangible commodity. The spoken word. A whispered rumor. It all had value to the right person, or the wrong one.

Sabine could hear Tracy let out a breath on the other end. *That's right you greedy bitch, you owe me.*

"Look, Sabine, all I can say is that her name is Rebecca Cartwright. She's single. Her husband died recently and she got a large insurance pay out. She's from Connecticut."

Sabine's ears pricked up at this piece of information. Insurance payout? Now that was interesting.

Sabine walked to the edge of the garage. The bright morning sunshine cut a diagonal across her torso. Honey-tanned legs, long and supple, illuminated by the wedge of light, her face still hidden in shadow as she continued to watch the workmen. She could see no one else. Maybe the new neighbor was inside directing where the boxes and furniture were to go.

"Keep talking, Tracy," Sabine said, her eyes trained on the house. She couldn't believe it was only one person, a woman, a widow who had bought next door. The place was huge, the same size as the other houses on Mill Point Road. The developer, who had acquired the land when it was still a small farm, had the foresight to build all the houses the same sprawling size, to blunt any competitive squabbling by those who could afford such opulence in a once impoverished town.

None of the owners along Mill Point Road, past or present, were locals. They all had fled the chaotic bustle of Washington, preferring a more sedate life among the rolling hills and country lanes.

"She's young, mid-thirties, no kids. She sold their home in Connecticut, said it was filled with too many memories and she's looking for a fresh start. She wants peace and quiet, a place where no one knows her so she can start anew."

"No pets?" Sabine asked.

"No pets," Tracy replied.

Sabine was pleased. She disliked pets almost as much as she disliked children. Both were dirty, messy, and noisy and had to be fed and cleaned up after them. For Sabine, she had to be the focus of constant attention, not some yapping furry ball of teeth or some doll-dressed, overpraised performing seal of a child.

"How much did she buy it for?" Sabine asked the question that had been at the forefront of her mind ever since she had returned home from her yoga class to see the moving van parked in the street.

The place had been on the market for almost a year, and Sabine knew the previous owner, Garrett Mason, a ferret-faced academic who taught political science at Georgetown University, wouldn't have dropped the price just to move the place.

"I can't tell you that, Sabine," Tracy replied. "You know the prices along there are confidential."

Sabine pursed her lips, her anger rising. "You told me what Maggie and Hank paid for theirs a few years back. Remember?"

Tracy sighed. That had been a mistake, but Sabine Miller had the distinct ability to hound people until they gave in and gave her what she wanted.

"Sabine, I could lose my license. It's confidential information. The seller insisted."

Sabine rolled her eyes. "Fine," she snapped. "Then I'll just have to tell Mark if he has any more clients to buy or lease properties he'll have to send them elsewhere."

There was an awkward silence on the line for a moment.

Sabine let the threat hang for a while. She could almost feel

Tracy squirming down the end of the line. Tracy Vanderschoot may be a seemingly sweet, honest and likeable real estate agent in these parts, but she was just like all of the rest of them. They say never come between a rabid dog and a bone. Well, don't come between a real estate agent and their commissions or marketing earn. For Sabine, they were all tarred with the same brush, bristles of greed, self-interest, and utter entitlement.

"OK, Sabine," Tracy finally conceded. "But you can't breathe a word of this to anyone."

"Of course, darling," Sabine purred down the line, her tone switching instantly from threatening and aggressive to warm and life-long friendly. "You know me, my lips are sealed." Sabine's lips were never sealed. She always displayed a slight gap between them so that her sharp perfect row of little pointed teeth were always showing.

Sabine licked her lips in anticipation, like a lioness about to feast on an antelope or a manipulative wife about to perform oral sex.

Quid pro quo. Something for something.

Tracy told her the price.

Sabine's eyes went wide. "Fuck me!" she blurted into the mouth piece. "That's less than what we paid five years ago!" Now Sabine was mad, really mad.

"It's a sign of the times, I'm afraid," Tracy said, somewhat apologetically and somewhat gloatingly. She knew the price history of every house on Mill Point Road. "The seller was happy to take the first offer and—"

Sabine ended the call, cut Tracy's annoying voice off with a press of her thumb. She had heard enough.

She stepped out of her garage into the full light and glared at the house next door.

"Bitch," she murmured under her breath, taking an instant dislike to her new neighbor already.

Chapter 5
Maggie

It had only taken five minutes before the first argument broke out.

You couldn't really call it an argument, more like a disagreement as to who the newest residents of Mill Point Road were.

Most mornings at 10:00 a.m., they gathered at someone's kitchen to drink coffee, discuss the recent goings on in their exclusive gated community, share information, subconsciously compare their indulgent lives or plan their next extravagant purchase. It was an ingrained almost daily ritual that they all looked forward to even if it was just to bond as a collective of diverse women. By 10:00 a.m. husbands, lovers, or both had left for work, crept home in the shadows of dawn to their own wives, or were busying themselves well out of earshot, doing whatever men did when women didn't want them around to listen in on important things that needed to be discussed.

This particular morning there was plenty to discuss, and they were holding court in the newly renovated kitchen of Maggie Vickerman's home.

"The new countertops look nice." Paige Hamill sat next to Maggie, admiring slabs of metamorphic rock, the clean white custom cabinetry, molded ceilings, recessed lighting, and a curved slice of watershed-finished walnut that formed the breakfast bar area where they sat.

"Vermont white quartzite," Maggie Vickerman replied, then innocently said, "I met Ricardo last night." She had that faraway look in her eyes that Paige had seen many times before. It was the look Maggie always had the morning after indulging in great sex from the night before. Maggie gazed into her coffee cup, the rich, velvety mocha surface, smooth and steamy, thinking about the previous evening she had spent with her personal trainer while Hank lost himself for two hours among the aisles of The Home Depot.

Paige regarded Maggie. She didn't know how the woman did it. "I thought you weren't seeing Ricardo anymore."

Maggie gave a smirk as she took a sip of her coffee. The warm liquid slid down her throat, the sensation coaxing up more memories of last night. "A girl needs a decent fuck once in a while."

"Once in a while?" Paige rolled her eyes in disbelief.

Maggie had a string of young, sweaty, shirtless tanned young men in tow, most of whom worked outdoors with their hands, meaning their bodies were "taut, tight, and terrific" according to Maggie. She had an entire library of photos of her various male liaisons on her cell phone that she proudly showed. She could recite verbatim when she last had sex with each of them, where they had been, and how long it had lasted.

Maggie caught Paige's disapproving look and protested. "Hank lost interest years ago. Now he's too busy tinkering around in the basement all the time. He simply can't keep up with my demands."

"Perhaps you should get a hobby, like Hank has," Paige suggested, a little jealous. She and Scott had a good sex life. But recently it had become mundane, pedestrian.

"I have a hobby," Maggie countered with a mischievous smile. "It's better for you than chocolate or alcohol or a workout at the gym and actually burns more calories than jogging. It's called Ricardo."

Paige shook her head but couldn't begrudge the woman. After all she had turned fifty last year and still looked amazing for her age. Sure Maggie had some procedural help, they all had, but Maggie managed to look like a woman fifteen years younger than she actually was. And she had a weakness for younger men. Much younger.

"What happened to Jacob, the pool boy?" Paige asked.

"I'm not fucking the pool boy," Maggie replied. "Because I'm too busy fucking my personal trainer."

The two women burst out in laughter.

"Christ," Maggie said, thinking about last night. "He fucked me for nearly an hour straight before he finally came. Nearly broke my FitBit, went right off the charts."

"My cousin uses Tinder," Paige said, "when she wants a casual fling when George is out of town."

"Can't blame her," Maggie agreed. She had met Paige's cousin and her husband, George, once. She and Hank had been invited over for dinner at Paige's place when they were visiting. The man sat at the dinner table the entire evening and spoke about climate change and how we as a society were consuming too much and ruining the planet. Self-righteous prick, Maggie had thought. She was glad to see the back of them as they drove off in their little Prius.

"Then again," Maggie said, "who needs Tinder when I've got

Ricardo's big log burning in my fireplace."

The two women let out another burst of laughter.

Just then Sabine walked in through the open kitchen terrace doors, grabbed a mineral water out of the fridge and leaned against the kitchen counter. "Sorry I'm late. Did I miss much?"

Paige and Maggie exchanged looks then laughed again.

Sabine shook her head, not disappointed at missing the first agenda item that they always discussed at their daily catch-up. "Spare me the details today, please." Sabine took a swig of the water then scrunched up her face in disapproval. "What the hell is this shit?" she asked, staring at the label on the bottle. "Where's the Acqua Panna?"

"Margarita is out doing the grocery shopping. She'll be back soon," Maggie replied.

Sabine placed the bottle of water on the counter next to her. "Mark told me to tell you your next distribution from the investment fund will be coming at the end of the month. Should be more than last month as well."

Maggie raised her eyebrows. She was impressed. She and Hank had invested a sizeable chunk of their retirement savings with Sabine's husband, Mark, who ran his own exclusive hedge fund. It was invite only and Maggie and her husband had to wait three months to get in.

"We made eighteen percent last month," Maggie said. "Hank and I couldn't believe it. Tell your lovely husband he works too hard and we are very grateful."

Sabine pushed the bottle of water farther away from her, like it was toxic waste from a nuclear reactor. "Didn't I tell you and Hank over a year ago you should invest with Mark? He's a financial genius."

Maggie and Hank had procrastinated for nearly a year before finally taking Sabine's advice.

Sabine turned to Paige questioningly, as if to say, *I told you so.*

Paige just smiled. Sabine could be very convincing. She and Mark were like the perfect professional couple. While Mark spent most of the week days in his D.C. office, commuting there and back daily, Sabine, who seemingly had no occupation at all, was clearly the more ambitious of the two.

Sabine had dragged Paige to a few of her yoga classes in town, and Paige had seen her in action firsthand. Sabine was a smooth, astute operator who constantly cultivated her expansive circle of friends and acquaintances. Paige believed no one was really a "friend" of Sabine Miller unless they had something to offer.

Sabine's approach was subtle, silky smooth, and strategic. She carefully selected certain yoga studios, fitness centers, and day spas that had the highest composition of well-to-do women, women who had money to flaunt or to invest. Sabine had told Paige once that it was women, not men, who controlled the purse strings by controlling what happened in the bedroom. They were the financial decision makers and that suited Sabine just fine.

So while Mark spent his days staring at multiple flat screens following the colorful lines of the stock market indices, Sabine spent her days downward dogging, socializing, shopping, lunching, and dining with potential clients. Sabine preferred the indirect approach, to let her new Rolex, her car, the pictures on her Instagram page of their latest ski trip to Aspen, or the vacation to the Bahamas do the convincing for her with her potential clients.

Sabine never posted a picture, hosted a dinner party, or had a luncheon date without careful consideration of how the invited guests could enhance Mark's growing investment firm.

Paige couldn't begrudge them though. They both worked

feverishly hard, and consistently made money for Mark's clientele.

"Where's Zoe?" Sabine asked, changing the topic. She would have to work on Paige some other time. She knew from past conversations it was Paige not Scott, her doting husband, who was the problem, holding them back.

"She's not feeling well," Maggie replied. "Said she has a migraine and needs to lie down for a while."

Just then Zoe Collins breezed through the terrace doors, all smiles and flowing auburn hair. "So who's the new neighbor?" she asked, helping herself to the coffee machine before sitting down next to Paige then looking around expectantly.

Paige and Sabine exchanged looks.

"I thought you weren't feeling well," Maggie queried.

Zoe held the coffee cup between both delicate hands and regarded everyone over the ceramic curve. "It was nothing, took some Advil."

Maggie nodded. As it was her house, she held court. "So who are they, these new people?" Maggie's eyes wandered to each person around the kitchen, but lips didn't move. "Has anyone seen them? Spoken to them?"

Sabine watched everyone closely, her face a mask of uncompromising concealment. She certainly wasn't going to relinquish the information Tracy Vanderschoot had provided to her, no matter how scant.

"I haven't seen anyone," Zoe offered. "Just the moving company guys hauling boxes and furniture into the place."

Maggie glanced at Sabine. "Have you spoken to Tracy Vanderschoot? Did she tell you anything?"

Sabine gave her a flick of her hand, "Haven't spoken to Tracy in months."

Quid pro quo. Something for something.

Maggie held Sabine's innocent gaze, knowing it was a lie. She knew very well that Sabine kept tabs on almost every property that was bought and sold in the town of Ravenwood, especially the luxury properties. As if Sabine wouldn't have sent word out into her wide and affluent network as to who had just purchased the house right next door to her own place.

"Maybe I'll make a batch of muffins and take them across this afternoon," Paige suggested. "A kind of 'welcome to the street' gesture."

Sabine could almost feel the muscles of her face tighten as she struggled not to roll her eyes at Paige. Paige was so fucking Martha Stewart to the point of being nauseating, a perfectionist with an obsessive-compulsive disorder.

Sabine smiled sweetly. "That's a lovely thought." *And maybe you can choke on one of your shitty muffins as well.*

Chapter 6
Hank

He could hear them through the floor above his head, women murmuring punctuated by bouts of laughter. Hank was certain that they were laughing at him.

Pathetic bunch of useless bitches, he thought to himself as he moved around the basement. It wasn't that he had been exiled here, banished because he wasn't important enough or the topic of conversation was too sensitive for his male ears to hear, but the idea of spending time surrounded by women who all they did was talk about themselves, wasn't appealing to Hank at all.

Ignoring the noise from above, Hank sat down at his desk, his laptop in front of him, powered on and ready. Maggie didn't know his password, thank God she didn't. Hank liked being in the basement. It was like his own little private domain, away from the gossiping women and other prying eyes. Maggie rarely came down here, and if he found her down here poking around, he would quickly chase her away. She had the rest of the entire house to keep her busy little mind occupied.

The basement was comfortable and clean, a picture of order

and neatness, a testament to Hank's days spent in the Navy as a ship's engineer.

He quickly logged into Facebook and finished a quick post he'd been working on, making sure the pictures he had selected were appropriate and suited the location. When he was done, he pressed "post" then opened another window, and started up the video player, before glancing over his shoulder to make sure no one was coming down the stairs. He usually locked the basement door from the inside when he wanted privacy, and that was exactly what he wanted right now.

The computer screen came to life, opening a window into another world, a bedroom scene, as viewed from the top of a chest of drawers, opposite the foot of the bed. The video was clear and so were the sounds, though the angle was slightly off. Part of the large bed was out of shot. Hank made a mental note to make adjustments next time.

Hank glanced over his shoulder one more time before settling in to watch the twenty minute footage.

A woman lay on the bed, flat on her back; legs splayed wide, the back of the man's head, wedged between her thighs, his face burrowed deep into the folds of her womanhood. The man's head slid up and down, wet sucking sounds coming from deep within the woman's cleft, like the man had spilled a Slurpee and was using his mouth and nose to lick and snort it up.

Pigs in the mire, Hank thought. Some young college kid, groveling in the slippery muck.

Hank glanced at his lap to see a growing fold at the front of his trousers that wasn't there a few minutes ago. He gave a snort and continued watching as the two pigs went at it.

"Filthy bitch," he murmured.

Hank wasn't one to suffer in silence, instead he raged in his loneliness as he continued to watch the video.

After about five minutes the young buck in the video transitioned to his knees, wiping the slop away from his face with the back of his hand before plunging his hips headlong into the murky hole where his face had just been groveling.

Hank's arousal grew even more intense. Even though he despised what he was watching, it gave him a weird feeling of sexual gratification that he couldn't explain.

The woman in the video squealed and gyrated on the bed with delight, her thighs and ankles wrapping around the man's buttocks, urging him on faster, drawing him in deeper with each thrust, a praying mantis holding its victim between its limbs.

The young man needed no encouragement. His bony ass and pale skin quivered and tensed, his hips moving in and out like a steam piston.

The fold in Hank's trousers reached its peak, a solitary vertical pole holding up a circus tent. Hank's breath shortened, his anger lengthened, his patience wearing thin. He gripped the edges of this desk with both hands, his nails digging deep into the wood, his own hips grinding in unison with the young man in the video.

"Filthy whore," Hank hissed through clenched teeth, then a guttural growl escaped the rictus snarl of his mouth.

The well-worn scene reached its climax on the bed, two bodies convulsing, one older and one much younger.

The entire bed was shaking now, the headboard thumping into the wall behind, the bed frame groaning, hinges creaking, joints straining under the onslaught until finally the young man arched his back and dispelled his seed in one long monotonous groan then collapsed between welcoming thighs.

The squeals, the shrieks, and copulating tremors of the

woman slowly subsided to soft moans and delirious whimpers.

After what seemed like an eternity, the young man freed himself from the clutches of the woman and rolled off the bed. Pale in his nakedness, he walked around the foot of the bed, flaccid and swinging like a pendulum. The screen darkened momentarily as he walked past the chest of drawers.

Hank had seen enough. There's no need to edit the footage. It was as incriminating as it was vulgar. With one click of the computer mouse he closed the screen, and then added the date and the title to the latest video file: #82.

He dragged and dropped the video file into a folder marked, "Bedroom" where it would take its rightful place in chronological order in the library alongside the other eighty-one videos stored there. There were three other folders, three more incriminating video libraries of anger and contempt labeled: Car. Motel. Bathroom.

Next Hank took a square of paper towel from a roll he kept in the desk drawer, and laid it across his thigh. Unzipping his trousers he wrestled and bent himself out. With deft clicks of the computer mouse he called up another folder from the hard drive and selected another video file.

An image leapt onto the screen, a twelve-year-old drowsy looking girl sitting on a small single bed in what looked like a loft, the walls were skinned with grime and the bed coverings filthy. Then against the backdrop of the child's screams and cries for help, Hank coaxed his hatred and contempt for his wife out and onto the paper towel on his lap.

When he was done he folded the paper towel once, wiped himself down and tossed it into the trash bin next to his desk.

Tucking himself away he leaned back in his chair, his mind in silent contemplation.

His wife was a pig, a sow, a breeder that rutted and wallowed with all and sundry. She hadn't always been that. She had once been a caring, compassionate woman who doted on Hank. A woman with virtues and high moral standing, loyal and enduring. Now all she seemed to dote on was herself, her string of lovers, and their son, Adam.

Maggie didn't know that Hank knew about her lovers, and definitely not about his video library of her brazen betrayal.

Taking a set of keys he opened one of the desk drawers and reached inside. He pulled out a large hunting knife and placed it on the desk in front of him. All pigs eventually go to the market. Hank had decided he had seen enough, collected enough proof of his unfaithful, debauched wife.

It was time to lead this pig to the slaughter.

Letter #1

My Darling,

You are the sweetest, most caring person I have ever known and I am so glad that you are part of my life.

I'm sitting right now in a crowded restaurant and I feel like the loneliest man on the planet. I wish that you were here now, right next to me. Pretty pathetic, huh? I get so lonely when we're not together, even in a big city like New York. Who would believe? But I'm lonely for you, no one else. I just miss you, that's all. I miss your smile. I miss how you smell, the smell of your hair, the smell of your skin, your scent. It's intoxicating. Christ, I'm getting turned on just thinking about you, and I haven't even ordered a drink yet!

So to overcome my loneliness, I thought I'd write you a letter and tell you how much you mean to me. Not an email. Not a text message, but good old-fashioned handwritten words on a page. Forgive the hotel stationery but it's all I could find.

Sometimes I think we've lost the art of communicating. We get too caught up in our busy lives, and we've lost the value of deep and meaningful conversation or expressing the feelings that we have for someone. Pixels of text somehow doesn't have the same impact, LOL!

Words mean more to me, and I hope they do for you too. Spoken words eventually fade with time, or get lost from our memories, and eventually forgotten. But I never want you to forget my feelings for you, and how much you mean to me.

That's why I've decided to commit my feelings to paper so you will never forget them. When you're feeling down, missing me, or are depressed, you can always pull this letter out and read it again and again.

Everything I write has come from my heart, written in ink, so that my love for you will never fade.

I knew from the first moment we met that you were the one I wanted to spend the rest of my life with, together, with you and only you. I want you to know this and to never forget it. When I'm feeling lonely, like I am now, I just think of you and all the great things I truly love about you. The warmth of your body next to mine when you curl up in bed beside me. How you wrap a solitary leg around me, like I belong to you, like I'm your property, wanting me to never leave your side. And I never will. I will always belong to you. I am yours for now and forever.

I love how when we make love you look deep into my eyes, unblinking. You make me feel like I'm the only man in the entire world at that exact moment, and when you climax, your kiss is hard, crushing, like you have given me everything in that precious moment, all of you, unselfishly, completely. I feel like we're the same biology, entwined. Melded together in the heat of our passion.

I know things have been tough lately that I'm away a lot with work. I know you hate these work trips I go on and it breaks my heart to leave you, it really does. Please know that I count the days, the minutes, the seconds until I'm home again with you. Things will get better my love, I promise. I'm working so hard for our future that I can be a little obsessive, a little distracted. But I want you to know that it has nothing to do with you if my attention drifts or if it seems like I'm miles away. I have so many dreams and aspirations for us, together, that I want to share with you and only you. Please be patient my love.

I know you want to start a family. I want children too, even though at times it may seem like I don't. But I do. Please believe me. I said this from the very beginning and I meant it. I still mean it. And when we have children I don't want you to work. That's why I'm working so hard for both of us now. I want you to focus on our children, our young family. I know you will make the best mother in the world. All I ask is that you grant me some time so I can get work under control. I'm not putting it off, even though at times you think I am. It will be worth it in the end, I promise. I want to make sure that I can provide for our family when the time comes and for us not to worry at all about money or paying the bills.

Your happiness and the happiness of our future children are what I treasure the most. I think about it every day. I can see us taking long walks along the beach, a beautiful daughter and a beautiful son swinging between our arms, chasing gulls, or building sandcastles with them. A boy and a girl. I want all of this and more with you. You deserve nothing less.

I can see us building a new home together, filling it with the laughter of children and fond memories, and all those special moments we will have together. I can see us growing old together, sharing the joys of watching our own grandchildren growing up one day. I can see it all, with you by my side.

You are a special person and every day you give me such hope and such joy.

I will always love you because you are the love of my life, my soul mate and I cherish every day that we spend together, and I hate the days when we are apart.

Always yours,
Michael xxx

Chapter 7
Becca

"Ma'am, where would you like this dresser?"

Rebecca Cartwright looked up, a solitary piece of paper in her hand, tears touching the corners of her eyes. "Oh, just put it along the wall, opposite the bed."

The two burly men nodded, and then, juggling the heavy dresser between them, they placed it gently into position against the wall. They walked back out the master bedroom and down the stairs to retrieve the rest of the furniture, personal effects and boxes that were designated for the upstairs.

Rebecca, or "Becca" as she preferred, glanced down again at the single sheet of paper in her hand, the ink dull and faded, the edges creased and torn. The letter was dated three years ago, the hotel watermark at the top.

She must have read this particular letter at least a hundred times before. It was one of her favorites.

Whenever Becca felt sad or overwhelmed or unsure of herself, which had seemed like a lot lately, she would choose one of the letters to read to herself, to remind her of Michael, of the past.

She knew she shouldn't. It would just drag up all the emotions again of how she had felt. But every so often she needed to bolster her spirits, to reminisce. Reading the letters made her strong, gave her courage, and at times, they were the only things that got her through some days, days where she would spiral downward into the depths of a black hole. And the only thing that gave her comfort and solace was reading Michael's letters.

Becca wiped the corners of her eyes, carefully folded the letter and placed it neatly into the shoebox along with the others.

She had experienced plenty of upheaval and uncertainty in the last twelve months, when self-doubt and perhaps a little regret crept back into her thoughts. Whenever she read one of Michael's letters, she always came away feeling better, grounded, more invigorated, less uncertain. Michael's words were reassuring to her, like a dose of medicine that she could turn to when she needed it the most.

For months Becca wrestled with depression and anxiety. The doctor had prescribed medication, they all do. And the pills had certainly helped. But they made her feel doughy, sluggish, and dulled her senses. "Happy Pills" her doctor had called them. Take one and all your troubles would disappear, brushed under the carpet. Just don't lift the carpet and take a look.

Then there was the overeating. Becca had stacked on forty pounds in six months. It was the depression her doctor said. Another visit. Another pill, a stronger dose this time. Soon her morning routine was getting up, having her morning coffee on the back porch and popping the lid on a Sunday-to-Saturday pill box.

But as the months passed, the dark clouds that had once covered her sky all the way to the horizon, blocking out all the warmth and sunlight in her heart, slowly began to part until eventually the clouds disappeared altogether.

The medication was dialed back progressively until Becca didn't need the pills anymore. She began to get out of the house, go for long walks, cutting back on sugars and fats. Started running. Soon the extra pounds she had previously piled on melted away until she became what she was today.

The odd dark cloud would come back now and again. That's when she would read the letters.

Taking the shoebox, she went into the huge walk-in closet and placed it high on the shelf for safekeeping.

Returning to the bedroom, a stack of packing boxes arranged neatly in the corner glared at her, demanding her attention. It was going to take her weeks to unpack everything. There was no rush. She had plenty of time, and she wanted to make everything in this house, her new home, just perfect.

Before the move, Becca had been brutal when she had gone through all the things she had accumulated, throwing out the majority of it. It was as much about decluttering her past, the bad memories, as it was starting anew.

Becca wandered back out of the master bedroom to the mezzanine upper floor balcony and the sweeping stairs that curved down to the entrance below. Standing there, looking down over the balcony rail she got a true sense of the size of the house that now surrounded her: six thousand square feet, four bedrooms, three bathrooms, gourmet open kitchen, acres of stone, wood, Italian tile, a huge triple garage and paved outdoor area with a volcanic-rock fire pit and manicured gardens. Not to mention the breathtaking views for miles in all directions of rolling green hills dotted with barns and picturesque farmhouses nestled in the distance, a view afforded from owning a house in the most exclusive gated enclave in Washington County, if not in the entire state of Maryland. Through the tall floor-to-ceiling windows in front of her, she could see the center of Ravenwood just a few miles away, nestled between the folds of the smaller hills and open plains in the distance.

Downstairs was nearly done, most of the furniture and larger pieces had been placed where she had directed the men.

As she took in her surroundings, Becca knew that she was going to need more furniture, furniture that suited the house, pieces that would transform it into a home.

Some rooms had no furniture whatsoever; others had just packing boxes hastily placed there for the time being.

And time was what she had plenty of.

Chapter 8
The Gatehouse

It was a beautiful Saturday morning, warm and sunny, the sky an expansive canvas of blue.

Becca decided to take a walk down to the gatehouse. Ribbons of paved driveways snaked down the front of each house, linking up to a wide paved road that ran parallel before following a gentle curve to the gatehouse entrance at the bottom of Mill Point Road.

Sprinklers threw out lazy arcs over lush carpets of dark green with perfect razor edges, and squared corners. The air was heavy with the earthy smell of freshly cut grass, recently turned soil and fertilizer.

Becca decided early that she wanted to get her hands dirty in her own garden, not to employ an army of gardeners unlike the other residents.

She would get someone to do the heavy lifting, to mow and to prune and to hedge. But she wanted to plant, to grow, to feed and nourish and to shape the terrain and foliage around her home as she wanted.

Topiary bushes of white hydrangeas and azaleas lined the footpath, bees spinning and hovering, and it took only five minutes to walk down to the gatehouse.

She passed no one. Perhaps Saturday mornings people slept in or did whatever they did, warm and sleepy under the sheets.

Becca immediately noticed the CCTV camera pointing at her as she approached the gatehouse and another camera was angled toward the main road on the other side of the barrier.

The gatehouse was a small but solid brick affair, white mortar and dark slate roof, tastefully built to be subtle, to blend in with the style and architecture of the mansions up on the ridge top. But without the look and feel of a Baghdad checkpoint.

The gatehouse was nestled among a perfect plot of green, edged with curves of manicured low hedges and clusters of brightly colored flowers.

A man wearing a gray uniform and ball cap came out of the open door of the gatehouse. Was Becca mistaken or did his uniform match exactly the slate color of the gatehouse roof?

His nametag said "McIntyre." She guessed he was perhaps mid-sixties, maybe a retired cop or security guard. Becca knew the gatehouse was manned between 8:00 a.m. to 5:00 p.m., six days a week. After hours the gate would open automatically to the push of a remote control that every resident had.

The man was thin and wiry with shrewd, alert eyes, closely cropped gray hair, a finely trimmed moustache, and the aura of someone who lead a life of discipline and watchful attention. Someone perfectly suited for the community.

He greeted Becca with a friendly smile. "Hello, Ms. Cartwright."

Becca smiled back. "Please call me Becca."

"Then please call me Mac. Everyone does."

The man reminded her of a warm and friendly grandfather, someone dependable, someone you could rely on. He instantly made her feel at ease.

"I hope you've settled in. I saw the moving van yesterday," Mac said.

"I still have a lot of unpacking to do, but I'm in no rush. It's such a lovely day I thought I would go for a walk, you know, familiarize myself with the area."

"Well if there's anything I can do to help, then please let me know," Mac offered. "In the meantime you haven't given me a visitors list."

Becca looked at him questioningly, and then she remembered. Part of the induction paperwork she had been sent after she had purchased the house was to provide a likely list of relatives, friends, and visitors that were permitted entry.

Mac went back inside and came back out with a clipboard and began to rifle through the pages. "Here we are, Rebecca Cartwright, Number 8."

Becca thought for a moment.

Mac looked up at Becca, a pen in hand expectantly.

Becca felt embarrassed even though there was no need to be. "To tell you the truth, there's no one really."

Mac looked at her for a moment, an awkward silence stretched between them, like he hadn't heard correctly. He didn't know whether to feel surprised or feel sorry for her. "No one?" This was something new for Mac. All the other residents had a visitor list. Mark and Sabine Miller, as expected, had the longest list. Sensing her slight embarrassment Mac quickly said. "I'll tell you what, Becca, if someone comes to visit you, I'll just buzz your house on the intercom. How does that sound?"

"Great," Becca nodded. "Let's just do that. Although I really don't expect many visitors. Perhaps the odd delivery driver now and then." That reminded Becca. She looked at Mac and asked, "Can you recommend a good handyman, perhaps someone you know?"

Mac smiled. He disappeared back into the gatehouse and returned moments later and handed Becca a business card. "Josh Daniels."

Becca looked at the card, black and orange, crossed hammer and wrench motif, gloss finish.

"He's a local handyman in town. Grew up here, spent all his life here," Mac explained. "He looks after most of the properties here. He's reliable and trustworthy. Had good reports from your neighbors too, and he won't rip you off."

Becca knew the deal. Some contractors saw a big house and a nice car as an invitation to overcharge.

Becca thanked Mac and turned to leave when he said, "Why don't I give you a quick tour of the gatehouse and the surroundings so you're familiar with how things work."

Becca already had an automatic key to operate the gate after hours as well as a separate key to open and close the side access gate. "Sure," she said. "I'd like that very much."

Inside the gatehouse there was a small office with a desk, a well-worn chair, and two computer screens that were linked to the CCTV cameras. Mac explained that there were two CCTV cameras, one pointed out at the street for visitor identification and the other pointed to the road that led up to the residences. The cameras run twenty-four hours a day, seven days a week and logged the time and date of everyone entering and leaving.

The office was cozy, spotless, and everything was in order, a testament to the meticulous care and serious approach that Mac took in his job, a job that others may have seen as token, or boring or mundane. But looking through the office, Becca could see that Mac believed ensuring the privacy, security, and overall well-being of the residents was more than just a job.

There was a small kitchenette off the office and, like everything else, it was immaculately maintained. Becca felt a lot safer after what she had seen.

Even though Mac said it was a straightforward job with set hours and that most of the residents didn't have a lot of visitors, except the Millers, of course, Becca knew he was just being humble. Becca took an instant liking to him, almost like a fatherly figure, minus the overbearing, know-it-all nature.

Mac explained that her business was her business, but to keep him informed of anything out of the ordinary. "Not that much out of the ordinary ever happens around here," he remarked.

Becca already knew how to use the key fob for the gates but Mac showed her how to use the entrance key for the side gate.

"The previous owner, Garrett Mason, used to come and go all hours of the night. He was a nice enough chap," Mac said. "I didn't see him that much other than on the CCTV footage. He tended to keep to himself, a bachelor, wasn't married nor did he have any kids or many visitors, come to think of it."

"I've never met him," Becca said. "My lawyer handled the purchase. I believe he already purchased another house before he sold his home to me."

"I believe he bought another house in town, not far from here. I think this house was too big for him," Mac said. He looked at Becca, thinking that the house was probably too big for her as well. He knew from the information he'd been provided that Becca had no husband, no kids, and no partner whatsoever listed on the information sheet.

As though reading his thoughts Becca said, "It's just me, by myself. But I like the space. In my previous home I didn't have much room. It was tired and cramped. I'm looking forward over the coming months to slowly fill the house, make it a home, with pieces I want."

A past life being let go, Mac thought as he regarded Becca.

"Is there any other helpful information you can give me?" Becca asked.

Mac smiled thoughtfully. "There are no unwritten rules if that's what you are thinking," he said. "The regulations are fairly simple, and I'm here to ensure the safety and privacy of all the residents of the community."

Becca could tell Mac was genuine and honest. She could also tell that discretion was part of his nature. He was in the perfect position to see everything, and know everything that went on in the community, having worked here for ten years. In fact he had been the only security guard since the development was completed ten years ago. He gave off the impression he didn't know much, yet those twinkling shrewd eyes never missed a beat. She was certain he was a wealth of information about the place, including the town.

"The only word of advice I can give you, Becca, is don't go into the woods behind your property. It starts at the top of the ridge along the back of the properties and runs down the hillside all the way to the rear fence."

Becca thought it was an interesting comment to make, almost like the line out of a nursery rhyme warning her to stay out of the dark nasty woods or something bad will happen. "Why is that?" Becca asked curiously.

"The slope up there is fairly steep in places. A lot of loose rock and shale, bare tree roots, old scrub. Plenty to twist an ankle on or something worse. There's also an old trail that runs down the back of your property to the main road below." Mac saw the slight alarm in Becca's eyes. "Don't worry," he reassured her. "No one uses it. The whole community is fully fenced so there's nothing to worry about. I just wouldn't want you getting hurt, that's all. The underground power cable that feeds supply to the entire place runs up that side of the ridge. There's nothing really there other than a junction box and a drainage ditch. Contractors were up there a few weeks back, replacing cable. But they had access from the road on the other side where there's a locked gate."

"I'll be sure to stay away from there," Becca said.

Becca thanked Mac, left the gatehouse and headed back toward home, a little more than curious as to what was in the woods at the rear of her property. Despite what Mac had said, she might take a look, and go exploring.

Chapter 9
An Invitation

The daily coffee meet-up at 10:00 a.m. only happened during the weekdays.

Weekends were usually reserved for relaxation and taking a reprieve from sharing gossip and tidbits of juicy information.

However with the arrival of the new resident on Mill Point Road, exceptions were made. It was an occasion that warranted a Saturday morning meet-up for the first time ever, and an invitation would be extended to the new resident.

So plans were hastily set in motion to hold an extraordinary coffee meet-up, and an invitation was quickly scripted, written, and delivered among a feverish burst of text messages back and forth between the existing residents of Mill Point Road.

So it came to pass that when Becca returned to her front porch after her tour of the gatehouse, unaware that not so candid eyes were watching her progress up the footpath, she discovered a small square of folded note paper jutting out from the doorjamb of her front door.

She unfolded the piece of paper and read the handwritten note.

Dear New Neighbor,

We would love to invite you to morning coffee at my house at 10:00 a.m. today. I hope you can make it as we would love to meet you and welcome you to our little community.

Best wishes,
Paige Hamill.
No. 2, Mill Point Road.

Becca stood staring at the note. She glanced up and down the road. Obviously people didn't sleep in on Saturday mornings around here and were too curious to find out who she was.

She checked her watch. It was just after 9:00 a.m. That would give her an hour to shower and get dressed, more than enough time to confront the inevitable.

———————～⁓—————————

"Maybe she's a lesbian?" Paige Hamill said.

They were all clustered around the kitchen table in Paige's house. Scott, her husband, had gone into town at Paige's insistence. It was Paige who had come up with the idea to hold a special coffee meet-up this morning and invite Becca to attend.

Paige had seen Becca through the slit of the bedroom blinds upstairs. She had been standing there, next to the window, naked, her breasts crushed against the smooth wall, her palms pushing back against the force from behind, her legs slightly parted, hips raised, Scott standing right behind her, *inside* her. The only sound that could be heard was the cut and hiss of the sprinklers on the front lawn and the rapid slapping sound of

Scott's flat stomach thrusting against Paige's buttocks.

For some strange reason Scott preferred sex standing up, had done so ever since they were married five years ago. He could control her better from that position, she imagined. Wrap his fingers around her mouth and jaw from behind, yank her head, arch her back like a banana. On more than one occasion he had been a little too vigorous, a little too rough and she had to elbow him in his stomach to remind him that she wasn't a contortionist. It seemed lately she had to remind him of this fact more often. Paige put it down to the stress Scott thought he was under, from the perfectly reasonable expectations she had of him. Nothing more.

At times their love-making had regressed into just raw sex, fast and furious, not unlike the movies of the same name: pointless hollow entertainment, minimal dialogue, senseless violence.

And it was in those moments of lost intimacy that Paige felt like nothing more than Scott's whore.

Becca walked past, heading down the road just as Scott grunted in Paige's ear as he shuddered in release. The idea came to her in that same moment.

She quickly showered, dressed, went downstairs to the kitchen, and made a batch of her famous apple pecan muffins. The muffins now sat on a cake stand in the middle of the kitchen table.

"She's not a lesbian," Sabine said. Sabine had shared with the group only select details about their new neighbor that she had gleaned from Tracy Vanderschoot. And she hadn't revealed her source, preferring to tell everyone it was just a rumor around town.

"She obviously has no children," Zoe said, eyeing the tantalizing muffins in front of her, calculating in her head the fat, sugar, and calories each one contained. *Fuck it.* She grabbed a muffin, broke it in half and shoved it into her mouth none too daintily, savoring the warm spongy sugar rush. She'd do an extra ten minutes on the treadmill today as penance.

"Usually you can hear them screaming first thing in the morning or see them playing in the backyard if she did. I haven't seen or heard a peep from her house at all this morning."

"I don't think she has children. Or a husband."

Everyone turned and looked at Maggie.

Maggie just shrugged. "Just my womanly intuition." Despite Maggie being two doors down from Becca's house, she had kept a watchful eye on the proceedings the day before when the movers were scooting back and forth unpacking the truck. She saw nothing that would indicate the newest neighbor was married or even had a partner. There was none of the usual manly clutter that Hank had stored, collecting dust in their basement. No golf clubs. No sporting equipment. No ugly boring boxy furniture.

"Well, if she is alone and there's no man in her life then good for her," Sabine chimed in. "If men didn't have dicks, we wouldn't give them a second look."

Sabine's comment brought a few laughs from around the table.

Suddenly the front doorbell rang.

All heads turned at once and stared toward the front of the house.

No one moved.

Finally Paige got up and ambled out to answer it. Moments later she returned.

Becca looked around looking slightly uncomfortable, not

expecting such an audience.

Paige ushered Becca to a spare chair between herself and Maggie. Sabine sat opposite Becca and Zoe preferred to remain standing, her back against the kitchen counter.

Paige went around the table and did the introductions. After the smiles and nods, a stony silence descended on the group, all eyes focused expectantly on Becca.

"So welcome to our little community," Paige finally said, breaking the uncomfortable silence. "We don't really get new residents. I think the last was you and Jason." Paige glanced at Zoe.

"That's right," Zoe replied. "Some of us have lived here for ten years. No one really leaves. We all like it here too much."

"It certainly is a lovely place," Becca said as Paige poured her some coffee.

"We usually get together during the week at 10:00 a.m. on most days," Paige continued. "Taking turns at each other's house. Just to talk, shoot the breeze, share the news."

"Mainly talk gossip," Sabine scoffed. "Who's sleeping with who. It's a small town, and we women have to pass the time somehow." Sabine watched Becca carefully.

"So you're all married?" Becca asked.

"Unfortunately, yes," Maggie replied with a hint of disdain.

Paige waved her off. "Ignore Maggie. Yes, we are all *happily* married."

Becca looked around at the faces that were watching her intently. It was obvious she was now considered to be the latest "news" in the enclave.

The women spent the next five minutes going round the table sharing their backgrounds with Becca: their husbands, what they did, occupations, and some of the local history.

Then it was Becca's turn and all eyes returned to her. Coffee cups went untouched.

"There's not much to say, really," Becca started. "I used to live in Connecticut."

"Doing what?" Sabine butted in.

Paige rolled her eyes and placed her hand on Becca's arm. "Sabine, let the woman speak."

"I'm a journalist by trade," Becca continued. She explained how she used to work for a small local newspaper until it was taken over by a global conglomerate and all the staff were promptly "downsized" and let go.

"Any men in your life?" Maggie leaned forward intently.

"Why Maggie?" Paige asked. "Looking for another? Aren't four enough?"

Becca gave a confused look. Inside gossip, she deduced.

"You can never have enough men in your life," Maggie retorted.

"Just for your own information," Paige looked at Becca. "Maggie is the local cougar."

Becca frowned. "I believed you were all happily married."

"So?" Maggie said. "Doesn't mean we have to eat the same meal each night does it?"

Paige patted Becca's arm again. "Like I said, just ignore her. Maggie has an insatiable appetite for young men."

"Good-looking, taut young men," Maggie corrected her. "Life's too short, and I have my needs." Maggie's eyes went to each face around the table. "Just think in a few more years' time when you're all in a nursing home, wearing a diaper, having to be spoon fed custard for dinner and getting your ass and mouth wiped for you, you'll all be regretting that you passed on getting some while you were still capable. You'll all have regrets. All except me. Mark my words."

"Go on, Rebecca," Paige urged.

"Becca. Please call me Becca."

Paige just nodded.

"Well," Becca looked at the women. "I was married. Up until last year."

The room fell into silence. Eyes narrowed. Breaths were held back.

Becca gave a slow nod. "My husband, Michael, we'd been married barely ten years. He died. He was killed in a motorcycle accident."

Chapter 10
The Past

No one spoke for a few moments.

Becca was surrounded by faces of sadness, faces of shock.

It was Paige who spoke first. "I'm so sorry to hear that." She gave Becca's hand a gentle squeeze. "You poor thing. It must've been such a shock."

The other women around the table leaned in, offering their condolences.

"I can't possibly imagine what it would have been like," Paige continued.

Becca explained how Michael was riding on his way to work one morning, a route he must have ridden a million times before, when he was hit by a passing car coming the other way. He was killed instantly, the motorcycle a mangled wreck.

The other women listened intently, not speaking, not moving, hanging on to every word Becca said.

Maggie shook her head slowly when Becca was done. This certainly wasn't like any other of the morning catch-ups they'd had in the past.

Then Becca smiled. "Life goes on, and I have to move on."

"Good for you," Zoe said. Still the news had come as quite a shock to the group. None of them had suffered such a loss.

Becca didn't feel awkward or uncomfortable explaining her past. It would have eventually come out anyway, and she was prepared for it. But it was the first time she had really opened up to anyone about the tragic death of her husband, Michael. Especially to a group of strangers, which these women were. But she wanted to put it into perspective, so they would understand why she was alone, and maybe stop prying.

After the funeral there were the usual offers of help, phone calls, unexpected visits from Michael's parents, checking in on Becca, making sure she was doing OK.

However as the months passed, the contact dried up. Becca's own parents were both dead and she had no other siblings or close relatives to offer support.

Becca continued. "So I sold the house in Connecticut. I wanted to move to a more rural location. A place where people didn't know me, where I could just blend in."

The women sat in silence, and continued to listen as Becca described her past.

"It's not that I didn't like my old home, or the town where we lived. It was just that it was filled with too many painful memories. I wanted to escape, to start a new life somewhere else, far away from there."

Sabine spoke up. "Believe me, Becca, I imagine there's quite a few people in Ravenwood who have moved here for the exact same reason." No one around the table picked up on the cynicism in Sabine's comment.

Becca went on. "I desperately wanted children with Michael. However for some reason he didn't. When we were first married, he welcomed the idea of starting a family. Then as the years went by he seemed to have lost interest in it."

"Most men do, honey," Maggie said with an understanding smile. "They say anything just to get you into the sack. Don't want their bride to breed."

Paige ignored Maggie's crass comment. "But you still have time. You're young."

"You just need to find a decent man. And I know that can't be easy." Maggie said scornfully, her comments about men a reflection of her own disappointment in her marriage to Hank.

Zoe pushed off the counter and came and sat down on one of the spare chairs at the table. "Jason and I don't want to have children. It's something we discussed before we got married. We've got nothing against children; it's just a choice we made. We don't see children fitting into our lives."

Becca looked around the table. "Do any of you have children? It's just that I have this maternal instinct and believe I would be a good mother. I know Michael would have been a good father and perhaps given enough time he would have come around to my way of thinking."

"I know exactly what you mean, Becca," Paige said. "Scott and I are trying. I'd love to have children and I've been going to a fertility specialist in town. I'm charting my cycles and targeting when it's best for me to conceive. Scott is very understanding about it all and he said he wants nothing more than to start a family."

Sabine felt like vomiting. She turned to Maggie, keen to change the subject. Of all the women in the group, Sabine was the least maternal and all this talk of children was getting more than slightly annoying. "Maggie, how's your son, Adam?"

Maggie and Hank only had one child, Adam, who was

nineteen years old. He had graduated from high school and decided to take a year off and travel overseas to Europe before deciding if he wanted to go to college or not.

While Hank seemed disinterested in whatever their son did, Maggie kept up-to-date with Adam on Facebook. "He's great," Maggie beamed. "Thank you for asking." Maggie absolutely adored her son and took great delight in talking about him. "He's been away for a few months now, but we stay in touch on Facebook."

Once a week Adam would post on his Facebook account photos of his latest travels, places he had visited. However in the last few weeks Maggie hadn't heard from him. Adam had said he was going to a remote part of northern France, up into the mountains, and the Internet connections would be weak.

"It was kind of sudden, wasn't it, Maggie? Him going overseas?" Sabine asked.

"It was unexpected," Maggie said, thinking back. "He never mentioned anything before about traveling or going overseas. But he had just graduated from high school and seemed very restless, didn't know what he wanted to do with his life. He'd saved some money so I guess he could go. We didn't even see him before he left. We just got an email from him at the airport saying he was about to board a plane and had decided he wanted to travel for a few months. Came as a complete shock."

"Did he go with anyone?" Becca asked. "Girlfriend?"

"Oh, Adam doesn't have a girlfriend," Maggie said with a defiant shake of her head.

"Maybe that's just what he told you, Maggie," Sabine said with a devious little smile on her face. "To keep you happy. Didn't want to upset you." Sabine knew how clingy Maggie was toward Adam. It was almost sickening.

Maggie ignored Sabine's not so subtle jibe. "He said he had some friends in London and they were going to meet up once he arrived, maybe travel together around Europe. He'd packed some of his things, so we've left his bedroom as it is," Maggie said. "He said he would be back in a few months, maybe longer. He messaged me a few weeks back saying that money was running out but he'd find a part-time job somewhere in Paris. He said that there were plenty of signs in cafés and bars for help needed."

"Might find a nice little French girl to shack up with." Sabine was relentless, enjoying watching Maggie squirm slightly.

Paige shot Sabine a glare. "I think it's great that he left home for a while to spread his wings," Paige said. "Too many kids these days stay at home for far too long. They need to get out and experience the world, show a bit of independence."

Maggie agreed. "I'm really glad he's gone, to tell you the truth. Adam wasn't a very social person and I never really met any of his friends."

Sabine yawned a little too obviously then turned to Becca. "So it's just you, all on your lonesome in a big house?"

"I like the space," Becca said. "Our other house was small. Over the next few months I'm going to enjoy picking out furniture, decorating the place, filling the spaces as I want."

Sabine leaned forward. "If you want a shopping buddy, I'm your person. I know all the best places in Hagerstown to buy furniture, special decorative pieces, anything you need. I know the owners of the businesses really well too. I'll get you a great discount off anything you want. Just let me know."

Paige and Zoe glanced at each other briefly. Sabine was positioning herself as Becca's new best friend. It was the tactic she employed when she was courting a new client for Mark's investment business. Sabine would shower her prospects with attention, flattery, take them out for coffee. Then it would escalate to lunch at an exclusive restaurant. Next she would introduce them slowly to her own network of colleagues, hairdressers, spa owners while all the time sizing up their bank accounts to see if they had enough money to invest funds with Mark.

"Thanks," Becca replied.

"No problem, honey. Just let me know any time. It'll be my pleasure." Sabine smiled like a hyena eyeing its prey.

There was an obvious question that all the women wanted to ask. But they left it to Sabine, knowing she couldn't resist. Then as if by clockwork, she spoke up.

"I don't mean to be nosy," Sabine said her best fake smile on her face. "But did your husband, Michael, have any life insurance?"

Paige groaned, "You don't have to ask that Sabine!" But secretly, Paige was glad Sabine had.

Becca smiled. "It's fine, honestly. And to answer your question, yes. Michael did have life insurance, and I'm very grateful that he did. Without it, I couldn't have bought in such a lovely community like this."

There were smiles and nods of agreement around the table.

"I guess you don't have to work then?" Sabine continued her covert assault, ticking off a mental interview checklist in her head. So far Becca was a prime candidate, ripe for the plucking: Single. No kids. Big insurance payout. No obvious debt or other financial commitments.

Paige shot Sabine another glare.

Becca shrugged. "Look, for the time being at least, like I said, I want to take my time, get settled in first. Explore the town. Maybe later, after six months I'll think about perhaps doing freelance work but I have no immediate plans. I might write a few articles and submit them to online news services or the local newspapers."

"There's a local newspaper in town," Paige said. "Given that you're a journalist by trade, I'm sure they would be interested."

Becca considered it for a moment. It hadn't entered her mind before. She was too busy with the move and the upheaval. But she knew she couldn't sit idle for too long. She wanted to keep her mind active and her pulse on the craft of writing. It would definitely be something she would consider.

"There certainly wouldn't be the stress or pressure compared to a big city newspaper," Paige added.

"I think the only news worth knowing gets discussed here," Sabine laughed, "between us. I can't imagine anything else interesting happening around town that would be worth writing about."

Chapter 11
The Woods

Ever since she was a child, Becca had shied away from authority.

It wasn't that she was deliberately defiant by nature. It was just that from a very early age Becca had discovered a strong vein of self-reliance and independence ran through her. She didn't like being told what she could and couldn't do.

Her mother was an alcoholic and her father, whenever he was home, ignored her mother's condition.

Becca had plenty of friends at school, and she used to play with the local kids in the street outside her house well into the early hours of the evening.

But when her mother drank, which was most days, Becca would withdraw into her small upstairs bedroom. Ensconced in what was familiar and comforting, she would find solace between her storybooks and drawing pictures until it had grown dark outside her small bedroom window.

Then she would creep downstairs where she would find her mother passed out on the floor. Becca would gently coax her mother to her feet, and then the two of them would stagger up the stairs, a grown, barely lucid woman supported by her five-year-old daughter. Ignoring the slurring protests, Becca would put her mother to bed.

On school days, Becca would rise early while her mother was sleeping off another drunken binge from the previous evening. Becca would go downstairs to the kitchen and make her own school lunch and pack her backpack. She would then leave the house, closing the door behind her, and walk the ten-minute route to catch the school bus.

When she came home after school, her mother would be in the kitchen preparing dinner for her. Her mother would kiss Becca on the forehead and ask how the day was. There was never any mention of the previous evening even though her mother knew it was Becca who helped her into bed and had tucked her in. What she wouldn't know was that Becca would then check on her every couple of hours during the night to make sure she was fine.

There was no remorse, no real spoken apology, even when she used to beat Becca during one of her drunken rages. Perhaps she didn't know what she was doing, Becca would reason.

Apologies would come, however, in other forms. Her mother would buy Becca small, unexpected gifts. A new pencil case would suddenly appear next to her plate at the dinner table. Or she would find a new coloring book on her bed when she got home from school. Or her mother would take Becca out for a cheeseburger instead of cooking dinner.

In the back of her mind Becca knew that these were not acts of kindness, but acts of guilt, a coping mechanism her mother adopted to apologize in her own way for the abuse she dished out.

Becca's father was in denial, even though he witnessed firsthand the alcoholic rants of his wife. Rather than seek medical help for his wife, the family simply moved homes and towns several times while Becca was growing up.

This meant her education suffered, because she never really settled into one school before being uprooted to the next.

It was an endless parade of new towns, new faces, new schools, all done in the hope that his wife would get better, would change. But despite the changes, nothing changed. Things never got better.

Then one day, Becca's mother declared she would never change. She was what she was.

At least she was being honest, Becca thought.

So hence, Becca spent most of her young life running away from something. Her upbringing had made her strong-willed, determined, and shaped her into the independent young woman she was today. She wasn't disobedient. She immensely disliked people telling her what to do or giving her advice as to how she should act or live her life, as though they had walked a day in her shoes or had seen the world through her eyes when she was a child.

Becca stood at the edge of the ridge at the back of her house, her feet almost buried in her lawn, luscious and green. A wall of trees and tangled undergrowth sloped away in front of her.

She hesitated, wondering about the warning.

Mac's comments only fueled her curiosity to take a look at what was on the other side of the ridge. After all, it was part of her property; she owned everything all the way down to the fence line at the bottom of the hillside.

She took one step down, leaving behind the verdant lawn and stepping onto dry earth where the water sprinklers didn't reach. The ground was cracked, littered with rocks, and covered with a stubble of weeds. Vines and creepers fought among themselves in a slow race to nowhere.

With deliberate care she descended down the rocky slope, each step taking her farther away from the bright sunshine and manicured harmony and into the shadowy gloom of overgrown disorder.

She used small saplings and branches to steady herself, placing her feet carefully between fractured rocks, pausing every so often to look back up the slope to see how far she had progressed. Slowly the world behind her disappeared as she trekked farther into the gloom and silence of the woods.

The air was distinctly cooler down here, but that didn't stop a bead of sweat trickling down the groove of her spine.

The sun filtered down as best as it could through the canopy above, casting small pools of blotchy light on the forest floor.

Then a sound.

Becca stopped, one hand grasping a small tree trunk.

She looked around but could see no one.

Onward she went.

The ground began to level out to a small plateau of scraped and graded earth. Through the undergrowth appeared the boxy shape of a cement drainage ditch in front of a gaping round dark hole of the drain pipe that burrowed into the hillside.

The ditch was ten-feet wide and three-feet deep and choked with leaves and a sodden mush of forest debris. A heavy steel grate was hinged across the entrance of the drain pipe and locked securely in place with a thick padlock. A small rivulet of water bled out of the pipe, under the steel grate and into the groove of the ditch.

Something fluttered under the canopy of the trees above; Becca glanced up, momentarily distracted. A chorus of insects broke out, hissing and clicking around her.

Hunkering down, Becca stared into the dark hole of the pipe but could see nothing, the sound of trickling water echoing somewhere in the darkness inside the smooth walls of the cement pipe.

She stood up and looked farther down the slope to where a thin trail of worn dirt snaked its way through the forest. This must be the trail Mac had mentioned that led all the way to the bottom of the hill where the access gate was.

Becca picked up the trail and continued down the slope.

Ten minutes later she reached the base of the hill, the ground flattened out, and she emerged out of the woods and onto a narrow strip of cleared land with a chain-link fence in front of her. More vines and creepers threaded themselves through the wire, a deserted two-lane road beyond.

The fence was tall and solid and there was a padlocked double gate to one side.

This is where electrical contractors could gain access into the enclave to carry out the work Mac had mentioned. Becca tested the padlock. It was strong and locked securely. She regarded the fence, imagining that it ran all the way around the base of the hill, effectively sealing off the entire enclave to intruders. But then again if someone wanted to get in they could just as easily cut the wire or scale the fence.

With her curiosity satisfied, Becca started back up the slope again and, as expected, the uphill journey was a lot harder than the downward one.

She arrived back at the drain pipe breathing hard and paused to catch her breath, more beads of perspiration trickling down her back, the inside of her shirt clinging to her skin and her legs were starting to ache from the exertion. As she stood bent over, hands on her thighs, Becca silently cursed. She needed to get more hill work and trail running into her training, instead of only pounding flat sidewalks.

She looked up the slope, and then let out a sigh before setting off again.

If Becca hadn't been hunched over as she climbed, staring at the ground instead of looking up the slope to where she was going, she wouldn't have seen it.

Something glinted at her feet.

Becca stopped, frowned then crouched down and pushed back the shrubbery. Draped over the leaves of a twisted vine was a thin ribbon of gold.

Becca picked up the object and held it up to the light.

It was a delicate gold bracelet with a name tag smudged with dirt. She turned it over in her hand, rubbing away the dirt.

Amber.

Instinctively Becca stood up and looked around at the surrounding woods. It was quiet, the air had suddenly grown still. Even the insects had stopped chattering. In the distance she heard a car pass along the road below, before the sound of its engine faded into the distance.

She stared at the bracelet again.

There was no one named Amber who lived in the enclave, and Maggie and Hank only had a son. Perhaps the bracelet belonged to one of the contractors who had carried out work on the hillside? It wasn't unheard of to have female contractors. But it was rare. Maybe a visitor hiking in the woods had lost it. The bracelet could have easily come off, snagged on a branch.

Becca pocketed the bracelet and continued her climb.

Chapter 12
Algiz

It was only after Becca had returned to her home and was standing in the kitchen looking at the chain bracelet that she realized there was something else engraved on the reverse side of the name tag.

Taking a coffee cup, she filled it with warm water, added a few drops of washing detergent, and dropped the bracelet into the solution to clean. She let it soak a few minutes while she made herself coffee. When she returned to the cup, she rinsed off the bracelet and studied it closer.

The nametag was reversible, and unlike most nametags on bracelets that were curved to the shape of the wrist, this nametag was flat. There was a second name on the reverse side of the name tag.

Adam.

There was also a strange symbol engraved next to the name. Becca had seen it before or a variation of it but didn't know what it meant. It looked like some type of Celtic or runic symbol.

So Adam did have a girlfriend, and her name was Amber.

Obviously the bracelet represented their commitment to each other, and he wore it on his wrist as a constant reminder.

The clasp on the bracelet was broken, likely caught or torn away without Hank and Maggie's son knowing he had lost it until it was too late.

All the houses backed onto the woods, unfenced, to keep with the natural look of the environment. Adam must have used the trail off the ridge and down through the woods to come and go from his parents' home that was two houses down from Becca's own home.

But why? Did he have a key to get through the locked gate Becca had seen?

Becca dried the bracelet with a paper napkin then sealed it in a plastic bag for safekeeping. She wondered why Maggie was so adamant that Adam didn't have a girlfriend. Perhaps Adam was keeping it from his parents? Becca couldn't imagine why Adam would keep it a secret. Most parents would be happy that their teenage son had a girlfriend, instead of them hiding in their room all day, playing computer games or surfing the Internet. It was no secret that teenage boys didn't possess the social skills or confidence that girls did at that age. Boys could be withdrawn and reclusive.

Unless...

Maybe this "Amber" was a bad influence on Adam? Maybe Hank and Maggie didn't approve of her.

Sitting at the kitchen counter drinking her coffee, Becca stared at the bracelet in the sealed plastic bag, the cogs in her mind slowly turning.

She considered giving the bracelet to Maggie. But then thought otherwise. If Adam did have a secret girlfriend he didn't want his parents knowing about, Becca needed to respect that fact.

Becca didn't want to cause any trouble between Adam and his parents, or cause a long distance argument to happen between them when they were already separated by so many miles.

Becca decided to return the bracelet to Adam discreetly, when he returned from Europe. She opened a kitchen drawer and placed the bracelet inside so it wouldn't get lost a second time.

The rest of the day Becca spent setting up her home office. She had set aside a large spare corner bedroom upstairs, at the rear of the house that overlooked the backyard, the woods beyond and the rear of Sabine and Mark's house on the right.

She positioned her desk so it faced the window, giving her an uninterrupted view of the trees and rolling farmland in the distance.

She set up her laptop and arranged everything on her desk just as she liked it, knowing that she would change the configuration probably a thousand times in the coming weeks until she was completely happy. In the corner of the desk she placed a vase filled with water and a single white rose she had cut from her garden.

She sat back in the desk chair and surveyed everything, adjusting the angle of her main flat screen slightly and relocating the pen containers.

Satisfied for now, Becca began unpacking the boxes that were neatly stacked in the corner of the room, taking out the multitude of books, some paperbacks but mostly hardcovers, and began filling up the bookcases the movers had brought upstairs.

She wanted to make her home office functional yet homey. Even though she wasn't thinking about looking for part-time work straight away, Becca needed a space where she could plan and organize her life, do research if needed, and keep her mind occupied.

She made a note to get more bookcases or maybe see if there was a local carpenter who could make some built-ins. She had more books than places to store them and she really wanted to fill this room with her books to make it cozy. It would just have to be a work-in-progress for the time being.

Becca went downstairs, grabbed a coffee and the plastic bag with the bracelet inside, then returned to her office and began searching the Internet for the engraved symbol.

She found websites that discussed ancient symbology, unique alphabets, and pictures of inscriptions on large monolithic rune stones from 7th century in Sweden. Most of the symbols had Germanic origins mixed with Latin meanings that referenced Norse and Anglo-Saxon culture. There were references to gods, man, and horses.

However she couldn't quite exactly find a match for the symbol that was on the bracelet. It looked like a tree, with three branches, but then, after a while of searching, all the symbols began to look the same, like trees with their branches at varying angles.

Becca was about to give up when a website popped up on her screen that listed runes and their meanings. Becca stared at the screen but this time she saw the symbol. She glanced at the bracelet in the plastic bag on her desk.

Yes! Finally. It was a match.

"Algiz."

Becca scrolled down the page and began to read. Algiz was described as a "powerful rune," whatever that meant. Maybe she could use it to cast spells or turn people into cats?

The rune represented the divine might of the universe. Once again, more hocus pocus. The shape of the symbol itself could represent a flower opening to receive the sun, or the branches of the tree, or the antlers of an elk.

Great. Nothing definitive. She continued reading.

There were so many interpretations listed for the same symbol that it was confusing, had no singular meaning, like looking into someone's palm and seeing twenty different futures for them. You could basically read any interpretation, modern or historical, into what the symbol meant. However a "divine plan" was mentioned several times. Becca made notes on a pad on her desk.

Divine plan? Becca had no idea. The word "Divinity" had definite religious connotations to it. It meant godliness, sacredness, holiness. Perhaps Adam was a religious person?

More questions than answers. Maybe she was reading too much into the symbolism. Maybe Adam just saw the symbol in a book or as a tattoo on someone's arm and thought it looked cool. Becca then did a search on the name "Amber" in Ravenwood and came up with a number of women's names. She searched Adam Vickerman and found her way to his Facebook page, which fortunately was public. There were the usual pictures of tourist locations in the United Kingdom and Europe. She scrolled through his timeline for a while but the posts became slightly monotonous. Next she did a quick search for local jewelry stores and found some matching styles for the bracelet with a reversible nametag. Gold did seem like an odd choice, though, for a young man.

After a few hours of further searching on the Internet she needed a break. The vertebrae in her lower back and neck cracked and popped as she got up and stretched.

She didn't know Adam Vickerman, and for reasons she couldn't explain, Becca got the feeling he was a sensitive, thoughtful young man. A thinker, someone like her, not prone to rash or impulsive behavior. Someone who was different from a lot of the other younger men his age. Maybe it was how Maggie had spoken of him, that faraway look she got whenever she talked about him.

Becca tilted her head side to side, more cracking and popping, and stared out the window at the woods. The sun was setting on the day, the sky a simmering burnt orange with darkening edges.

Adam Vickerman had used the trail through the woods up to the ridge. What Becca couldn't understand was for what purpose? Unless it was for some reason where he didn't want to be seen going through the main entrance of the enclave.

Becca thought back to the CCTV cameras that were mounted at the gatehouse, the comings and goings of everyone being recorded, blocks of data laid down on a hard drive.

What was so secretive that Adam Vickerman didn't want anyone else knowing or seeing?

Chapter 13
The Last Victim

The cell phone camera clicked. A concentrated flash of light bounced off drab gray walls inside the confined room then faded.

"Adam David Teal." Detective Marvin Richards spoke into his cell phone, nitrile gloves on his hands dictating what his eyes saw.

Later tonight, in the quiet semi-darkness of his small, crammed office at home, he would upload the photos to his laptop. Then while his neighbors slept warm and safe in their beds, he would descend the dark and twisting staircase searching for the floor he was last at. Once there, he would pause and relive the horror of this latest crime scene, slowly arranging the pieces he had already placed there the night before and the night before that and the night before that. He would then add more pieces to the puzzle, making the picture a little clearer, but less sane. For no one in their right mind could comprehend the picture that Richards was building of a villain who always seemed to be one victim ahead of him.

Some parts of the puzzle were taking shape, but it still looked like a wide, fractured picture that made no sense. Perhaps Richards had tried to force some pieces to fit. It was an occupational hazard, when trying to assign motive and method to a crime, especially a homicide, forcing pieces to fit, to suit your view, to get a quick conclusion.

Richards didn't know where the bottom of the spiral staircase led. But he knew it ended somewhere. They all did. He just hoped it ended in his lifetime and he reached the bottom before it was too late.

Downward he would go, sometime inches at a time. Sometimes giant leaps. But always downward, a journey away from the surface, from the light, from the air. Deeper and deeper. Always downward. Because farther down in the deep dark depths of the earth, at the very bottom lived the killer Richards was hunting.

Richards would listen to the audio he had just recorded, replay it in his mind, over and over again, while scribbling down notes in a simple flip notebook. Forensics had done their thing, and Richards would have their report soon enough to cross reference his own conclusions with. He preferred to make his own observations, a different set of eyes, desensitized as they were to the countless scenes of horror and destruction he had seen during his career.

This didn't happen in a town like Ravenwood. Just didn't.

The cell phone clicked again, the loud fabricated sound of a camera shutter opening, the momentary bleaching of color, then the shutter closing again. The photos were of what the latest victim, a young man named Adam Teal, had been wearing when he was found dead: designer jeans, oxford shirt, college ID, and blue canvas converse sneakers, scuffed, and worn.

Slowly Richards was acquainting himself with the victim he

had never really known when he was alive. The first time they had ever met, Adam Teal was dead. It was through these painstaking initial steps in the investigation—visiting his mother to tell her the shocking news that her son was dead, going through the victim's personal items he had on him in the last moments of his life, talking to his family and friends—that Richards was slowly getting to know, and understand the young man.

Richards often said to the younger detectives and police officers that in situations of homicide, it was the dead they worked for. Not the families or the police department or the town. They owed their allegiance to the dead to do everything possible to find who killed them.

Motive and method.

There was always a motive, and most cases where one person killed another, it could be boiled down to just three: greed, jealously, or rage.

Being a cop first, then a detective for more than fifteen years in Lower Manhattan, New York City, Richards had seen the worst of what people could do to each other. Ugly, senseless violence.

Most cops said it doesn't rub off on you. But it did. It left its mark. Wading through the filth everyday always left a stain that couldn't be removed, even years later.

Richards donned a pair of nitrile gloves and carefully pulled the jeans out of the plastic evidence bag and laid them out flat on the table.

Expensive, skinny cut, quality denim, fashion label. Made in some sweat shop in Haiti for a fraction of what they sold off the hanger in the upscale stores.

The camera clicked again. The walls of the room blinding

white before fading back to drab gray.

Richards did the same with the shirt and shoes, laying them out carefully. Forensics would have already photographed and swabbed everything, including the clothing on the body and off the body.

Three previous bodies. Three men. Two white. One black. Adam Teal was the fourth victim.

Method and motive.

Richards already knew the method. It was like all the others. The coroner had just confirmed that fact a few hours ago with Richards. Strangulation was such an intimate, raw, up close and personal method of killing. Staring right into your victims' eyes while you squeezed the life out of them, taking joy in knowing that the last person, the last image they would ever see would be your face.

Richards took another photo, describing a few more details into his cell phone.

He still didn't have a motive. Motive always revealed itself last, when you had finally reached the bottom of the spiral staircase, and had finally pieced together enough of the puzzle or interviewed the perpetrator and they decided to tell you why they did it.

As much as he didn't want to admit it, Richards knew there wasn't going to be a normal motive for this case. There would be elements of rage as part of the motive, he was certain. The excessive ligature marks around the throats of each victim were testimony to that as well as fracturing of the hyoid bone, the horseshoe-shaped bone located below the chin. It was a crushing relentless grip that went beyond what was required to produce cardiac arrest or asphyxia.

But it was his own conclusion of what the motive was that

concerned Richards the most: enjoyment.

Someone was deriving immense enjoyment from killing young men whose first names were "Adam."

When someone killed for enjoyment, it made the leads, the clues difficult to find. Because in most cases, the perpetrator didn't know the victims. They were randomly selected to fit some predetermined preference.

The known statistic that in most cases victims knew their killer didn't apply in cases like this.

"The Eden Killer." That's what the police had already labeled him. His victims, all males, all named "Adam" like Adam and Eve from the Book of Genesis.

After the first body was discovered twelve months ago, Richards thought nothing of it. Just a one off homicide. Then the second body was discovered and Richards found himself transported back to the mean streets of New York, Fifth Precinct, the southeastern edge of Manhattan. Little Italy. Chinatown. The Bowery.

He saw himself back among the labyrinth of low-rise brick buildings, darkened alleys, fire escapes, narrow streets piled high with trash, the constant drone of sirens, traffic and the urgency of eight million people condensed into one of the most heavily populated cities on the planet.

Richards finished taking his photos, returned the evidence to the locker room, and walked outside into the fresh air.

Chapter 14
Searching

Meddling bitch.

He parked his car down the road, in the parking lot of a picnic spot. Being the dark of night, the lot was deserted and there were no lights. No one would see his car from the road.

Then he walked back, keeping off the shoulder of the road, and well hidden among the dark trees of the woods that lined both sides.

Headlights appeared in the distance, swung around the curve of the road. He sank farther into the shadows until they passed, then he continued.

The access road appeared on the right, just a smudge of dirt through the woods. He cut inward and moments later he reached the fence line and double gate at the base of the hill. The woods around him were dark and silent, the moonlight throwing a scatter of shadows and silhouettes.

He glanced over his shoulder, just to make sure no one had seen him.

Careful and cautious was his motto.

Taking out a key, he undid the padlock, opened the gate, closed it behind him, and then locked it again securely. The gate hinges were well oiled, he made sure of that. Don't want some screeching sound alerting anyone. Sound traveled farther at night.

He'd brought with him a small flashlight.

Just to make sure.

Didn't need it though. He had traveled this trail numerous times, especially at night, knew every rock and crevice, branch and tree, groove and undulation, could walk up the hillside blindfolded in the dark too, he reckoned.

Slowly and carefully he began his silent trek up the hillside, eyes up, looking ahead, ears tuned to the nighttime whispers and clicks. He wore soft shoes with plenty of grip.

There was nothing cerebral about his decision, this course of action he had chosen. He simply laid out the facts as he knew them, and when the calculated risk reached an uncomfortable threshold, he made his decision. The woman had found the bracelet in the woods. That fact was undeniable and later confirmed when she started searching about the unique piece of jewelry and its design.

He didn't like making mistakes. Mistakes meant carelessness, and carelessness meant being caught. And he was never going to be caught. He enjoyed it too much. It was better than anything he had ever felt or experienced in his life.

There were only a few possible locations where she could have discovered the bracelet. What he needed to do now was to make sure there was no other evidence left behind, and if that also meant going inside her house to look as well, then so be it.

The ghostly shape of the drainage ditch and outlet pipe materialized in front of him.

This time he needed the flashlight. Crouching down and with the beam pointed downward, close to the ground, he scoured the dirt and undergrowth, pushing aside foliage as he went, moving in a grid pattern in one direction, then crossing over and covering the ground from the other direction.

Slow and meticulous, because he was never going to be caught.

He stood up again when he was finished.

Nothing.

Was it good or bad, that he'd found nothing else? Nothing foreign, nothing that shouldn't have been there?

He tried to remember the exact location of where he had been that evening, months ago. He was certain this was the exact location, the only location other than the trail he had followed.

Good or bad? The question bugged him.

Slowly and carefully he searched again, on his hands and knees this time.

Just to make sure.

His fingers rummaged through leaves and twigs, plowing softly through muck and debris, grit and dirt getting under his fingernails.

As expected, the second pass took longer. However now he was certain nothing else had been left behind by accident.

Next he made his way over to the outflow pipe and shone the flashlight deep inside, circling the beam around the smooth inner walls. The sound of dripping water could be heard somewhere deep within.

Something else may have dropped here, been washed away by the rain. It would be hard to tell, searching for something that wasn't here.

He moved to the concrete drainage ditch and resumed his

search, once again pushing aside muck and mud with his fingers, the ground soft and wet, digging through the wet soil with his hands.

Thirty minutes later he was done.

He checked his watch. Luminous dials told him he still had time and he wasn't in the mood to come back another night and finish what needed to be done.

Meddling bitch, he mumbled again.

Because of her, he'd given up a warm evening in front of the fire with a good book and a bottle of red wine just to go out into the cold darkness and forage in the dirt like a raccoon.

All that was left was to scour the trail the rest of the way up to the top of the ridge, following his previous footsteps. It was risky, but he needed to be certain.

He continued his trek up the slope, using the flashlight for this particular leg of the journey, making sure the beam was pointed low and at the ground, his eyes slowly searching the trail, left and right. If someone came, he was prepared.

As he moved upward he contemplated killing the woman. That would be simple. But it didn't fit into his plans, and it would raise immediate suspicion. It was too close to home, literally.

When he neared the top of the ridge, the trees thinned. He paused, covered the beam of the flashlight and waited a few moments for his eyes to adjust. Patchy silvery clouds tore across the moon, a dull light reaching down toward him. He hung back in the shadows, an arch of light bleeding over the edge of earth above him where the ground flattened, the woods ended and the backyard of her house began.

He could tell the backyard lights were off. If they weren't, the edge of the woods would be bathed in more light, not just dull moonlight.

He slowly stepped forward, up the incline and toward the house above.

Becca rubbed her eyes.

It was getting late and she'd seen enough cryptic symbols and runic stones for one evening.

The bracelet sat in a plastic bag next to her laptop, a notepad next to it, the page covered with scribbles, doodles and sketches of runic shapes. After dinner, she'd spent another two hours searching Internet sites, trying to decipher the symbol.

Perhaps she was reading too much into it, that it was just a symbol chosen based on looks alone.

Yet somehow, something niggled at the back of Becca's mind. Maybe it was her journalistic instinct that was making her antennae twitch, as it had done in the past. She could be a dog with a bone, her past editor had told her once, and that was a good thing.

She leaned back and stretched her arms and shoulders. Grabbing her coffee cup, she turned off her laptop and the desk light, plunging the room into darkness.

Becca stood at the window for a moment, looking out into the darkness. She could see the silhouette of the edge of the woods at the end of her backyard. She was about to turn and call it a night when something caught her eye, a glimmer of light, through the trees, near the edge of the ridge.

Becca moved to the edge of the window. Her eyes were too tired, maybe she was seeing things.

And there it was again, a slight dull flicker of light, in the tree line.

There was someone outside, past the edge of her backyard, in the woods. Becca rushed downstairs, and into the laundry room. She quickly slid on a pair of sneakers, and grabbed a flashlight from its wall charging mount next to the backdoor. She was tempted to turn on the external lights but decided against it. It might spook whoever it was.

It angered Becca that someone would have the nerve to sneak around at night out there, in her backyard, so close to her house.

Chapter 15
Chase in the Dark

He paused and listened.

It was definitely a sound, the soles of feet on grass coming toward him from above. He immediately flicked off the flashlight and crouched low among the scrub below the lip of the ridge, twenty feet from the top. He was certain no one had seen him.

Through the trees he could partially see the second story of the back of the house. It was in darkness, but the lights were on at the neighboring houses on both sides, the light however, fading before the tree line. Slowly he reached into a side pocket, his fingers finding comfort in the shape of the object he had brought with him.

He wouldn't hesitate to use it if he needed to, especially on her.

Becca kept her flashlight off, the moonlight painting her backyard in ghostly grays. She could see the start of the woods in front of her, tall dark brooding shapes of trees, a solid wall of darkness beyond where the land fell away steeply down the hillside. She held back in the shadows waiting to see the light again but nothing appeared. Slowly she edged toward the tree line, the light around her fading with each step.

Then she stopped. This was crazy. Suppose the person had a knife or a gun? Unless... Could it be the same man? The one she had seen in Connecticut and then Allentown? Had he followed her all the way here? She'd first seen him at Michael's funeral, a stranger, tall, late fifties she guessed, willowy and dressed in a raincoat. He hung around at the back, near the trees, away from the main crowd, watching proceedings, watching her. God, was he stalking her?

The atmosphere in front of Becca took on a sudden malevolent feel to it, like something wasn't right. She glanced back over her shoulder and could see the light in her laundry room, a warm comforting glow that was only a few feet behind her if she needed to go back to the security of her home.

Then she looked back at the woods in front of her. This was the spot where she had seen the glimmer of light, she was certain.

Becca switched on her flashlight and a thousand lumens of super bright LED cut down the darkness in front of her, pushing aside the shadows and trepidation she now felt.

She panned the wedge of intense light left and right, bleaching everything white that it touched before she stepped off the edge of the lawn and into the first row of trees.

The ground started to slope downward; the feel of the woods felt different at night compared to when she was last here during the day.

Becca descended slowly, using the flashlight to light up the ground.

She paused and panned the flashlight around and down the slope in front of her. The woods were quiet and still, no insects, no sounds, just a kaleidoscope of darkened shapes and vertical lines pressed in around the beam of the flashlight.

Maybe she should turn around, go back, and call the police. Mac at the gatehouse would be long gone by now. *Perhaps I should call him*, she thought. There was an afterhours number. Then Becca realized in her rush to leave her home she'd left her cellphone charging on her desk upstairs. She decided to go down a few more feet then turn back. Whoever it was, they had gone, scared off no doubt by her.

Something moved above him, farther up the slope, at the top of the ridge, darkness moving over itself. Someone was there, just a few feet inside the tree line, looking down the slope, looking toward him. The shape moved forward again, slow and deliberate steps. Then a burst of bright light lit up the woods to his right.

Damn it! She was coming down the hillside toward him. His hand tightened on the object in his pocket as he shuffled around to the other side of a wide tree trunk. A blinding beam of light scanned the woods above him, searching for him.

The beam stopped, perhaps twenty feet from where he lay hidden. He crouched lower, then went to his belly, pushing himself farther into the dirt, burrowing into bracken and scrub around him. The beam swept directly over his head, then back again.

More footsteps. She was heading past him, on his left. All he needed to do was just wait, sit tight.

Through the trees below drifted the bellowing groan of a

large truck as it struggled up and around the bend of the road. The sound grew louder.

He used the opportunity to mask any sound he would make as he crawled sideways along the ground away from her.

He could hear the truck engine reach its zenith, as it cleared the slight rise on the bend of the road below, before trundling down the other side of the hill, the sound then fading.

Becca heard the truck too. She glanced to the left, and saw movement farther up the slope of the hill this time. It was definitely a person, hiding among the scrub, fronds and leaves moving. Somehow she had gone past them in the dark. She began moving up again, grabbing branches and saplings to steady herself as she went, making a line directly to where she had seen the movement.

She reached the spot, panned the flashlight around the ground.

Nothing.

The darkness shifted behind her, parted, and a dark shape lunged out at her.

Becca sensed movement behind her, went to turn, then felt bone-crushing pain at the back of her skull, before the darkness all around her exploded into pure white.

Chapter 16
Allentown

Shapes swirled behind Becca's eyelids.

A solitary dark outline, someone's head, warped, featureless, no mouth, no eyes. The featureless head regarded her for a moment, studied her. Slowly the head transformed into a face, waxen, drawn. Eyes and a mouth appeared.

Then the face was gone, whipped away.

Multiple voices, dull and distant crowded her head, mumbles of concern. The voices spoke to her. Then to each other.

Then someone took a power drill, placed the drill bit against the back of Becca's skull and squeezed the trigger. Sickening pain cut into her skull, into the bone, then deep into her brain. The pain was excruciating. Becca squeezed her eyelids tighter, trying to block it out. Nausea swept over her. The blackness came and Becca drifted off again.

"Becca." Someone called her name, a voice soft and gentle but far away. Becca floated below the dark surface, suspended, light seeping in from above. She kicked up, reached up and broke the surface.

"Becca." The same soft and gentle voice again but this time closer, inches from her face.

Becca opened her eyelids. She saw a face looking down at her, like she was lying in a grave, a rectangle outline above her, someone peering down at her. Another face appeared at the edge of the grave. This one she didn't recognize. Hands worked with quiet efficiency, taking a pulse, applying ice to the back of her head, the sun came out, a brilliant ball of white that flooded each eyeball. Pupils dilated.

Becca lifted her neck, tried to sit up. Then the drilling started up again at the back of her head.

A gentle hand rested on her shoulder, easing her back down, more soothing words.

"Becca. It's me, Maggie. You've had an accident."

Becca closed her eyes and tried to remember what had happened. But it was like a handful of her memory had been ripped away, a break in the song where the needle had jumped.

Now three faces crowded the edge of the grave, all staring down at her.

Then another voice, a young woman. "Becca, my name is Officer Haley Perez. You've been injured. Can you remember what happened?"

Becca took a deep breath, her lips parched, her throat sore. "My head hurts."

Perez looked at the paramedic who was leaning over Becca, checking her eyes, monitoring her vitals. Another paramedic was kneeling next to the sofa, packing things up into a medical hard case.

The paramedic leaning over Becca nodded at Perez. "She'll be fine. Just a mild concussion. Just needs some rest. I think she still needs to go to the ER for a scan, just to be sure with any head trauma."

Upon hearing this, Becca struggled upright again. This time hands helped, not hindered her to sit up. Slowly things came into focus and Becca looked around. "What happened?" She was sitting on the sofa in what she guessed was Maggie's living room.

"You tell us," Maggie said. "We found you in the woods."

"Who found me?" Becca asked, her mind still groggy. Her head throbbed.

Perez stepped forward. "Mr. Vickerman found you in the woods at the back of your house, unconscious. He carried you up here, then called the police."

Becca's mind swirled, fragments of her memory spinning in a web, trying to form into some logical sequence. Images and feelings flashed in her head. The woods. Darkness. The feeling of something, someone, there among the trees. Sounds. Someone behind her, evil rushing toward her. Then nothingness. Someone had hit her, she was certain.

Then she remembered and questions flooded her mind. Was it him? The same man she had seen in Connecticut who had been following her just days before she had left. She recognized his car again when she was filling up at the gas station on the outskirts of Allentown, Pennsylvania. It was only a six-hour drive to here when she had moved. Becca had taken I-95 after skirting around the Bronx and cutting across the Hudson River. She'd stopped a few times for coffee and she was certain he was following her. Maybe she was imagining things. Why would he hit her then? It seemed over the top if he was just spying on her and she had caught him in the act, on her property, in the woods.

Becca looked up for the first time at Perez. She couldn't tell them the truth, not yet anyway. It would attract the suspicion of the police and she didn't need that. "I slipped in the dark. That's all. I hit my head on a rock when I fell."

The two paramedics exchanged looks with Perez, a faint smile there.

Becca continued. "It's my fault I shouldn't have been out in the woods. I don't need to go to the ER."

"Ma'am, can I ask what were you doing in the woods wondering around in the dark?" Perez asked.

Perez had already made some initial inquiries with the Vickermans. Becca had no dog so she wasn't taking anything for a walk at night. There was no logical reason for the woman to be in the woods alone in the dark. Then again Perez had seen stranger things at night.

"I went for a walk," Becca said. "That's all. I wanted some fresh air so I thought I would take a stroll." Becca was starting to get annoyed with all the questioning. She gazed at Perez. "I had a flashlight with me. So I didn't plan to slip and hit my head if that's what you're asking. It was an accident, pure and simple."

The female police officer searched Becca's eyes, trying to figure out if she was being completely honest with her. If being a patrol officer had taught Perez anything, it was that people always lied to the police. Always. Even the innocent. And right now she knew Rebecca Cartwright wasn't being completely honest with her. "You live alone, Ms. Cartwright? There is no one else who can stay with you? A relative I can call, family friend?"

"You can call me Becca. And yes, I live alone."

Maggie touched Becca's shoulder. "It's a good thing Hank found you, dear."

"How did he find me?" Becca looked around, but Hank was nowhere to be seen. "Where is Hank?"

"He saw a light in the woods from his backyard," Perez said.

Maggie chimed in. "Hank was checking on the storage shed

in our backyard when he saw a light shining up through the trees. So he went to take a look and found a flashlight resting against a rock, pointing upward into the trees, with you lying unconscious next to it."

Just then Hank appeared from the kitchen carrying a tray filled with steaming coffee cups. He placed the tray on the table and looked at Becca. "You are quite lucky, young lady," Hank said. "I was checking that the shed was locked when I glanced down in the woods below and saw your light."

Becca looked up at Hank. "I must have a guardian angel then," she said. "Thank you, Hank, for finding me and bringing me back here."

Everyone was clustered around Becca, eyes on her. "Look, I'm sorry to cause this much trouble. It was an accident. I should have not gone walking alone."

"Especially not in the dark and certainly not down in those woods," Maggie said. "That hillside can be very steep and dangerous, especially at night."

Becca looked from Maggie then to Perez. "I'll keep that in mind from now on."

The paramedics finished packing up their equipment and Perez thanked them and walked outside with them.

"Like I said, she should be fine, it's just a mild concussion," the senior of the two paramedics said, while his younger partner loaded the equipment into the back of their truck.

"And what about the head injury?" Perez asked. "What can you tell me about that? Is it consistent with her story? Of falling and hitting her head on a rock or a log?" Perez had waited to ask this key question outside, when she had the paramedics alone and away from the others.

"Look, I'm not the medical examiner," the paramedic said.

"But you've seen and treated enough injuries to know the cause most of the time." Perez wanted an answer. "Off the record. I'm not going to hold you to it, but what's your professional opinion?"

The paramedic glanced back at the house, making sure no one was standing at the front door listening. "She could've slipped down the hillside," the paramedic said. "Hit the ground pretty hard with the back of her head."

Perez wasn't convinced, and neither was the paramedic. "But?"

"Don't quote me on this. But I think she was deliberately hit from behind by someone. There's evidence of swelling on the back of her head, but no abrasions, no tearing of the skin or cuts. Her injury is consistent with what you would expect from someone being struck with a blunt but not solid object. Where she was struck on the back of her head, the cerebellum region, is the exact spot where you would hit someone to knock them out. Either she slipped and was incredibly unlucky, or someone else was in the woods and decided to put her to sleep for a while and knew how to do it cleanly."

When the paramedics were gone, Perez walked back inside the house, thinking about what they had said.

Becca had a cup of coffee cradled in her hands and Maggie offered one to Perez. She thanked her and took the cup, her eyes watching Becca carefully. Perez was tempted to sit down, take out her notebook again and start questioning Becca directly now that she was conscious. But there was no point at the moment. If the woman wasn't going to be completely open and honest, she couldn't force her to tell the truth.

After finishing her coffee, Perez stood and thanked Maggie and Hank again and repeated that Becca should go to the ER to get a scan done.

"I will in the morning," Becca promised.

Perez nodded. As she was about to leave she turned to Becca one more time. "Just a word of advice Ms. Cartwright."

Becca looked up at her.

"Perhaps next time you decide to go into the woods at night, either take someone with you, or don't go at all."

Letter #2

My Darling,

Chicago is cold and gray today. I'm sitting here in a café, rain beating off the window panes, watching people outside, bundled up, heads down, scurrying like rats along the sidewalks. The city is just a mass of depressing cement streets and an icy flurry of leaves. Everything about this place matches the melancholy I feel right now. Depressed, desolate, and empty.

Christ, it was only two weeks ago we were on Nantucket with the warm sun beating down on our backs, soft sand under our feet and the air fresh and salty. I miss being there right now and I miss you.

It was a wonderful week we spent there. I wish it was longer. Those long lazy afternoon walks we took hand in hand along the deserted beach out to that lighthouse. How we huddled together under the bed covers on those cool nights creating our own heat. How we drank wine sitting on that old picnic bench in front of our small cottage, watching the sunset, with the seagulls spiraling above, my arms wrapped around you, nuzzling your hair, the smell of the ocean on your neck. It seems like a lifetime ago.

It was the best week of my life, not because of where we were. I know it was so romantic, so removed from everything else. I wanted to surprise you, steal you away for a week. I want you to know that it was the best week of my life because you were with me, in my arms, in my dreams, in my bed, under me. I never wanted it to end. It's how things should be between us. But yet we have to go back to work. Too quickly we get caught up in the daily grind, but I won't forget that week with you.

I've got a week here at this stupid conference. It's only been the first day and already I hate this place. I hate this town. I hate the weather. I hate the people. Most of all, I hate being away from you. I miss you and miss the time that we had together on Nantucket. So much so that I'm already planning our next trip away together, just the two of us. The thought of it is the only bright light in this otherwise dreary place.

Until then I have to act like a grown-up and not like a spoiled little child. You know, suck it up and try to enjoy the drudgery of this place.

On the flight out I stared out the window at the clouds, thinking back on what we had done on Nantucket. Those cold misty mornings, the shoreline shrouded in fog. How we would make love under the blankets in a sleepy haze until the sun came up and burned off the fog, turning the day into something bright and beautiful, just like you. I know it sounds corny but it's how I felt, still feel.

I still laugh about that old couple along the beach that day. Christ, we must've given them a real shock! I honestly thought the beach was deserted at dusk that no one would be around, that the little hidden place among the dunes we had found would be secluded. When you laid out the picnic blanket, took my hand, then pulled me down to you, imagine my surprise when I realized that under your dress you had no bra or panties on.

In that exact moment, I didn't really care who saw or heard us. We could have been lying in the middle of a football stadium during the Super Bowl and I wouldn't have heard the noise of the crowd or seen a single face other than yours. It felt like it was just the two of us, the last two people on earth, making love for hours in the fading glow of the sun, to the crashing sounds of the waves until darkness covered us and the moon came out and shone down on us.

Pretty poetic huh? But it's a memory I will never forget. I don't have to die to go to heaven. You make me feel so alive that it feels like heaven has come to me!

It makes it all the much harder now when you're not with me. What about that little beachfront restaurant we stumbled upon? How good was that! And that table out on the terrace overlooking the ocean where we sat under paper lanterns with the stars above. I don't think I once let go of your hand the entire evening. I couldn't care who was watching us, but I knew people were, wishing they were as much in love as we are. I'm sure men were staring at me thinking "who's that lucky bastard?" And I am lucky. I'm the luckiest man alive to have you.

Christ I miss you! You're like a drug, my new addiction I can't get enough of. Right now it feels like I've hit an all-time low, like I've got withdrawal symptoms, stuck in this windy place going cold turkey.

I miss the time we spent together. Have I said it enough? LOL.

I hope you feel the same way. I'm sure you do. The things we did together among the dunes that night, and again in that tiny secluded rock pool we discovered on that hot day. Intimate, personal things that no one has ever done to me. Your hands, your mouth, your lips on every part of my body. Places and things that no woman has touched or ever tasted. I guess we're more familiar with each other now for you to do those kinds of things. That moment you took me, all of me, every last drop. No one has ever done that before. I want you to know that. No one, just you.

It was a selfless act that showed me how much you truly love me.

Always yours,
Michael xxx

Chapter 17
Haley Perez

The incident report was nothing remarkable, well written, concise, only the salient points mentioned.

Detective Marvin Richards had no idea how it had ended up on his desk, though. He wasn't the supervisor of the officer who had written the report, but somehow the report had made it into his in-tray for follow-up.

On the surface, the incident report seemed like the routine call out to a disturbance at a house in a gated community on Mill Point Road. However it was the last line of the report that caught his attention.

Taking the report, he got up from his desk and went in search of the author. He soon found her alone in the squad room sitting at a table writing in her notebook, a styrofoam cup in front of her, something black inside. She looked up when Richards entered the room. He saw her shoulders visibly tense, and she sat a little straighter in the chair.

"Have you got a second, Officer Perez?"

"Yes, sir," she said. Haley Perez was twenty-two years old,

came through as a cadet, obtained an associate degree in law enforcement, then was offered a probationary position as a police officer in the Uniform Patrol Division. She was the top of her graduating class, the only female in an otherwise all-male class. After that, she fell through the cracks, was assigned downtown on foot patrol duty and got quickly lost among policing jaywalking, parking violations, and community initiatives.

Maybe it was office politics. The senior police officer who was her supervisor seemed to take most of the exciting and interesting assignments for himself and passed the dregs he didn't want to deal with to Perez. That was understandable. She was a new officer, starting at the bottom of the ladder. Her mother was Puerto Rican, her father came from Colombia, and she had moved to the United States when she was twelve years old. Perez had pitch-black hair, which she pulled back in a tight ponytail, and striking hazel eyes that had an intense and mysterious quality to them. Her fellow officers said Perez was a loner, tended to keep to herself, didn't socialize with them after hours when they went out to the bar across the street, a place frequented by off duty officers. Some said she was abrupt at times, abrasive, behavior that could be misinterpreted as rude. Maybe it was just sour grapes, spread by a few officers who had struck out when they made advances toward her.

Richards sat down opposite her and placed the folder on the table. "It's about your report from last night. And please don't call me 'sir' Detective will be fine."

Perez nodded. She hadn't had much contact with the senior detectives in the Criminal Investigation Division, other than a cursory glance at best. "Is there something wrong with my report?"

Richards regarded her for moment. Truthfully he hadn't

really noticed Perez in the department until just then, even though she had been a uniform patrol officer for nearly twelve months. Even though her patrol area was downtown, last night someone called in sick so Perez found herself out on the road solo in a squad car in Ravenwood when the call came through. She was the closest mobile unit to respond to what seemed like a prowler.

Richards angled the report at her. "I just wanted to ask you about the last line in your report."

Perez gave a concerned look. She thought her report was thorough and complete, needed no explanation.

"You mentioned that this Rebecca Cartwright said she had slipped and fell at the back of her property, in the dark, in the woods." Richards looked at Perez over the frame of his glasses. "But you also mention in your report that you didn't believe her statement. Is that correct?" Richards could tell Perez was rigidly coiled like a spring.

"It was just a feeling I got, detective, when I spoke to the woman. It's all in the report. She was adamant that she slipped and hit her head on a rock or something."

"But you don't believe her?" Richards held her gaze. He could see indecision behind her eyes.

Perez looked at the pages of the report in front of her. No one had taken this much interest in any incident report she had written in the last twelve months. Her supervising officer just signed them off before tossing them into a file for safekeeping.

"Just instinct, I guess," she said. "Do you want my honest opinion?" Her hazel-colored eyes bored into Richards, unflinching.

"I expect nothing less," Richards said.

"I went back," Perez said.

"You went back and saw the woman again?" This was a surprise for Richards. Perez was certainly dedicated and thorough.

"Just a follow-up, not to see the woman. I went back to the scene, the hillside, this morning before my shift started." Perez left out the fact that there was a locked gate at the bottom of the hillside, so she climbed the fence. "I found some footprints near a drainage ditch about halfway up the hillside. Size eleven, probably a man's. They looked fresh."

Richards sat back for a moment. He didn't know what to make of Haley Perez. Other young officers wouldn't have given the incident a second thought. Put it down to injury by misadventure. And yet this young woman sitting in front of him saw something else. She bothered to go back and follow up because her gut was telling her something wasn't right with the scene or the statement that this Rebecca Cartwright had given her.

"A woman, late at night, taking a walk out in the woods behind her house didn't make sense to me," Perez added.

"So what do you think happened?" Richards said. "You think the woman is lying?"

"In my opinion, I believe she isn't being completely truthful."

Richards smiled. She had a lot to learn. "Get used to that fact. Everyone lies to us."

Perez just nodded.

"I spoke to the paramedics too, about her head wound. They believe she was deliberately struck on the back of the head. She went down the hillside at night, for some reason I haven't been able to determine yet, came across someone, and, again for unknown reasons, that person knocked her out."

Richards said nothing for a moment. Perez was observant, focused and strong willed. She had a determination about her. Street smarts.

Six months ago, there was a situation, a call out where she and a senior officer attended to a domestic dispute. A drunken man was holding a knife to his wife's throat in the front yard, threatening to kill her. Guns were drawn and they were ready to shoot him dead if they could get a clear line of sight. More officers arrived and soon there were four squad cars, lights blazing, crammed into the narrow street. Richards had read the report. The situation was slowly escalating out of control and the officers didn't want to shoot the man but they would. Perez then took it upon herself to holster her gun, calmly approach the man to convince him to put the knife down, which he eventually did. The police arrested the husband, and no one had been shot. And yet somehow Richards couldn't understand why Haley Perez has been overlooked, and was still stuck on patrol duty.

"So if you disturb an intruder or a stalker on your property, why cover it up?" Perez asked. "Why lie to the police?"

"Exactly," Richards said. "She has something to hide."

Richards placed the incident report back into the folder, stood up and looked down at Perez. "Thank you." He nearly made it all the way to the door.

"Detective."

Richards turned and looked back.

"I'm sorry if I did something wrong. It is private property after all, the gated community up there."

Richards just smiled. "Don't ever apologize for taking initiative. You did good to follow it up. It's not an issue of what is right and what is wrong." Richards turned to walk out when Perez spoke up again.

"Detective, one of the residents up there, the Vickermans, I believe. They have a son."

Richards stopped again, unsure of the relevance.

However what Perez said next made his blood turn cold. Something that wasn't mentioned in her report. "And his name is Adam."

Chapter 18
An Offer

They sat in a twenty-four-hour diner across the street because the coffee was better there. That and the fact that Richards needed to get out of his small office. He was feeling slightly claustrophobic and was never one for sitting at a desk for long periods of time, surrounded by shelves crammed with fat files, the floor space fighting a losing battle with storage boxes.

He was a beat cop at heart who had risen through the ranks to detective only after paying his dues in man-hours spent knocking on doors and wearing out shoe leather on the sidewalks, grimy streets and trash strewn alleyways of Lower Manhattan.

They say New York cops have strong leg muscles from all the stairs they have to climb in apartment buildings with no elevators when they canvas the neighborhoods, going door-to-door asking people if they saw or heard anything.

Despite his old-fashioned approach to policing, trolling through social media sites for clues about the victims and possible perpetrators was nothing new to him. What was new to him, however, was a rookie cop doing it on her own time based on a hunch about a case that she wasn't involved in or knew anything about other than what was reported in the press.

"So tell me about Facebook," Richards said. He was content to drink coffee, sit back, and just listen as Perez explained the method to her madness. He concluded it was either that or she simply had too much time on her hands after her shifts ended.

Perez explained how, after she left the scene last night, she went home and did some digging on Facebook. She wanted to know more about Rebecca Cartwright, but she ran into a dead end. There was no Facebook profile for the one living on Mill Point Road in Ravenwood. "What sort of person doesn't have a Facebook page?" Perez asked. She had one, but it was private.

"Me," Richards replied.

Undeterred, Perez then did a search on Maggie Vickerman and was directed to her Facebook page. It was there, on her public timeline that Perez saw numerous shared posts from her son, Adam. Perez explained that in the past few months Adam Vickerman was backpacking through Europe and the United Kingdom and had posted every few days on his own timeline pictures of tourist attractions where he was. "It was only through his mother sharing his posts on her timeline that I was able to determine that she had a son called Adam," Perez explained.

"There are plenty of men around town with the name Adam," Richards said. "And as you said, Adam Vickerman is overseas, traveling around Europe."

Perez was silent for a moment. It was not a secret that all the victims of the Eden Killer were named Adam. It was a tenuous leap, but Perez thought she should at least mention it.

Richards could see it in her eyes, that troubling glimmer. She slid out her cell phone and began scrolling down the screen. She handed it to Richards. "The son has a public Facebook page, meaning anyone can see what he posts on his timeline."

Richards took the phone and began to slowly scroll through the various posts and photos. There were photos of the Eiffel Tower, Buckingham Palace, Tower of London, what looked like a German beer garden, the glass pyramid outside the Louvre Museum in Paris. There was a photo taken of Piccadilly Circus crammed with tourists sitting around a famed statue of Eros.

Richards continued along the timeline. The River Seine. Notre Dame Cathedral, parts of the roof charred and burnt. Mona Lisa hanging on the wall above a sea of heads.

Richards frowned, his finger pausing for a moment before scrolling forward then backward again.

Perez smiled. He had noticed it too.

He looked up at Perez.

She gave a slow nod. He had worked it out, seen what she had seen. Or more importantly, seen what wasn't there. A good police officer needs to be a good observer, and being a good observer is more than just trying to spot a face in the crowd, or looking for something odd and out of place. It was also about trying to spot what was missing from the scene in front of you. Something that should be there.

"Plenty of photos," Richards said, his voice slow and deliberate. It could be nothing, just a coincidence. But like Perez, Richards had the same tingling feeling in his gut, that suspicious intuition that separates an average cop from a good one.

Perez leaned forward. "But not a single photo of him, Adam Vickerman. It's all just scenery, monuments, tourist attractions."

Richards leaned back in the booth and thought for a moment. It may be something, or it may be a worthless chase. But somehow a little voice inside his head was telling him otherwise, to follow up on the lead, to see where it eventually ends. He gave the phone back to Perez.

"What about the footprint you saw up on the hillside, at the back of Rebecca Cartwright's property in the woods?"

Perez scrolled through her phone again and brought up the series of photos she had taken and showed Richards. Various footprint indentations in mud and soil, chunky pattern, perhaps hiking boots.

She certainly is thorough, Richards thought to himself as he studied the pictures. "So what can you tell me about the Eden Killer?" Richards asked, handing back the cell phone.

"Not much. Other than what's in the newspapers. And the fact that you are the detective heading up the case."

Richards studied Perez for moment. He saw in her eyes that spark of enthusiasm that belied her sometimes deadpan and overly serious demeanor. She was intense, there's no doubting that, and maybe she had fallen out-of-favor with some of her fellow officers because she didn't partake in idle banter or socialize with them. However what she had shown Richards today, made him look at her in a new light, not just a rookie cop stuck on downtown patrol, busting people for misdemeanors and issuing fines.

Tucking a few bills under his coffee cup, Richards slid out of the booth, and then extended his hand towards Perez. "Welcome to the team," he said.

Perez looked at his hand and felt a twist of excitement in her stomach. "I'm a rookie cop in the patrol division," she said.

"Let me worry about that. From now on, you're working on my team. Patrol officers are still required to investigate, without having to be a detective."

"How many are on your team?" Perez asked.

"As of now?"

Perez nodded.

Richards smiled. "Two."

Perez took his hand, her grip firm, uncompromising. Then she did something she hadn't done for a long time on the job.

She smiled.

Chapter 19
Cold Shower

It only took Becca five minutes of standing naked in the corner of the shower, with her hand under the stream of freezing cold water to realize that something was wrong with the water heater.

She tied a robe around herself, grabbed a flashlight and went down to the basement, cursing. The basement was dimly lit, and she made a mental note to replace some of the dead florescent tubes and install more lighting.

A few packing boxes were stacked against the wall and the water heater was hunkered down in the corner. Pipes ran out of the sides and there were levers to pull, and taps to turn but Becca had no idea what to do. It was stone-cold to the touch, inert, lifeless.

She went back upstairs, into the kitchen and found the handyman card that Mac had given her. It was stuck to the refrigerator.

It was just after 10:00 p.m. and Becca certainly didn't expect anyone to pick up the call. She was rehearsing what to say to a voicemail message when the call was answered just after the second ring.

"Hi, this is Josh." The voice was rough, gravelly but with a smooth edge to it.

"Hi, my name is Becca Cartwright—" Becca fumbled, not expecting the call to be answered this late. "I live up on Mill Point Road, and I think my water heater has died." In the background Becca could hear the sounds of a football game on the television. *Typical.*

"When did you last have hot water?" Josh asked.

She explained she'd taken a shower this morning and it seemed fine then. She was resigned to the fact that she would have to wait till tomorrow morning for the handy man to come out to take a look.

"You must be at Number 8? Garrett Mason's old house."

The question caught Becca by surprise. "That's right. I only moved in a few days ago."

"No problem," Josh said. "I can be there in about twenty minutes."

Becca subconsciously tightened the robe around her body. She certainly wasn't expecting the handyman to make a house call this late on a Sunday evening. "Are you sure?" she asked. She was certainly grateful.

"Yeah," there was a pause. "My team is losing anyway."

She thanked Josh, ended the call and dashed upstairs to change.

Exactly twenty minutes later, Josh buzzed her intercom from the gatehouse and she let him in. Moments later came the throaty roar of a large pickup truck pulling into her driveway.

She was expecting a gray-haired, cranky, gruff man, weathered and old. But when she opened the door, what she got was a young, tall, good-looking man with blond hair and the bluest eyes she had ever seen.

Josh Daniels stood in her doorway, six feet tall, lean and powerful looking, broad shoulders, tanned forearms, just the right amount of muscle hardened from manual labor rather than pumped up gym bulk. A large red steel toolbox held by one hand completed the picture.

Josh looked at Becca with those deep blue eyes and for a moment she forgot what he was doing standing at her front door. Becca fussed with her hair, wishing she had taken the time to run a brush through it and at least apply some makeup even though it was foolish, girlish, and out of character for her.

Josh offered a warm smile. *He was too good-looking to be a contractor,* Becca thought, and he certainly didn't look like any contractor Becca had ever met before. Not that she had met many. It was Michael who usually took care of things like that, doing odd jobs around the house and contacting handymen when required.

Becca followed Josh down to the basement and he quickly got to work with smooth and rapid efficiency, prodding, poking, turning valves, and checking pipes, his strong hands grabbing wrenches and screwdrivers from his toolbox.

As Becca watched him work, a mental checklist began to form of other jobs that needed Josh's attention around the house in the coming weeks.

"The thermostat is busted," Josh said, looking up.

Becca said nothing for a moment, her mind elsewhere, her eyes lingering over Josh's butt as he bent over the base of the water heater. Then she said the only thing that a woman could say when told that the thermostat of her water heater was broken. "Can you fix it?"

"Luckily I've got a spare one in my truck. It'll take me just a couple of minutes to swap the old one out."

Becca offered Josh a cup of coffee and he accepted. While he went out to his truck to grab the new part, Becca went upstairs to the kitchen and turned on the coffee machine. Ten minutes later they were both standing in the basement, drinking coffee and watching the water heater as it slowly ticked and hissed, heating up again.

"How hot do you like it?" Josh asked as he adjusted the dial.

Becca stared blankly at him for a moment.

"The water, how hot do you like your showers?" Josh waited.

"Oh—" Becca spluttered with a mouthful of coffee. "I prefer really hot showers."

Josh nodded and set the thermostat to one hundred forty degrees. "So how do you like living here on Mill Point Road?" Josh started packing up his tools and double checked the thermostat one more time to make sure it was working properly.

"It's very peaceful and quiet," Becca replied. She still couldn't get over how Josh Daniels looked. She was certain he was close to the same age as her, maybe a smidgen younger.

Josh flipped the toolbox shut and turned to Becca. "You seem different from everyone else."

Becca gave Josh a puzzled look. "Different? How so?"

Josh shrugged and drank his coffee. "Well by now I'm sure you've met all your neighbors. I do most of the handyman work around here, have been for more than five years." Joshua looked around the basement.

"I see," Becca said thoughtfully, wondering if Maggie Vickerman had gotten her cougar claws into him already.

"Didn't do much work for Garrett Mason, though. He tended to keep to himself." Josh frowned and walked to one of the walls. He stared at it for a moment, running his hand over the plain surface.

"What's wrong?" Becca asked as she stood beside him.

"Looks like he had some dry rot, some water damage as well. This piece of drywall looks new."

Becca glanced around. The walls all looked the same to her; then again, she didn't have a handyman's eye.

Josh shrugged it off and turned his attention back to Becca. "You seem different—nicer."

Becca smiled, more than happy to take the compliment from him.

Josh continued, "I find most of the people up here can be stifling, a bit stuck-up at times."

"How do you mean?" Becca asked.

"You know, pretentious. I guess you have to have a lot of money to live here."

"I don't really know everyone that well," Becca said. "I just met them."

"Maggie and Hank are a nice enough couple," Josh said. "Even if Maggie has tried numerous times to come on to me." Josh laughed.

Now why didn't that surprise Becca?

"Zoe and Jason Collins I don't really see that much. Fixed a few things around their house for them. They seem to be too much in love with each other, which is nice, but I find it a little gushy at times."

The more Josh talked, the more Becca liked him. Sure he was a bit rough around the edges, but in Becca's mind just the right amount of "rough" was a good thing. Too many men these days were a bunch of sissies, grooming their hair or slurping down kale smoothies.

"You gotta be careful of Sabine, however," Josh said. "She can be a real shark."

Becca had a fair idea about Sabine Miller: ambitious, pretentious, self-obsessed, and used to getting her way. Maybe that explained why Maggie and Hank had invested money with Mark's investment firm. Paige had warned Becca it wouldn't take long for Sabine Miller to come calling on Becca as a likely candidate.

"She's a slick operator," Josh said. "Before you know it she'll be hitting you up to invest in her husband's investment firm. Sabine hit me up a few times but I'm a simple person. I don't understand financial markets or how stocks work. I just keep my money in the bank. I find it is the safest place these days."

"What about Paige and Scott?" Becca asked. "I like Paige, I think she's honest and everything is black and white with her."

"I agree," Josh said. "They seem like a nice enough couple. I see Paige around town but I rarely see Scott that much. The wives around here seem to stay at home and spend their husband's money." Josh laughed. "But I think Scott just lives off Paige's money. It is just a feeling I get."

He certainly had a direct way about him, Becca thought.

Suddenly Josh drilled his blue eyes into Becca. "Is your husband not home today?"

"I'm not married," Becca replied. "Actually, I'm the only single person on Mill Point Road."

"I guess that's why you're different," Josh said. "But like I said, you seem nicer, more down-to-earth than the others."

"How can you tell from only knowing me for a few minutes?" Becca asked dubiously. "You must be a good judge of character."

Josh gave a mischievous smile that Becca liked. Confident too, she mused.

He tilted his head, making a show of appraising her. "I usually get a good vibe about people when I first meet them.

Either I like them or I don't."

"I might be a bad person," Becca said. "I might be a serial killer. Or a murderer."

"I doubt that," Josh said, looking at Becca seriously for the first time. And he liked what he saw: short raven black hair, petite, five three, she came up to his chin, intense hazel eyes that could turn fierce in a heartbeat he guessed, narrow waist and hips, doll-like. He stole a quick glance at her breasts. Not much up top, too much silicone already in this community. But somehow it worked for her, and Josh found it unusually appealing. Becca wasn't pretty in a made-up way, more alluring though, how she held herself, the way she stood, confident but not aggressive. He could crush her like a flower in the palm of his hand. Definitely not a serial killer.

Josh handed Becca his coffee cup. "Thanks for the coffee."

They stood on the porch for a moment. The street was quiet.

Josh slid out his cellphone. "Give me your email address and I'll send you the bill."

Becca rattled off her contact details. "I suppose there's going to be some huge call out fee for this?" she said with a fake smile.

Josh punched the last of Becca's details into his cell then pocketed it. "Of course," he said. "I was sitting at home watching the football game on TV looking forward to having a few beers when you called."

Becca couldn't tell if he was joking or not.

Then he smiled that confident smile again. "But coming here was far more entertaining than watching grown men bashing into each other," he said before turning and walking down the porch steps to his truck, leaving Becca standing there deciphering what he had just said. Was it a compliment or was coming here to fix her water heater just slightly better than boring?

Becca watched him back out of the driveway before the truck disappeared down the hill. She turned to go back inside then noticed movement in Mark and Sabine's house next door. The blinds in an upstairs window were parted, fingers poking through, a shaft of light cutting out into the darkness. Slowly the blinds closed as the fingers withdrew.

Becca went inside and closed the door, looking forward to having, at last, a nice long hot shower before going to bed, with thoughts of a blond-haired, blue-eyed, good-looking man on her mind.

Chapter 20
Perez's First Task

It took less than twenty-four hours for the paperwork to be done and signed off. It was more like a temporary transfer; Perez didn't relinquish her patrol duties entirely.

Instead she was now required to split her time between uniform patrol shifts and more in-depth investigative work for Richards. To make it easier, her patrol area was shifted from Hagerstown to within the city limits of Ravenwood itself, closer to where the crime scenes were for the Eden Killer case.

Her supervising officer was glad to see the back of her. He complained to Richards that she lacked tact and finesse around her fellow patrol officers, and she displayed an air of superiority, like she was better than everyone. Perhaps she was. She wouldn't be missed in the downtown patrol. Budgetary cutbacks together with a newly installed CCTV camera system meant less feet on the ground were required around the city streets. *A sign of the times*, Richards thought. Either way, Perez now reported directly to him as her supervisor.

There was a backlog of cases in the Criminal Investigation

Division, and for the last two months, Richards had been pushing the powers that be for additional resources so he was happy to take Perez, even if she was a first-year officer. Somehow he felt, based on the initiative she had shown so far, she wasn't going to hinder the investigation or burden him with constant hand-holding. Her talents seemed wasted in the patrol division; she just needed something more challenging. So for her past sins and because he was more than a little curious, Richards decided to throw her in the deep end to see if she could swim.

To bring her up to speed, Richards gave her full access to the case files on the past victims. Perez eagerly poured over them, not just during work hours, but during every spare waking moment she had.

She was also tasked with making discreet inquiries with local utility companies, to see if any of them had carried out recent work up on the ridge along Mill Point Road. But there had been no work orders in that location for more than three months. Anyone who had been up on the ridge the other night was either a resident or an intruder.

Richards didn't want to arouse suspicion with the residents, so no direct queries were made to Maggie and Hank Vickerman about their son, and Rebecca Cartwright was left alone as well.

It had been twelve months since the first victim had been discovered.

Adam Bailey, a twenty-two-year-old worker from a local water treatment plant, and they were no closer to finding who the killer was. The MO was the same with all four victims: death by asphyxiation. All were young men aged under twenty-five. All had been bound, as evidenced by ligature marks on their wrists and ankles. There were no signs of sexual assault, torture or mistreatment. Just abducted, plucked from plain sight, usually in public places, held for a period of time, usually three to four days, then killed within a twenty-four hour period prior to being dumped according to the county coroner. The locations where the bodies had been found were not well hidden, like the killer wanted them to be found sooner rather than later, a statement being made. No grave, no ground coverage, just dumped like trash.

Adam Bailey was hog-tied with cable ties and dumped in a wooded area behind a cluster of picnic tables in Greenbrier State Park, four miles northeast of Boonsboro and three miles east of Ravenwood where he lived.

Adam Thurston was a twenty-one-year-old who worked as an associate at a Wal-Mart Supercenter. His body was found covered in trash and rotting food scraps in a dumpster in an alleyway behind a bar and grill in Funkstown, five miles west of his home in Ravenwood. The rats had taken their toll on his body according to the county coroner. He'd been inside the steel box for almost a week, and it had been a particularly hot, oppressive week.

Adam Drake, a twenty-four-year-old black man with a diploma in Hospitality Management, worked as a duty manager at a Courtyard Marriott in Hagerstown and lived in San Mar, a small community one mile north of Ravenwood. His body was found among the scrub in the woods near a soccer field, four miles northwest of his home.

And so for her penance, Perez was given Adam Teal.

Chapter 21
Adam Teal

Adam Teal was the latest and youngest victim, a nineteen-year-old college freshman who attended Hagerstown Community College.

Adam was studying for his associate degree in Teaching in Early Childhood Education. He had two younger sisters and a younger brother, and according to statements given by his distraught mother, Adam was the hub of the family who doted on his younger siblings.

Marvin Richards went with a uniformed police officer to Adam Teal's mother's house to tell Valerie Teal that her son, who had been missing for three days, was found by a jogger, bound, strangled and left in a ditch on the side of the road within sight of her driveway.

Scattered around the living room of the Teal family home in Beaver Creek, a small community three miles north of Ravenwood with a population of three hundred, were framed pictures of the family. Richards noticed that Adam, the eldest, took center stage, his arms wrapped protectively around his other three siblings. He was a good-looking kid with blond hair, blue eyes, and a smattering of freckles around his nose that hadn't faded despite him flourishing into a tall, broad-shouldered young man with a warm mischievous smile and smoldering eyes.

Richards imagined Adam Teal would have attracted his fair share of attention from the ladies, young, old, single, and married. It didn't matter. However, Adam Teal had drawn the attention of someone else, a predator who had been attracted enough to stalk, abduct, restrain, then murder the young man. It was now up to Richards, with the aid of Perez, to find out who that person was.

Through tears and heartache, Adam's mother had told Richards her husband, Adam's father, had walked out on them soon after their youngest daughter, Connie, was born.

Richards sat on a well-worn sofa in a plain living room with wood-paneled walls. From observing his surroundings, Richards got a sense of who Adam Teal was. No words were needed, no explanation required. To his siblings and his mother, Adam had assumed the role of absent father and husband, and for that, the loss was made even more distressing.

As well as completing his studies at community college, Adam had a part-time job at one of the local outlet centers where he was a store associate. It was a job Adam had taken, not so he could earn money to waste on frivolous things, but to support his mother, brother, and sisters, Valerie Teal had said.

Somehow this tight-knit, unassuming family had built up resilience from enduring the adversity of Adam's father walking out on the family when Adam was just ten years old. Now that carefully built resilience was shattered by the senseless death of a son and brother.

Perez and Richards found themselves standing on the

shoulder of a small back road off Route 66, a few hundred yards from Adam's home in the small community of Beaver Creek. It was almost like the killer deliberately dumped his body here, within sight of the family home, taunting his mother and younger siblings.

Perez leafed through the pages in the folder she was holding. She was standing at the bottom of a small embankment in a narrow drainage ditch that ran parallel to Black Rock Road, a narrow ribbon of blacktop that curved around the northern perimeter of the Beaver Creek Country Club before doglegging to the left under the Dwight D. Eisenhower Highway. After his shift at the outlet store, Adam texted his mother that he would be staying at a friend's place that night and would be home in the morning.

The road was hemmed in on both sides by heavy woodland, breaking every so often to reveal open fields and modest houses that backed onto the road. In the distance you could hear the hum of the highway to the east.

Three days after disappearing, at around 7:00 a.m., a jogger pounding the blacktop where Black Rock Road met the creek of the same name came off the shoulder and down into the bushes near the drainage ditch to relieve themselves. It was then the jogger discovered the body of Adam Teal.

Marvin Richards stood on the side of the road looking into the ditch, the sun at his back.

Adam Teal was so close to home but never made it that fateful evening when his dreams of becoming an early childhood teacher were destroyed.

Shielding her eyes, Perez glanced up at Richards, a featureless silhouette framed by an endless blue sky. "This is the exact spot?"

The silhouette nodded, "Right where you're standing."

Perez searched through the photos in the file, until she found the right one. Fishing it out she positioned it in front of her, rotating it until it matched the background of the ditch, the contours of the land, the line of the scrub and height of the weeds.

Then she went back in time, picturing if she were standing in the exact spot, and then realized that the toes of her feet would be six to eight inches from Adam Teal's left shoulder.

She studied the photo some more. He was face down in the ditch, his head partially submerged in a mix of mud and shallow water, arms secured behind his back, cable ties around his wrists, skin scuffed red raw. Perez took a step back and to her right, and then rotated the picture like a gimbal. The background shifted slightly but the foreground—the photo she held in her hand—remained despondently the same.

Up on the top of the embankment, the featureless face of Marvin Richards smiled down as he watched Perez do the exact same thing he'd done a week ago. Richards had seen the body in situ, as intended by the killer. He had also returned here afterwards, as he had done with all the victim locations, crime scene photos in hand, alone, sometimes in the dark, recreating the moment the body was laid to rest.

The search for DNA, God's contribution to forensic science to exert some control over the Sodom and Gomorrah that mankind had regressed to, had proven pointless. The body was clean.

They found Adam Teal's cell phone shattered on the side of the back road a hundred yards from where they were standing. Someone had taken a hammer or rock to it after removing the SIM card. Richards doubted Adam Teal actually sent the final text message to his mother saying that he wouldn't be home that fateful evening.

Being young, social, and outgoing implied that Teal would've been active on Facebook, and that's where Perez intended to start her digging after she was done with this case file.

She climbed out of the ditch, stood next to Richards, then looked both ways along the road, taking in everything. Their car was parked a hundred yards away. The only instructions he had given her when he had handed her the folder was to tell him what she saw, envision the world through the eyes of the killer when he had dumped the body here.

Apparently Adam Teal had no steady girlfriend but a string of admirers according to his co-workers at the store where he worked and the group of college friends he hung out with.

The area around Beaver Creek was dotted with a litany of small Lutheran and Catholic churches, yet the Teal family was not religious. If in hindsight they had faith in God, they now had a reason to demand answers.

Richards wanted to show Perez this particular crime scene first, given that it was the most recent. Over the coming days, Perez would visit each of the other crime scenes alone to get a sense of the loss, develop a feel for the loneliness, and to fuel her belief in redemption. Richards would focus his attention on the other three victims, not Perez. They would meet daily to compare notes, dispel theories and to formulate motive and linkages between the victims. At the moment they had a debris field, scattered with the dead, bound and strangled bodies of young men and not much else. This anomaly was a clue in itself: the killer was meticulous, thorough, and highly intelligent and wasn't going to stop any time soon.

They spent the next half hour searching the banks on either side of the ditch, looking under bushes, pulling back weeds, Richards kicking stones and rocks with his feet in frustration.

The crime scene, like all the others, had already been thoroughly scoured for any clues, but Richards never stopped searching, looking, rehashing: habits he wanted to instill in his young apprentice, Perez.

On the way back, they passed a fly fishing store along Maple Road, a church spire in the distance, and the flying saucer shape of a water tower farther beyond.

"I don't want any special treatment," Perez said as she sat in the passenger seat watching the undulating landscape creep slowly by. "I know the department has a policy about minorities."

Richards glanced at her, the driver side window down, his arm resting out the window, one hand on the wheel. "But you are a minority," he said. Richards kept his eyes on the road ahead but could feel Perez glaring at him. Then he began counting off on his fingers. "You're intelligent. You have initiative. You're not rash to making judgments. You are devoted to finding out the truth. And you're impatient."

Perez's gaze softened at the string of compliments, not used to or expecting such words used to describe her.

Richards continued. "In my opinion, for these reasons, you are a minority." He turned and smiled at Perez. "Maybe not the same reasons you perhaps were thinking about."

Perez appreciated what he said and the mutual respect that was developing between them. Maybe at times she was guarded, a closed book. But she had reason to be. "But you're African-American," she said.

Richards slowly shook his head. She still had a lot to learn, to see things that weren't there. "I prefer black man," he said.

"Not a black person?"

Richards looked at her skeptically for a moment before

replying. "I'm pretty sure I'm a man last time I checked." He let out a sigh. "The only victims here, Perez, are the dead ones, and the living who we can still help. Just remember that."

Perez contemplated the advice as she stared out the window and the higher calling Richards was implying. To focus on the others, not yourself. "So where to now?" Perez asked.

Richards drummed his fingers hard on the steering wheel and thought for a moment. They had literally no clues in any of the four cases, and pressure from above was mounting. "I want you to do a deep dive into Adam Teal, pull apart everything we have so far."

He made a turn and headed back toward town.

Chapter 22
Rinse and Repeat

As the days flew by, Becca occupied herself sourcing more contractors, with Josh's help, to take care of the garden and how she wanted it to take shape.

There were shopping trips to furniture and housewares stores in Hagerstown and farther afield, all carefully orchestrated by Sabine Miller with the military-like efficiency of an invading force. With a Hermes Birkin handbag draped casually over one arm and clutching her cellphone, Sabine would go forth and conquer. There was no shortage of store associates who followed behind her like little lambs while Sabine pointed one way then the other at pieces of furniture and decor for Becca to consider.

Becca soon realized she had different tastes compared to Sabine. She still valued her sage advice but made her own decisions on the pieces she wanted. Sabine organized heavy discounts, which was just as well, given that Becca was more used to putting furniture together from Ikea.

Afterward they went to lunch at some high-end restaurant. There were more kisses on cheeks, acquaintances were introduced, leaving Becca wondering just how many people Sabine actually knew. Over homemade pasta and a glass of chilled white wine, they talked about Becca. Sabine seemed to be fascinated about her past life, what Michael had been like, where they lived, her job as a journalist and how she was coping on her own now. Subtly the conversation would steer toward Becca's financial position. Sabine voiced her motherly concern that Becca, given her sudden good fortune, needed sound financial advice. No guessing that she put forward her husband, Mark as the perfect candidate to guide Becca through the minefield of charlatans and con men who no doubt would try and part Becca from her small fortune. Becca did a good job of deflecting Sabine's curiosity as to the amount of the insurance payout, which was close to five million dollars.

Sabine told Becca she was envious of her in some ways; she was an independent woman with no "baggage" such as a husband or boyfriend.

Becca could only imagine what Sabine would be like if she wasn't married. She would no doubt have a string of lovers following her around almost as big as the network of friends and acquaintances she had already introduced to Becca.

Josh visited the house regularly, working through the list Becca had given him to progressively tackle. For a start she had him replace all the external door locks, something she didn't consider when she took possession of the property.

Gradually the house was beginning to take shape into a home, her home. It was a beautiful house, filled with beautiful but tastefully chosen pieces, not too garish or opulent, as perhaps Sabine would have liked. Where Sabine was into the overstated and obvious, Becca preferred understated, minimalistic but quality, supporting local manufacturers where she could.

She was also getting more comfortable with Josh, bringing her defenses gradually down with him, more than she had previously. What Becca liked most about Josh was that he listened to her, her suggestions and ideas about the house, without treating her like some dumb woman who didn't know anything about hardware, carpentry, or the wrong end of a power drill. Josh wasn't intrusive. He didn't take liberties. He always buzzed through at the gate of the enclave, even if Mac was happy to let him go on up.

And whenever he pulled in her driveway, he always knocked on the front door, even if it was ajar and he had a pile of lumber thrown over one shoulder. He always asked to come inside, requesting permission. Becca liked that. She had had enough of presumptuous men in the past.

Josh also respected Becca's privacy. He never asked or mentioned again about her past or why she wasn't currently married or why she didn't have a boyfriend. He just went about his work, efficiently and quietly.

He was all lumber, screws, moldings, power tools, and hard work that he delivered with a genuine smile and an attitude where nothing was too much trouble. He never swore, even when he missed a nail with his hammer and slammed his finger instead. Becca remembered that day distinctly, him standing in the kitchen dripping blood on her white Italian tile floor, his powerful frame towering over her as she stood in front of him, holding a dishcloth wrapped tightly around his hand, his bodily scent engulfing her, a spicy mix of sandalwood, sage, sweat, and sawdust. She felt safe, like he would protect her if needed.

There is something to be said about a man who makes things with his bare hands. Who could fashion beauty and functional shapes out of raw materials. Who scribbled measurements on lumber using a pencil, then did the calculations in his head without the need for a calculator, and whose daily office attire was not a stiff suit and tie, but an obligatory white T-shirt, dark jeans frayed and stressed from hard work, and a leather tool belt that he wore low-style on his hips like a gunslinger from the Old West.

Officer Perez dropped by unannounced one day to see how Becca was doing. They sat and drank coffee, while Becca assured the young police officer that she was fine.

Becca attended the daily coffee catch-ups with the other women when she could. It was good to listen to what was happening, not that much really did. Becca's popularity temporarily spiked when her misadventure in the woods at night was the only newsworthy item of discussion within the group. But that soon faded to the back page after a few days.

Maggie's son, Adam, and his latest Facebook updates he posted of his European travels took center stage, until Sabine in her inevitable way would hijack the topic of conversation and steer it firmly back to her and her wonderful life. Such as the surprise vacation Mark had secretly planned for her to the Bahamas to celebrate their wedding anniversary. Or the new vintage handbag she had bought for a steal after twisting some poor store assistant's arm, literally. Or how fabulous Mark's investment firm had performed the last quarter.

Listening to Sabine, Becca would feel a little envious. She had often said to Michael they should escape for a few days, take a vacation to an island or just relax on the beach or go sailing on the ocean. She longed to go out to Cape Cod, stay in a beautiful beachside cottage and visit Martha's Vineyard.

But Michael detested salt water and hated sand, said the combination gave him a rash. He much preferred staying at home, not spending the money. Mind you, one year he did surprise Becca with a weekend away to Hartford, the state capital. They stayed in a fairly modest bed & breakfast, visited Mark Twain's House and walked around some of the historical buildings and the Museum of Connecticut History, which had free entry.

Zoe would mention Jason, how hard he was working and that he'd been away a lot recently. Becca noticed Paige taking a particular interest in Zoe during these coffee catch-ups, almost like she was scrutinizing the woman, watching her out of the corner of her eye. On one occasion a small argument broke out between Zoe and Paige when they had gathered in Paige's kitchen. Paige insisted that Zoe should sit down around the table with the others. Zoe said that she preferred to stand. For a few minutes it went back and forth until finally Zoe relented just to keep Paige happy and sat down.

It was then Becca noticed Zoe grimace slightly as she gently settled onto the chair.

Paige shared with the group how she and Scott had been trying so hard to have children. Every day she would track her ovulation calendar on a pregnancy wheel she kept on her nightstand. They had been trying for three months, and she couldn't understand why she hadn't yet conceived. She was thinking of looking into in vitro fertilization if nothing happened after another three months.

Sabine just rolled her eyes; grateful that she and Mark had come to an agreement long ago, before they got married, never to have kids. Maggie would then get teary-eyed, thinking about her son and how much she missed him, and then the whole cycle would repeat.

Sabine would give Paige a subtle prod, to see if she and Scott had decided whether or not they were going to invest in Mark's firm, quickly pointing out how well Maggie and Hank had done last quarter. Maggie would nod, saying that she felt almost guilty as to how well their investments were performing.

What Becca found curious though, but never said anything, was that if Mark's investment firm was doing so well, according to Sabine, why Sabine still was constantly touting for new investors. Becca recalled from their shopping trips together where Sabine seemed to personally know every store owner, restaurant maître d', and store assistant. She would constantly ask them if they had decided if they were going to invest in Mark's firm as well.

And yet during all the past weeks, during all the coffee catch-ups, trips to the stores, and discussions with Josh about the work around her home, at the forefront of Becca's mind was finding out who had struck her on the back of the head that fateful night in the woods.

Chapter 23
Escapades

"I see Josh seems to be spending more time at your house," Maggie said, her tone tinged with envy. "You must be keeping him very busy."

This time it was Becca's turn to host the morning coffee catch-up. They all sat around her new kitchen table, a plate of cookies and raspberry muffins Becca had made took center stage in the middle of the table. Becca filled everyone's coffee, pausing over Maggie's cup "It's strictly a professional relationship," she said before topping her up. "He's very talented, great with his hands, done some amazing things around here."

"I bet he's great with his hands," Maggie mumbled into her cup, taking a sip of the coffee, somewhat jealous at seeing Josh's truck seemingly always parked in Becca's driveway and not hers. Maggie was almost tempted to take a sledge hammer to one of her walls and say it was an accident just so Josh could come by and fill up her hole.

Becca just smiled. Mind you she did enjoy Josh's company. It was nice to have a man around the house at times, even if he spent most of his time busily cutting, sawing, and nailing things.

Paige picked up a muffin, scrutinizing it to determine how many calories it contained. "Scott's lost interest in sex lately. I don't know what it is. He's either too busy or would rather watch Netflix at night. By the time he comes to bed, I've fallen asleep."

"What about kinky sex?" Sabine asked innocently. The conversation had somehow veered off Josh and carpentry to the sexual antics of everyone at home. "You know, spice things up in the bedroom. Not that I've had to resort to that with Mark. He's so fabulous in bed, we don't need to. He's a real Trojan warrior, can go at it all night. Never a dull moment with him."

Now why didn't that surprise anyone? Becca thought. Sabine always had to be better, have better sex than anyone else. No matter what the topic of conversation was, Sabine always had to one-up everyone.

"I think it's disgusting," Zoe added her two cents. "If you have to dress up or play games or use toys to entice your partner."

Everyone turned and looked at Zoe.

"Love should be enough. Jason and I love each other so much that we don't need to resort to anything else."

Sabine turned away for a moment and rolled her eyes.

Maggie scoffed at Zoe's remark about love and devotion. "All of you are too young, your heads full of love and lust and nothing else. Believe me, it'll soon wear off in all your marriages."

Paige let out a deep sigh, her shoulders slumped. "Scott used to enjoy sex, he practically wanted it every day. Sometimes twice a day."

"Half your luck," Maggie said, with a mouthful of muffin. "The last time I think I had sex with Hank, Roosevelt was in the White House."

Everyone burst out laughing around the table, including Becca.

"I bought some new lingerie the other day," Paige continued, her voice sullen, "I'm hoping it'll rekindle Scott's interest, the passion we had in the bedroom."

Sabine turned to Paige. "By the way, how's his new book coming along?"

"New book?" Becca asked.

Sabine kept her eyes on Paige. "Scott's a budding bestselling author, isn't he, Paige?"

Becca picked up on the slightest slither of contempt in Sabine's tone.

"How long has he been working on that one book?" Sabine continued.

Paige fidgeted, her discomfort obvious, her eyes not meeting anyone.

"Must be at least two years now?" Sabine persisted.

"He'll have it finished soon. He just isn't in the right frame of mind at the moment," Paige said defensively.

Maggie cut in quickly. "Hank can't seem to get it up," she said, coming to Paige's rescue. "Even with Viagra. Not the spring chicken he used to be."

There was another burst of laughter from around the table.

Sabine turned her attention on Becca, switching to what seemed like a pre-determined agenda she had in her head. "I guess there's no lover in your life at the moment?"

"To tell you the truth, I haven't really thought about it much lately. Since Michael's death, I really haven't had time to think about anything other than sorting out the estate, selling the house, moving here, and settling in." Becca was interested in Josh, preferring to keep that little secret to herself. "I don't need a man in my life at the moment; I'm busy enough without one."

"I guess you must miss Michael," Paige said a look of sadness and empathy on her face.

"At times I do miss him," Becca said. "He was fine in bed. A little fast though. Like he was in a rush."

Maggie gently touched Becca on the arm. "You don't have to talk about Michael if you don't want to."

Becca shook her head. "I don't mind talking about him, sharing some things with you all."

All eyes focused now on Becca as she spoke. "Like I said, he was just really quick and direct. No foreplay, just straight in for the kill." Becca looked at the sympathetic faces around her. "I like romance," she said. "A man who takes his time, is there for me and not just for himself."

Everyone sat silently, somewhat shocked at Becca's blunt assessment of her recently dead husband. They had only known Becca for a few weeks and during this time she was always slightly reserved, held back. Now she was sharing with them some of the intimate details of her marriage. She felt she had to if she was to gain their trust, share something about her that was relevant to the conversation, a trade.

"I definitely agree," Sabine said, once again trying to one better everyone else in the group. "Mark is just so considerate—"

"That's OK, honey," Maggie said to Becca, cutting in again, glaring at Sabine to just shut up just for once. "Sometimes men can be very efficient in bed. Hank on the other hand, I've forgotten more times than I care to remember the number of times I've gone to sleep waiting for him to do anything at all."

Everyone laughed again, except Sabine, who just looked sour-faced.

These women were certainly blunt in their conversations about what happened in the bedroom, Becca thought as she looked around the group. Sexual desires had been the source of a few

141

arguments between Michael and her. Michael wanted oral sex but Becca wasn't willing to perform it on him, felt that it was disgusting. He kept pressuring her, telling her that if she truly loved him, she would do it, all of it, right to the end. Typical man, justifying his own need in the name of love. If *he* truly loved and respected her, he wouldn't have kept pressuring her.

Becca smiled at Maggie. She liked Maggie. She had a way of diffusing a difficult conversation or an argument before it would escalate.

Becca noticed Sabine looking intently at Zoe when she asked her next question. "Kinky sex is fine, but what if it ever gets out of control? Like out of hand?"

"What do you mean?" Maggie asked.

Sabine looked around the group, before her eyes settled back on Zoe again when she spoke. "You know, if it gets too rough. Violent."

Maggie choked back a laugh. "Well, if Hank so much as raises a finger to me, I'll cut his balls off."

Another round of laughter ensued.

Becca watched everyone carefully. Zoe was the only one in the group who didn't laugh at Maggie's serious but somewhat crude comment.

"There's no room for domestic abuse at all," Paige added.

Becca continued to watch Zoe and noticed that Paige was looking at her too. Zoe just sat there, staring at her hands in her lap.

The atmosphere changed, an awkward silence seemed to descend around the table until Becca suddenly jumped up, her chair almost falling down behind her. "Anyone for more coffee? She carried the coffee pot back to the machine and refilled it again.

Chapter 24
Devious

Sabine adjusted her hips slightly and settled herself lower.

That's better.

"I think Jason is hitting Zoe again," she said.

"What makes you think that?"

Sabine tilted to the left. "Just a feeling I get. I think I saw bruises on her wrists the other day. Looked like someone's fingerprints, where Jason had grabbed her, the same type of marks I saw last time." Sabine let out a deep contented sigh, letting all the stresses of the day seep from her body.

"I spoke to him last time, remember Sabine?"

Sabine remembered. Jason said that it was nothing, that Zoe tended to get carried away at the gym, banged herself against one of the machines.

Sabine settled into a slow, steady rhythm, easing herself into it. She used to go horseback riding when she was younger. As a child it fascinated her how she could control something much larger and much more powerful underneath her with just the slightest movement of her hips, knees, and heels. For her, horseback riding was about being in control, making a beast much larger than you do want you wanted. To make it turn and change direction with just your knees, how applying the slightest pressure with your thighs would make it comply.

The skills Sabine had mastered at an early age transferred effortlessly into her adulthood. Men were just like horses, an animal to be tamed, to be broken-in by her. Then they could be manipulated, made to change direction, follow her simple non-verbal instructions all with the same subtle movements of her thighs, knees, and hips.

Sabine leaned forward slightly, and she found herself back in the saddle again as a young girl, moving up and down to the rhythmic beat of a thoroughbred under her.

The response was instant and she felt him growing bigger inside her, if that was possible at all. She pressed her knees harder into the plush, soft mattress, the hinges and brackets of the four-poster bed protesting. Probably the most stress the bed had been put under since it was purchased, she imagined.

Slowly she began to gyrate her hips, controlled circles from the waist down, resisting the urge to increase the pace until she was ready to.

"So you want me to speak to him again?" The voice was more strained this time.

Sabine bent forward, her hands against his chest, her sharp fingernails digging into the hard flesh.

He groaned in painful ecstasy. He was nearly there, near the edge, feeling that intolerable itch that couldn't be scratched; only the sweet release would bring him relief.

Sabine dug her fingers in harder, relishing in the grimace on his face. She increased her pace, lifting herself higher, faster rhythmic pulses, drawing it out of him. She preferred to do the riding, rather than being ridden.

The body under her tensed, his climax building, muscles straining, nerves stretching, his hands gripping and twisting the folds of the sheets, soiled and damp with their sex.

He then grabbed her breasts with both hands, pushing them together and then upward toward her throat, harsh and rough, stretching them to the limit of their pliability.

"Not so hard," Sabine gasped.

He eased them back, but still held them greedily in his fists. His neck tensed, the grinding unbearable, thrusting deeper and harder into her.

Then Sabine stopped. Sat perfectly motionless astride him.

Disbelief then anger flared in his eyes, anguish then pleading. "Bitch!" he hissed through gritted teeth. She always did this, tormented him, brought him to the brink only to pull him back from the edge at the very last moment.

Sabine smiled, enjoying his discomfort, the look of distress on his face, his fear that his building torrent would fizzle out into an unmanly dribble. She had him exactly where she wanted him, to know who was boss. Her, not him.

He glared at her, hating the games she played, how she derived some weird sexual pleasure out of teasing him. He released her breasts and moved his hands up and around her throat.

Sabine gave him a questioning smile. *Really?* Then she began to slowly move her hips again, rhythmically up and down.

The look of torment faded from his eyes, his head fell back, smiling once more. "You're still a bitch," he whispered, his eyes shut in blissful splendor.

Yes, I am, she thought.

"We don't have sex as much as we should," Sabine said,

watching him now, increasing her thrusts, feeling him growing inside her again.

"You know how busy we both are," he said, eyes still shut, his mind adrift. "I wish we could spend more time like this."

They both lived busy lives and spending time together like this was getting more difficult.

Sabine lifted her hips higher, his manhood almost escaping before she thrust back down again engulfing him. His face became more pinched, his body tensing again, his hips moving up and down in time with her movements.

Sabine reached behind her splayed buttocks with one hand, her fingers finding then closing around two bouncing orbs of dangling flesh. Taking both she squeezed and twisted them at the same time.

"Christ!" His eyes shot open as he cursed. The pain of ecstasy almost too much to bear. He was at the brink.

Sabine tilted her head, an amused smile on her face. She squeezed and twisted a little harder.

His back arched, slamming himself into her repeatedly like the pistons of an engine at full speed, the muscles of his neck bulging, veins of his throat popping under the skin.

Then he erupted, wrenched and thrashed about in a sweaty mess on the bed, his hips and groin convulsing. The copious flow finally receded and he collapsed into a blithering stupor. "You're the best. You're the best…"

Sabine, equally satisfied, rolled off him and collapsed onto the mattress beside his heaving body, his chest rising and falling with each breath he took.

A few minutes later he turned and looked at her. She lay there, like a cat preening, her skin smooth, toned, covered in a sheen of perspiration, a body honed for one purpose. "I'll talk to

Jason again," he said, thinking that's what she wanted to hear.

Sabine propped herself up onto one elbow and gazed at him. She dragged one delicate long finger across his damp chest, then slowly down his abdomen, tracing the groove of each cobblestone of muscle until her finger reached the flatness of the lower stomach.

She paused.

It's a good thing he had a good body and the manhood to match, she thought. Because he certainly had shit for brains.

Sabine leaned closer and stared at Scott Hamill directly in the eye. "I don't want you to talk to Jason Collins again. I'll deal with him."

Good, Scott thought. That suited him. He knew Jason Collins probably would listen to Sabine more than he would to him. "So what would you like me to do?" Sex with Sabine was always transactional. He knew her all too well.

Sabine's solitary finger continued south again, until it found something flaccid but still surprisingly large even in its resting state. Then her solitary finger was joined by her other three fingers and her thumb, as they encircled then grasped what needed grasping—tight. She glared into his eyes. "As I've said all along, I want you to talk to your dumb fucking wife and convince her to invest in Mark's firm."

Scott Hamill tensed. "I've tried, Sabine," he insisted. "Numerous times. But Paige won't budge. You know the deal. You know she controls the purse strings."

Sabine wasn't going to give up that easily. A door slammed in the face meant that she just needed to apply less subtle tactics, like kicking it in. Her fingers squeezed some more. "Then try a little harder," she said, her voice a little firmer, like the thing she held in her hand.

Scott squirmed with discomfort, yet he could feel his arousal coming on for the third time this evening.

"Tell Paige to get the money from her father," Sabine whispered, coaxingly. "After all, he did pay for your house, didn't he? I'm sure she has plenty of money to invest from her father." Sabine knew exactly what "the deal" was that Scott was referring to. Paige Hamill was the only child of fabulously rich parents. Her father was Senator Brooks. The family was old money from Boston who now lived on a sprawling beach-front estate on Long Island, equipped with a pool, tennis court, and one-hundred-eighty-degree uninterrupted views of the Atlantic Ocean, when their luxury sailing yacht wasn't moored at their jetty.

Much to Scott's feelings of financial inadequacy, which Paige's father often reminded him whenever they saw each other, her father had bought the house on Mill Point Road for them. A "wedding present" he had called it. More like a handcuff, Scott thought resentfully at first. The house was a constant reminder to Scott that he would never be able to provide for his wife in the style she was accustomed to when she was growing up. Even if Paige had insisted she didn't care about money. People who don't care about money tended to be people who had a lot of money.

Paige's father also provided a generous allowance to his only child. Then as time went by, Scott griped less, became comfortable with the regular deposits into their bank account, even if it meant being tethered to her parents for eternity. Scott reasoned if someone was willing to dish out money to support him and his wife, then so be it.

In reality, Scott Hamill was a failed author who was simply living off his wife's support from her parents, parents who desperately wanted to become grandparents. Paige shared this burning desire.

But little did Paige or her parents know that Scott had secretly had a vasectomy. He had told all this and more to Sabine over the years.

Quid pro quo. Something for something.

Scott wasn't going to let the gravy train end, especially since Paige's mother detested him immensely, said he would never be a success at anything, and couldn't even impregnate their daughter.

Scott believed he was only being kept around to sire their grandchildren. He had tried to get published, had sent all three manuscripts to every publishing house and literary agent on the East Coast. And had them all promptly rejected.

While he did truly love Paige, Scott had an addiction that she alone could not satisfy. That's why he had turned to Sabine and her likewise insatiable appetite for sex. Scott had been fearful that once he got Paige pregnant, her libido would drop, and once kids came along, it would dry up altogether. He wasn't willing for that to happen.

"Talk to her again, Scott," Sabine said. "Hank and Maggie have made a lot of money. You could do the same. That way you won't need to rely on her parents." She let go of him and sat up. "Maybe get her to draw against the equity in her home, invest that. You'll have it paid back in less than a year. Then you'll be independent, not be tied to her parents."

Scott looked at Sabine for a moment. She always seemed to know the right things to say. She was right. Hank and Maggie had made a heap on their original investment with Mark. Maybe it was an opportunity to be less dependent on Paige's parents, have some capital of their own. "I'll talk to her again, Sabine. Promise."

"I'm just looking out for you, Scott. I know how you must

feel." Sabine gave him a concerned smile, kissed him on the cheek, rolled off the bed and walked naked into the bathroom carrying her panties, and closed the door behind her.

Sabine took a wash cloth from the rack, rinsed it in cold water and wiped the concerned smile from her face. She then wiped herself down. She would take a shower when she went back to her own house.

She looked at herself in the mirror, and gave a smile to her reflection. Scott was a fool, a weak little man backed into a corner and living under the beck and call of his pathetic lazy wife, who was getting adult child support from her parents.

Sabine certainly enjoyed having sex with Scott. Mark, her own husband, was always too tired when he got home from work. He was incapable of satisfying her anyway even when he did occasionally try. Bless his little soul, and his other little parts. That didn't stop her from assuring him that he was the best lover in the world.

But Sabine had a higher purpose in sleeping with her neighbor's husband. She needed Scott to convince Paige to invest. It was too great an opportunity to pass up. Sabine knew that Scott and Paige would not regret taking that initial step, that the returns would be significant to them. But they only served as an appetizer to the main course that Sabine had in mind. If Sabine and Mark could provide credibility, prove to Paige their legitimacy, then introductions would be made to the wider circle of friends and family including Paige's parents. The locked doors of the fabulously wealthy would be suddenly thrown wide open. Then the real money would flow. It was Sabine's intention through Scott to get to Paige, for she held the key to the locked vault.

It was late, and Mark was staying in D.C. for a couple of days.

Paige had gone into town with some girlfriends to catch a late night movie and supper.

Sabine tossed the soiled wash cloth into the laundry hamper. She paused, thinking, her panties in her hand. She lifted the lid of the laundry hamper, it was half full. She gave a slight smile then lifted the top layer of clothing and placed her soiled panties underneath, closed the lid and went back into the darkened bedroom to the sounds of Scott snoring.

After a quick glance at Scott to make sure he was fast asleep, Sabine gently eased open the drawer of Paige's chest of drawers. Inside bras and fresh panties sat neatly folded. Sabine rummaged around then finally found what she was after. She lifted out a new white lace lingerie set that still had the tags on. She tore the tag off the frilly panties, slipped them on, and returned the matching bra to the drawer.

Perfect.

She quickly got dressed.

Under the cover of darkness, Sabine let herself out via the back door of the house and slinked back to her own house, confident that no one was watching her intently.

But on this one occasion, someone was sitting in the shadows, watching her.

Letter #3

My Darling,

I know it was a bit premature but I knew you would love him as soon as you saw him, I certainly did. Those big sad brown chocolate eyes, his floppy ears and cute button nose.

They said at the animal shelter he had been abused. I can't imagine who would ever do that to a dog. Most of his hair has started to grow back. But as I said when I brought him home, he's had all his vaccinations and they assured me he has a good temperament. Good with children too, which is important given our plans to start a family soon. I've always wanted a dog and as soon as I saw him I knew he was the one.

I know space is tight and there is no backyard for him to run around. But I know how much you like to get outdoors and run and go for long walks in the park. So now you can take him with you! I'll let you think of a name for him, and I'm sorry if I kind of dumped him on you, but I had to catch my flight.

He'll make a great guard dog, someone to keep you company while I'm away. Please don't be angry. I know I said I wanted to get a dog only after we bought a bigger place, but I get worried when you're home alone all by yourself, especially at night.

It will only be for a little longer I promise. Like I said, we have plans, you and I in the next few years. A big house, big family, and pets, maybe two dogs. I can see it all clearly in my mind. I know you prefer cats, but they can't exactly deter an intruder, can they?

How about when I get back we start looking for places? Homes, maybe acreage, nothing too big, otherwise I'll be spending all my time mowing the yard! I know you want a big house, so do I, plenty of rooms so we can fill them with plenty of kids. Christ, I can't wait!

It's nice here in Boston. Better than cold windy Chicago that's for sure! Went for a walk down to the waterfront last night and thought about how much I miss you.

It would have been great if you could have come too, but I know you couldn't get the time off work at such short notice. Work sprung this trip on me as well. I wasn't supposed to be going to this trade show, but Ritchie, the other sale executive I told you about, got sick, and I know the product so well so I guess I was next in line. Good thing too. I secured three big orders on the first day, so I'm expecting a big fat commission check.

Some great restaurants and bars are here in Boston. I feel depressed because everywhere I look I see other couples together, holding hands walking across the common, sitting snuggled together in the restaurants, enjoying each other's company. Maybe next time we can plan the trip together, give you some warning so you can take time off work and your boss won't get mad. I can't believe you have all this vacation leave accumulated and they wouldn't give you a couple of days off. Your boss sounds like a real prick, if you ask me.

Like I said, I'll be back on Tuesday, and I can't wait to see you. I'll bring you back a Red Sox T-shirt, or maybe this really sexy tank top and shorts set for bedtime that I saw in a store window today.

It will just have to be a surprise...

Love you always,
Michael xxx

Chapter 25
Cats -vs- Dogs

Something brushed against Becca's calf as she sat at the dining table with the other women at Zoe's house. Glancing down she saw a gray cat threading its way between her legs.

"Oh, don't worry about Sam," Zoe said as she set down a plate of muffins on the table. She promptly picked up the cat and placed him outside. "If I leave him inside all day he'll just sleep," Zoe said, returning to the table. She looked at Becca. "You don't like cats, do you? I can tell."

"It's not that I don't like cats," Becca replied. "It's just that I prefer dogs. They seem more loyal, their affection is unconditional. Whereas with cats you don't really know who actually is the owner and who is the pet."

Paige laughed. "I agree. My father has dogs and he treats them like family. Someone once told me that a cat is just an animal that lives in your house. Eats, sleeps, comes and goes whenever it suits."

The cat stood by the sliding glass door staring daggers at Becca, its mouth wide open in a silent scream of protest.

"I was thinking of getting a dog," Becca said.

Sabine gave a frown. "Too much effort. You know, having to take them for walks, feed them, clean up after they have pooped on someone's front lawn. Leave me out of it."

"Sounds like having a husband," Maggie said, bringing a bout of loud laughter around the table.

Paige agreed. "I spend my days cleaning up after Scott. It's like he just drops his clothes a foot from the laundry hamper."

"It's the same with Hank," Maggie nodded. "He tends to wear the same pair of boxers three days in a row. They practically peel themselves off him and run to the laundry hamper out of desperation." This brought another bout of laughter from the women.

Becca could relate. "No, seriously, I'm thinking of getting a dog. Nothing big, maybe something from the animal shelter."

"Did you have a dog before?" Zoe asked. "When you were living in Connecticut with Michael?"

Becca shook her head. "I've always wanted a dog. But Michael didn't like them. We certainly had a big enough backyard, it was huge, but for some reason he really didn't like dogs."

Zoe smiled and gave Becca a wink. "Try a cat. They are beautiful creatures. Sophisticated, regal, and arrogant, which I like. Maybe something happened to Michael in his childhood. Maybe he was chased or bitten by a dog."

"Not unless he didn't tell me. Then again he didn't tell me everything," Becca replied.

Paige tilted her head at Becca's comment. "Scott tells me everything. Even about his childhood, which I know were difficult years for him. We have no secrets."

Sabine gave a sudden, spluttering cough, choking on a piece

of muffin. "Excuse me," she gasped reaching for a napkin. "Swallowed too quickly."

Becca tried not to laugh at Sabine's impeccable timing. There was nothing in the gated community bylaws that said pets weren't allowed. But the backyards were not fenced so she would have to keep any dog indoors and then take it for walks. Becca didn't mind. She enjoyed being outdoors in the fresh air and the thought of finally owning a dog, a companion whose love, loyalty, and affection cost no more than a bowl of dried food and the occasional milk bone, appealed to her.

Chapter 26
The Letter

It was an easy enough mistake to make; the way the number six was typed on the envelope could have been misread as an eight.

The letter wasn't addressed to a person, just a company name; Bickwell Investments LLC, and was jammed in with Becca's other mail, a rubber band holding the tight bundle together. Quick hands and careless eyes back at the post office, she guessed for the error.

Becca stood in her kitchen, envelope in her hand, wondering what to do with the letter that should not have been in her mailbox, but in Sabine and Mark's mailbox instead. Big red letters on the envelope's corner glared back at her, a warning, like a red stop sign: "Urgent Legal Documentation inside - Do Not Ignore." The return address a postal box in Baltimore.

Placing the letter on the countertop, she poured herself another cup of coffee, the third for the morning, then returned to the envelope, curious as to what was inside. The envelope seemed to ooze bad news, the kind of letter that demanded your attention, gave you a slight sick feeling in your gut when you saw it.

Becca picked it up again, tapping it on her knuckles contemplating. Should she? After all, no one would know. It was an honest mistake, not her fault it was in her mailbox. She could always read it then reseal it and no one would be none the wiser.

She turned the envelope over and studied the back seal flap, a thin rind of unused glue still there, the seal flap moistened quickly then pressed down at an angle. There were no security slits on the flap, no chance of damaging or tearing the paper if she gently teased the flap back with her nail.

No one would know it had been opened, tampered with.

The urge was too much, the envelope practically yelling at her to open it.

So she did.

Placing the envelope flat on the counter, she worked her nail under the corner edge of the seal flap and slowly along its length. It would be a simple case of pressing down the flap again to reseal it, or perhaps apply a smear from a glue stick.

Inside were two sheets of paper folded into thirds, thick and creamy to the touch, the type of heavy bond paper used by prestigious law firms. There was an imposing watermark, company logo, and a Baltimore street address for the law firm of Cullen & Co.

Becca scanned the contents of the letter then read it a second time to make sure. There was no mistaking the legal phrases, the threats, the blunt warnings. The second page contained a list of people's names, almost thirty in total, strangers bound together by common financial pain and suffering.

Becca placed the letter back on the counter, and stared at it for a moment, almost regretting that she had opened it. As they say, a bell cannot be unrung.

She folded the letter, placed it back in the envelope, resealed it, making sure the flap stayed stuck down.

Taking the letter, she went outside, looked both ways to make sure no one was watching, then quickly cut across her front lawn to Sabine and Mark's mailbox near the curb.

Becca was about to slip the envelope into the mailbox when Sabine opened her front door.

Half bent over, Becca looked up and froze.

"Hi, Becca," Sabine called out to her.

Becca groaned and quickly stuffed the envelope through the slot. She stood up and smiled as Sabine slowly made her way down the path towards her, a puzzled look on her face.

Becca backed away from the mailbox.

"What are you doing?"

"Just returning some mail that accidentally was in my mailbox." Becca gave an innocent smile.

Sabine frowned, then reached down, unlocked the back of the mailbox and retrieved the only letter that was inside.

Becca's heart dropped. She was hoping there was other mail inside the box, that way Sabine wouldn't know which exact letter Becca had seen, the one with the legal warning stamped so clearly on the front.

Sabine looked at the envelope then glanced at Becca.

An awkward silence ensued. Sabine finally gave a forced laugh. "Just my luck," she said absentmindedly. "Probably some stupid magazine subscription I forgot to pay." Sabine paused for a moment, her eyes scrutinizing Becca, peeling away her innocent look one skin cell at a time. *Did you open my mail, bitch?*

Then she smiled warmly, "Fancy coming inside for coffee?"

"Thanks, but got some errands to run in town. Maybe some other time." Becca said a little too hastily, like she couldn't get away quick enough from Sabine's probing glare. God, the woman would have made a great interrogator.

Sabine didn't move. Her eyes narrowed, "Sure, maybe next time."

Becca retreated calmly but briskly across the lawn to her own front yard.

It was then she saw Jason Collins in his driveway on the opposite side of Becca's house. He paused when he saw her, like a deer in headlights, car keys in one hand, next to his car. He was dressed in a suit and tie, like he was going to work, a leather briefcase in his other hand. He just stood there, staring at Becca.

Becca gave a forced smile and waved. "Hi Jason," Might as well do the neighborly thing. She walked over and held out her hand. "I'm Becca," she said. "From next door," she added because he looked so perplexed.

Jason Collins didn't move, just stared at Becca's outstretched hand like he was uncertain what to do with it.

"Hi," he said, his voice low and awkward.

Becca could tell he knew who she was, probably from his wife, Zoe. Jason was of average height, fit-looking, short dark hair and dark eyes that darted every which way guiltily.

"Look, I've got to get to work, sorry," he said, abruptly ending the conversation. He quickly climbed in his car, started the engine, backed out then roared off in a hurry.

Becca stood there for a moment, watching him leave. She turned and nearly jumped out of her skin. Sabine was standing right behind her.

"Christ, Sabine, you frightened the hell out of me."

But Sabine wasn't looking at Becca, instead her eyes were watching Jason Collins' car as it drove down the street before vanishing down the hill toward the gatehouse. "Yeah, run you bastard," she spat, before turning back to Becca. "He beats her, you know?"

"You mean Zoe?" Becca asked, looking down the street after Jason's car.

"He's a cunning little prick. And don't be fooled by his timid little act. He's a narcissist that one, I can tell."

Becca smiled on the inside, thinking like recognizes like. But to Becca, Jason Collins seemed withdrawn, timid almost. Maybe it was an act.

"I don't know how he does it. Leaves no obvious facial marks. But I can tell, just how Zoe sits sometimes."

Becca thought for a moment. Zoe did seem withdrawn at times when they all met for coffee. There was also that incident when Paige had insisted Zoe sit down at the kitchen table with the others. Yet, Zoe flatly refused. Becca suddenly felt disgusted, imagining all too well what Jason Collins may have done to her so it was painful when she sat down. "Son of a bitch," Becca muttered.

Sabine smiled knowingly at Becca. She now had an ally. Sabine placed a hand firmly on Becca's shoulder, a little too firmly perhaps for Becca's liking. "We have to confront Zoe, Jason as well. Will you back me up?"

"Like an intervention?" Becca wasn't too keen to be roped into this. After all she hardly knew Zoe or what had happened in the past.

"Exactly," Sabine said, squeezing Becca's shoulder some more. "I've been telling Maggie for months, saying I think something's wrong with Zoe, that Jason is abusing her. But nothing changes, nothing happens."

"And?" Becca asked.

"Maggie just says don't interfere, it's personal, it's between husband and wife. I say bullshit!"

Becca agreed. Sabine may be a lot of things—arrogant,

manipulative, forceful—but she had a protective streak in her, to stand up for women's rights. Not that you wouldn't want to stand up for someone if you had actual proof they were being abused by their husband. "Have you mentioned it at all to Zoe?"

Sabine just scoffed. "I keep asking her if everything is OK without pressing the point. But she says everything is fine between her and Jason. You know most women won't admit to it, that they're a victim of domestic abuse." Sabine shook her head. "They prefer to be in an abusive relationship than no relationship at all. I can't understand it."

Sabine looked intently at Becca. "We need to stand together, we women, right this wrong. Paige agrees as well but she's too soft."

"I agree but—"

Something suddenly distracted Sabine. She looked up, past Becca's head, towards a window on the first story of Zoe and Jason's home.

Becca turned back and looked up as well.

Standing there at the window, looking down at them, was Zoe. No smile, no expression at all on her face, not even a wave or nod of acknowledgement.

Then she was gone.

Chapter 27
Sadie

It had been a disastrous day for Scott. He didn't want to write. No matter how hard he tried the white-washed computer screen of harsh bright pixels remained blank.

This had been his worst mental block he could remember.

In an effort to get inspired, he grabbed the car keys and trudged defiantly out of the house in search of inspiration to solve his creative constipation.

Twenty minutes later he found himself in his favorite sports bar in Ravenwood, perched on a stool, an icy cold beer in front of him, gazing up at a multitude of flat screens catering to every sport fan's taste imaginable.

He didn't usually drink in the middle of the day, but what the hell? Paige had gone out to the outlets in Hagerstown and wouldn't be back for a few hours.

Paige certainly had been in a strange mood this morning, unusually chirpy, Scott thought as he nursed his beer. For the first time in a long time she actually cooked him breakfast. Normally, he was left to help himself to a bowl of cereal or just a piece of toast. But not this morning. Scott woke up to the tantalizing smell of bacon and maple syrup wafting up the stairs and through the open bedroom door.

Staggering downstairs almost like he was hypnotized, he found Paige busily moving around the kitchen, apron on, spatula in her hand, humming a tune to herself. She waltzed over to him, gave him a quick peck on the cheek, before waltzing back to the cooktop to finish making his favorite: thick French toast, topped with bacon and a generous drizzle of maple syrup. She hadn't cooked breakfast for him, certainly not like this, in ages.

Scott had asked her what the occasion was. Paige simply smiled, looked at him lovingly, shrugged then told him how much she loved him.

Scott promptly sat down but kept one suspicious eye on her as she poured fresh coffee into his cup. Surely she wasn't ovulating again so soon? It just seemed like last week when she insisted they have sex, twice a day for a five-day stretch. Paige tracked relentlessly her twenty-eight-day menstrual cycle on a color-coded wheel chart. Scott no longer felt like a husband. In his mind he was now reduced to a dot on a carefully plotted chart, a stud-bull who was wheeled out to do his inseminating duties when the dial on the chart rotated to the appropriate colored segment labeled, "fuck now."

After a few minutes of watching her fuss over him, Scott gave up worrying. If Paige wanted to play adoring wife for the next few days then the stud-bull would oblige.

Paige topped up his coffee and slid another piece of golden brown French toast onto his plate with another serving of bacon.

Scott smiled back. Maybe she thought he needed the stamina for the next few days of mattress pounding.

Things were looking up. Maybe she finally was realizing how

valuable he was even if he wasn't earning any money at the moment. He was contributing in other ways to the relationship, or at least his manhood was.

And as he sat there at the kitchen table dressed in his pajama bottoms, and an old T-shirt, scruffy and disheveled, he had to agree with himself.

He was a fine catch. He snuck in a quick scratch of his balls while Paige's back was turned. Might as well get the puppies warmed up for later.

Scott sat contented and worked his way through the second serving of French toast, glad she'd finally come to her senses. What he needed to work on now were Paige's parents, to get Paige to convince them if they could borrow the money to invest in Mark Miller's investment firm.

Sabine had texted Scott last night, stressing the point yet again. Christ, did that woman ever give up? She was like a dog with a bone, bashing people into submission. But then after talking to Maggie Vickerman, Scott was convinced it was the right thing to do. After all, Maggie and Hank had made a ton of money from investing with Mark, and they had been in his fund for only a short time.

Scott wanted to prove himself, not that he lacked confidence. But he needed to prove his worth to Paige's parents, show them that he wasn't some useless would-be bestselling author free-loading off their daughter's allowance, wishing for the day she got her full inheritance. Paige was an only child and that was a good thing. More Benjamin Franklins for him and Paige.

Scott drained his beer and recounted more of the day so far.

So while the day had started out on a good note with breakfast, it quickly went downhill from there. Scott spent nearly an hour staring at his computer screen trying to find inspiration. Then he decided to do a few chores around the house, anything was better than being chained to his desk, trying to force the words out of his head and onto the screen. He desperately needed to get his book back on track. Somehow arranging his sneaker collection and lining up his pens and pencils on his desk seemed more important.

By noon he had found himself back at his desk totally uninspired. It was then he decided he needed a change of scenery, to get out of this claustrophobic house that seemed to be pressing in and around him on all sides.

There were only a few people in the sports bar, and Scott liked it here. It was like a giant man cave, something that Paige would never allow in the house. He felt safe here, like a gazelle drinking at a watering-hole, camouflaged among the dark wood paneling, exposed brickwork, polished brass, and subdued lighting with an endless row of tap handles to choose from.

Mind you, Sadie behind the bar wasn't bad to look at either.

That low-cut top she wore, stretched tight over her ample cleavage was something to behold. She probably wore it especially for him, Scott thought as he ogled her right now.

The way her fingers clasped firmly around the shaft of the tap handle as she smiled up at him as she slowly pulled a beer into a glass, coaxing the amber liquid out of the tap, all cold and frothy. She was a true artisan in flirting.

Sadie made a show of doing an extra-long pull of beer into a glass right in front of him, dipping her chest slightly lower, angling her breasts a little more toward him. A little peep show just for him alone.

She placed the beer in front of him. "Here you go, hon," Sadie said suggestively as she swapped out Scott's empty glass for the new one, full and frothy, with just the right amount of foam dribbling down the sides.

"Thanks, babe," Scott smiled, his eyes lingering momentarily on her breasts. She had no bra on and he could tell both nipples were pierced. He could clearly see two little barbells under the tight fabric. *What an exhibitionist*, he thought as he slowly drank his second beer, savoring the spicy taste, wondering what other piercings she had on her body. Maybe a little tinker bell piercing somewhere down below. Scott imagined himself bent over, his face buried between Sadie's thighs, making it jingle just with the tip of his tongue.

Scott knew he could fuck her if he wanted to. Most women wanted to when they met him, wives included. He could smell it on Sadie, the wanting. She had some scrawny thing of boyfriend, a bean-pole who was all tattoos, black clothing and greasy black hair. What Sadie needed was a real man, someone who could dominate her in bed, satisfy her, not some creepy tattooed-covered freak who had the body of a pre-pubescent boy.

Sadie moved away to serve another customer and Scott looked up at one of the flat screens. It was showing a rerun of last night's Redskins game. Yawning, he went back to drinking his beer, watching Sadie again as she went back and forth behind the bar, her gravity defying breasts bobbing up and down.

As if reading his dirty thoughts, Sadie turned and gave Scott a knowing smile.

Scott returned the smile. *That's right, you dirty bitch, you want me, don't you?*

An hour soon became two and before Scott knew it, it was past 3:00 p.m.

But he felt good in the afterglow of the alcohol. The words and the writing could wait for another day, another month for all he cared.

Scott managed to chat some more with Sadie, relishing in the attention she gave him. Different from Paige who only gave him her attention when she wanted something from him.

Sadie told Scott she wasn't happy with the boyfriend. Scott nodded sympathetically, trying to suppress his delight, and before he knew it, he was confiding in Sadie like she was his therapist.

He told her about the pressure he was under with Paige, how she desperately wanted to get pregnant and her plans to have three children.

Scott complained that his only purpose in life now was to impregnate his wife, to provide her parents with grandchildren. Sadie nodded in sympathy. "I couldn't think of anything worse," Sadie agreed. "Knee-high in diapers and baby poop. All that dribble and effort."

This was the first time Scott could tell someone how he actually felt. Not just his usual griping, but reveal his deeper feelings. Sadie was the first person who understood him, the difficult situation he was in. Paige wouldn't understand. She was too caught up in her perfect house and her perfect garden and her perfect kitchen cabinetry. Now she wanted perfect children to go along with the whole façade.

"Despite all this," Scott slurred, bolstered by his fifth beer, "I'm still loyal. Never once have I cheated on her."

Sadie gave his hand a squeeze. "You're a good man, Scott. A great catch. Loyalty is a rare commodity these days."

Scott stared at her for a moment, her firm heaving chest, her pouting lips, her flirty eyes. He could feel himself getting aroused, more now than he had ever felt with Paige in the last few months. *Jesus*, Scott thought, looking at Sadie. *She really gets me.* Scott wanted to fuck Sadie here and now, hoist her up onto the bar among the pretzel crumbs and spilled beer and pound her senseless.

Sadie broke off and went to serve another customer.

While she was gone, Scott began to make a mental list in his head of all the things he disliked about Paige. How she was flat-chested. Her pale translucent skin. Her obsessive compulsive disorder with neatness and order around the house. How she scrunched up her nose in disapproval when Scott suggested oral sex. Scott was pretty sure Paige had never experienced an orgasm. No matter how hard he tried. No matter how many times he went down on her against her objections to the point of where his jaw and tongue went numb.

Maybe she was immune, inert to the normal sexual yearnings women had. It wasn't that Paige was shy, she was just insecure about her own sexuality, and it was really beginning to annoy Scott.

He checked his watch. Maybe he should go home now.

Scott slid off the barstool, and felt instantly woozy. He hadn't eaten anything since breakfast.

"You all right, Scott?" Sadie asked, returning to him.

"I'm fine." He told Sadie not to worry and thanked her for listening. She said anytime. He paid his bar tab in cash so Paige wouldn't find out then slipped a twenty dollar tip to Sadie. She promptly slipped him her cell number scribbled on a napkin and mouthed the words, "call me."

Full of confidence and beer, Scott found his way to the restrooms and doused his face with cold water.

Maybe it was time to taste the delights of more women, not just Sabine, he thought to himself as he looked in the mirror. He gave himself a once-over then gave a cocky nod, pointing his gun-shaped hand at his smiling reflection, clicking his tongue as he mockingly shot himself. Then he assumed a headmaster's haughty tone. "Life's a smorgasbord, son, and you've been eating the same meal every day. Time to sample the other dishes on the menu."

There was one tasty dish he wanted to sink his teeth into right now. He pulled out the folded napkin and looked at Sadie's cell phone number. She was a very tasty dish delivered straight to his door.

With his mind made up, he carefully folded the napkin and slid it back into his pocket.

Sadie was going to be the first new dish on his menu. And he intended to eat as much as he could stomach.

Chapter 28
Chugga Chugga Choo Choo

Scott closed the front door behind him and was greeted by the haunting breathless voice of Norah Jones, and a sweet smell of spices wafting from the kitchen.

Definitely ovulating.

That's why she had been so nice to him this morning, cooking breakfast and fussing like a bitch in heat. And now she was busily chopping, sautéing, browning, and stirring in the kitchen preparing a lavish meal. Scott's shoulders slumped, resigned to the fact that Paige's niceties correlated with her charts. Maybe he could feign impotence just for one night? Throw Paige's carefully crafted plans out the window?

Or maybe he would surprise her tonight when she least expected it. Add his own little pinch of spice to an otherwise bland and boring dish—flip her over onto her stomach and thread a different eye of the needle instead.

Scott gave a devious little smirk. Certainly would shock her. Prude bitch.

Standing tall and putting on his best "honey, I'm home" face he strolled toward the kitchen.

Paige was floating between the island counter and the stove, hair pinned up, apron wrapped around her, looking like Martha Stewart.

Scott paused, leaned against the wall, trying to hide how used he really felt.

"Hi, babe," Paige said, just a little too bright and perky. "How was your day?" She jutted out her bottom lip and blew at a loose strand of hair from in front of her eyes.

"Got a great start on a new book this morning," Scott lied. "Wrote about five thousand words. The book's coming along great."

Paige moved to the chopping board and was facing him, knife in hand ready to slice and dice some more. "New book?" She gave a look that best could be described as amused puzzlement.

"What happened to the one you had been working on? You know, the story about the man on a bus who had seen something—murder I think you said—on his daily commute to work?"

Scott dismissed the comment with a flick of his hand. "Meh... Man on a bus. Girl in the window. Boy in the car. The bookstores are full of crap like that." Scott pulled open the refrigerator and grabbed a beer. He threw the bottle top in the trash and waved the bottle around as he spoke, showing his annoyance at the recent saturation of what he termed "Girl this and that" thriller books. "Been done to death. Girl Gone. Girl not Gone. If I see another book with 'girl' or 'women' in the title, I'm going to go insane." He took a swig from the bottle. "This new book I've started writing is more literary," he lied. "More commercial, unique. A killer story with a twist at the end no one will see coming. Have it banged out in a couple of months."

This news pleased Paige to no end. "Dinner will be ready in about an hour," she said with another smile before turning back to the cooktop, where several pans were bubbling and simmering away, swirls of steam rising up into the humming extractor.

Upstairs, Scott felt very pleased with himself and the little charade he had pulled. He was on a good thing here with Paige and her family, so why spoil it? He'd pay some ghost writer to churn out some copy-cat thriller then pretend he'd picked up a deal with a publishing house. It would be another two years before it was published and any royalties come in. That would buy him more time to figure out the rest later.

He could continue the charade of an up-and-coming author for as long as it took, even if Paige's mother detested him and her father thought he was useless.

He stripped off then tossed his clothes into the laundry hamper and stood over the sink, smiling to himself, admiring his best asset. It hung heavy, long and bulbous like the clapper of the Liberty Bell. It was his ticket on the gravy train, and he wasn't going to step off any time soon. There was no need really. He could still play the field behind Paige's back, get the best of both worlds, and she'd be none the wiser. Women were so dumb.

Maybe in a few more years of trying to get pregnant, her biological clock will come to a grinding halt. By then she'd be too old to have kids. But until then, his little charade would continue: look to her with loving eyes and with a straight face, tell her how much he wants kids, a family of their own, how she'd make the perfect mother and how he desperately wanted to be a good father, a role model for all fathers.

Scott gave himself an admiring wink in the mirror. "You rascal!"

He had gotten away with it so far and kids were the last thing he wanted.

His cell phone vibrated on the sink.

Christ! Sabine again, pressing him some more, wondering if he'd asked Paige for the money to invest yet. "What is it with these damn women?" Scott mumbled. He felt like throwing his phone in the toilet and flushing it. Even then he knew Sabine could talk underwater with a mouthful of his testicles. But he needed to keep her on his side. She promised him she'd put him in touch with a few high-powered agents and editors in New York, other investors she had corralled into Mark's investment firm. That was one of the "perks" she had explained to Scott. Being an investor with Mark opened up all sorts of doors and opportunities within their network of influence.

He switched off the phone and hopped in the shower cubicle, lathering himself under the scalding jets of hot water.

He then began to whistle.

Life was good. A superficial wife. Filthy rich in-laws. No shortage of women around town. And no kids on the horizon.

Chugga Chugga Choo Choo!

Chapter 29
Meat

It was perfect. The table setting, the special fine bone china plates, the silver cutlery, the crystal wineglasses, dim lighting, tall fragrant candles. All carefully arranged to create the mood for seduction and eventual fertilization.

Paige sat at one end of the long dining table, Scott at the other.

Norah Jones had sung herself into silence, and had been replaced by the smoky, husky voice of Diana Krall.

Scott was already drunk before he even sat down, but that didn't stop him from drinking two glasses of red wine before the appetizer was served. Despite this, Paige didn't seem annoyed. Usually in the past she didn't like Scott drinking too much before they made love. She wanted him to perform.

On this occasion she even topped up his wine glass when she cleared away his plate on the way to the kitchen to bring out the main course.

Very strange indeed. *What the hell*, he thought draining the wine glass. She was obviously buttering him up as she had done at breakfast this morning so he could butter her up in bed later on in the evening.

Scott was confident in his plan. The more he considered it, the more he realized it was the right thing to do, stringing along Paige and her parents for as long as he could, milk them for every last drop. He deserved to enjoy Paige's allowance. He may even tell her that she should increase it. He certainly was going to be more forthright from now on with her.

If she wasn't going to ask her parents for the money to invest in Mark Miller's company, he would. Scott was feeling very sure of himself as he regarded the empty crystal wine glass, wondering how much the set had cost Paige, not him. He gave himself a toast, "Here's to you, old boy."

Paige returned with two large dinner plates and set one down in front of Scott. He eyed the beautifully marbled New York strip steak, fluffy mashed potatoes, and green beans. The steak had been marinating in the refrigerator all afternoon, while Scott's eyeballs had been marinating on Sadie's breasts at the sports bar.

Scott began to salivate just looking at the beautiful cut of meat and the delicious char-grilled aroma that wafted up into his face.

"There you go, my darling," Paige said. "Rare, just how you like it."

Paige filled up his wine glass again before sitting down and then she waited for Scott to start.

He looked at Paige puzzled. It was then he noticed that Paige's own wine glass was empty. In fact she hadn't drunk a drop of wine all night, no alcohol at all. She just settled for a glass of mineral water.

Maybe it had something to do with the ovulating, Scott

thought, grabbing a steak knife and cutting into the juicy piece of meat. He didn't care if he couldn't perform tonight. From now on he was going to set the ground rules and Paige was going to follow along. If she wanted his sperm inside her, then it was going to be on his terms, not hers.

The steak melted like butter in his mouth and Scott closed his eyes in pure ecstasy.

"I'm glad you're enjoying it," Paige said, watching the look on his face.

Scott opened his eyes, and muttered to himself just out of earshot of Paige, "It's better than sex with you at least."

Paige raised an eyebrow, "What was that, darling?"

Scott looked down at his steak, his knife poised. "Nothing, darling, I was just saying how beautifully cooked this steak is." He raised his wine glass. "To you, darling."

Paige raised her glass of mineral water, "No," she corrected him. "To *us,* darling."

"I can't believe the effort you've gone through just for me," Scott said, cutting a thick slice of meat.

Paige sipped her mineral water, her food still untouched in front of her. "I want you to feel very special tonight, darling."

Scott looked at her, "I do feel special." He waved his knife around. "This is wonderful. It's a very special evening, no doubt."

Paige gave a mischievous grin. She carefully dabbed the corners of her mouth with her napkin and set it aside. She couldn't contain herself any longer. The suspense was bursting her insides. Today had been the best day of her life, and it wasn't because of the idiot sitting across from her, her lazy fool of a husband. Well, it was partially due to him, his contribution to their marriage, not financially anyway.

Paige placed her hands on each side of her plate and sat up a little straighter, a beaming smile now across her face.

Scott glanced up at her, "What are you so happy about, darling?" he asked, a little too much emphasis on the word "darling" like he said it while dragging his finger nails down a chalkboard. He cut another large wedge of juicy meat and shoved it into his mouth, chewing it slowly, savoring each fiber of prime cut, blood pooling on the plate. He liked his meat rare, didn't mind a bit of blood now and then.

Paige pulled something out from under another napkin, and held it high. "I'm pregnant!" she screamed with delight.

Scott kept chewing, oblivious to what Paige had just said. Maybe his senses were dulled by the alcohol. Maybe it was because her words, the good news she had been trying to suppress all day until tonight, was just so scientifically impossible, from Scott's understanding of how biology worked.

Then his brain caught up mid-chew. Their eyes locked, then he saw what she was holding in one hand. He stopped breathing, just stared at it in disbelief. All the air seemed to get pulled out of the room.

"You're what—?" Scott's words cut off.

There, in her hand, was a home pregnancy test stick. She held it up gleefully like it was the Olympic torch she was carrying. She screamed again with delight. "I'm fucking pregnant!"

Chapter 30
WTF!

Scott's world distorted, wobbled, then tumbled completely off its delicate axis.

His mouth fell open, and the piece of meat he'd been chewing tumbled out and onto his plate in front of him with a resounding thud.

Confusion gave way to disbelief.

How can it be?

"What the—" Scott had to stop himself from screaming out, "But I've had a fucking vasectomy!"

Paige looked glowing. She hadn't been this happy since Daddy bought her a pony for her sixth birthday. She still had the pregnancy stick in her tight little fingers, a wide exuberant look of glee on her face. "Isn't it wonderful?" she squealed.

Paige spent the next five minutes heaping praise on Dr. Goodmyer, her fertility specialist, and how they were going to decorate the baby's room, and the baby shower she wanted to throw for all her family and friends, and how wonderful and complete their life would now be, and how she couldn't wait to tell everyone, and how, and how, and how…

Scott sat bolt upright, two revelations slicing into his brain at once: Either the vasectomy hadn't worked or, if it had, then Paige was fucking someone else. And… Sabine was the only other person he had told about his little sperm-stopping procedure. Why had he been so stupid as to tell the biggest mouth in town?

"Honey… that's great news." Scott's words belied the look of utter shock on his face.

Paige frowned, "You don't seem happy."

"Eh… well…" Scott stuttered. How could he not be happy? His wife could be pregnant by another man and his carefully constructed world of endless adultery and cunning play-acting had suddenly come tumbling down. Scott got up from his chair, knelt down next to his wife, taking one hand, and gave the academy-award-winning performance of his life. "Of course I'm delighted," he said with all the genuineness he could invent. "I'm just a little surprised, that's all." He kissed her knuckles. "All that plotting and temperature taking has finally paid off."

Paige beamed. "Dr. Goodmyer said it would, I just needed to be patient."

Scott gave a tight smile. "How pregnant are you?" He had to think fast.

"Just a few weeks," Paige said. "I don't really feel any different, but I took the test this morning. Before breakfast. I wanted to wait until tonight to tell you, make a special dinner, a celebration."

Scott looked around the table. The candles. The fine bone china plates. The carefully folded napkins. It wasn't to grease the path to get him to perform his end of the bargain. It was for them to celebrate as new parents, welcoming in a new life in their world.

Scott suddenly felt ill. Sabine would know he wasn't the father. It would be another piece of leverage she would have on him—and on Paige. Sabine had no scruples. She would blackmail them, Scott was certain.

The ice was cracking under his feet as Scott stood. "Look, how about we don't tell anyone just yet." Scott tried his best to sound upbeat, not sound like he was pleading to his wife. He could see a little of the excitement fade from her eyes, as she frowned at him.

Scott took the pregnancy stick from her hand. There were indeed two intersecting blue lines in the little window. This must mean she was pregnant. Scott waved the plastic test stick in the air. "Well, how accurate can these things really be?" he asked. He edged forward and squeezed her hand more. "Look I just want you to enjoy this moment, make certain, that's all."

Paige slowly nodded her head, trying to understand.

"Don't you want to be certain?" Scott asked. "It would be awful if this test thing was faulty." Scott waved the plastic stick like he was conducting an orchestra. "They must pump out millions of these things."

Paige's shoulders slumped, the wind taken out of her sails. "I guess you're right," she conceded. "I'll make an appointment with Dr. Goodmeyer first thing in the morning, get a proper test done in her clinic."

Scott breathed a sigh of relief then wrapped it up in a picture of husbandly concern for his wife. "I just want you to be happy, not disappointed. I want your parents to know for certain that they are now proud grandparents-to-be. That's all."

He bent down and kissed Paige on the top of her head, the fingers of both his hands subconsciously curling around her throat.

Chapter 31
The Other Woman

While it seemed small, the apartment was cozy, functional, and where Perez called "home."

Every space was utilized without the feeling of things being cluttered or claustrophobic. There was a small combined living and dining area, a bedroom area, a small kitchenette and separate toilet and shower. It also had a narrow balcony that overlooked the bustling street below, lined with small grocery stores, a deli, various cafes, and convenience stores.

It was a busy, vibrant little neighborhood block, and her apartment was above a grocery store, a family business that had been run for generations. The enterprising family owned and leased the apartment to Perez and also owned the liquor store across the street and a laundromat two doors down. They saw the benefit of having a cop living upstairs, a deterrent, a way of protecting their business interests. Hence, they offered Perez reduced rent and free unlimited use of their laundromat.

She soon became known around the block as the lady cop who lived above the grocery store, a tag she didn't mind. Old people would nod and say hello to her in the street. Teenagers and kids would keep her up-to-date on local gossip as they congregated outside the deli or on the street corners. They never saw her as a threat or feared her as a cop. She was nice, courteous, and most of all, respectful. She never wore her uniform around the neighborhood, preferring to change out of it as soon as she got home. It was these little things that allowed her to tap into the vibe of the local community and keep tabs on trouble before it escalated.

It was after 9:00 p.m. by the time Perez arrived home. She took a quick shower, changed into jeans and a sweatshirt, and walked a block to a Thai food restaurant to collect her take-out meal for one. It summed up her social life at the moment: home alone with a take-out meal for one.

She didn't want the complications of a man in her life right now. What she wanted, more than anything else was to be a detective, and it was too much of an opportunity to work with someone like Marvin Richards to jeopardize with frivolous distractions.

Perez didn't really like men either. Most of her life she found them either to be Neanderthals, primitive oafs who did nothing but eat, sleep, drink, and fornicate with the odd grunt and groan now and then. Or, the men she had known were at the other end of the spectrum: self-obsessed, groomed like poodles, taking selfies of their puckered faces and ranting on about their softer, compassionate sides. For Perez there was no middle ground. She wasn't a feminist either, and she couldn't stand women who were, especially the really radical ones who had emerged lately.

She didn't hate men, she just found nothing appealing about the species. Maybe she hadn't met the right type of man, not that she had met many men. Most men found her intimidating, abrupt or just plain rude, which she wasn't. She just couldn't see the point of pursuing a relationship at the moment.

The television was on but the sound was turned down. Perez sat cross-legged on the bed, her laptop open next to her, together with a plastic take-out container, a plastic fork, and the remnants of a half-eaten yellow curry.

Spread out in an arc around her were the case files notes for Adam Teal that she had copied back at the station so she could take them home to study.

The police IT guys had accessed Adam Teal's email and cell phone accounts and were processing them separately. So far nothing relevant had been found. They had also hacked into his iCloud account and had given Perez the access codes so she could search the photo files that were stored there. Adam Teal's Facebook page didn't reveal anything significant. His security settings were set to public, and after an hour of scrolling through photos of faces on campus or crammed in bars with his college friends, Perez had seen enough. There were also numerous family pictures, with his siblings and his mom, Valerie Teal, in happier times.

Her eldest son was the surrogate rock of the family unit, and was the reason for the sparkle in his mom's eyes, that sparkle now gone. All that remained, Perez imagined, was that perpetual vacant and washed-out expression one had when your life had been torn apart.

Apart from the photos, there was nothing that added to the mystery of who had abducted then murdered Adam Teal.

Perez finished the rest of her now-cold takeout meal in somber silence as she thumbed through the pages of statements, crime scene reports, forensic results, and the autopsy report.

She then logged into his iCloud account. There were over

two thousand pictures saved there and she wondered how someone's life was so interesting that warranted recording it on an almost daily basis. She started scrolling through in chronological order, with the latest photo uploaded just a day before he went missing. This most recent photo was taken of Adam at the store where he worked, a picture of him and a young black woman, no doubt another sales associate, squeezed together, smiling at the camera.

Slowly and methodically Perez began to wade through thumbnails of images, pausing now and then to open one up to take a closer look.

After a while the tiny images seemed to blur together, nothing different, nothing that stood out. Smiling faces, funny faces, like celluloid film, individual frames spooling in reverse, the clock of Adam's life ticking backward, getting further and further away from that fateful day that he died.

The pictures were more of the same that were already posted on Facebook. Photos of him at college with his friends posing with beers in hand at bars, or eating burgers and fries.

Perez took a break after half an hour, rubbed her eyes and stretched. It was just after ten and she was on an early patrol shift tomorrow morning.

She got up, made herself a cup of coffee, then returned to her little patch of murder and mayhem set among her pillows on the bed. She picked up the statements made by Valerie Teal that Richards had taken, and read them again.

In the weeks leading up to Adam's death, Valerie recalled seeing a car driving back and forth in front of her home a few times, usually when it was getting dark. Not every day, but perhaps once a week. It was odd. Black Rock Road was usually quiet that time of day. Then one night she recalled a car pulling up at the top of her dirt driveway. It just sat there for a few minutes, motor idling. Then it backed out and disappeared up the road. She thought it was someone who was lost, picked the wrong house. There were no street lights along Black Rock Road, she had told Richards, and once the sun goes down, darkness comes on very quickly.

Perez highlighted sections of Valerie Teal's statement in yellow. Perhaps the person in the car was not lost. Perhaps it was Adam Teal's killer, stalking him, seeing where he lived. Any tire marks on the shoulder of the road outside the family home or on the dirt driveway would be long gone by now, washed away by the wind and the rain.

The surrounding houses had been door-knocked by patrol officers. As expected, no one saw or heard anything that evening when Adam Teal didn't come home.

Perez scribbled in her notebook to ask Richards what he thought about the drive-by car. Her finger moved across the mouse pad again, as she continued her search through the photos in the iCloud account. More of the same, smiling faces, happy times, bright eyes, a bright future cut short. Photos of his naked mother—

The monotonous stream of thumbnails suddenly changed to a short burst of pale grays, milky whites and charcoals that disrupted the flow of bright colors. It was now all skin and flesh, and partial shadows.

Perez's mind caught up and she suddenly stopped scrolling, her tired eyes and fatigued brain suddenly wide awake.

She quickly scrolled back.

There. A cluster of thumbnails, different from the others, buried in the seemingly innocent minutia of a young man's social life.

Perez squinted at the screen then enlarged the first thumbnail.

Pale flesh, arms and legs, a body turned, the distinct curve of a woman's spine, her face obscured.

At first Perez thought she was staring at a close-up photo of a body, translucent in death. Then she saw the messy ruffle of bed sheets, torn from the corner of a mattress.

It was a woman, mature, her back to the camera, one heavy breast caught in the frame, saggy, no implants here. She had deliberately turned her face away from the camera lens. Adam Teal had taken photos of a woman who had wanted to remain anonymous.

Perez scrolled to the next photo and enlarged it. A bare leg, smooth, toned with a defined calf. A woman's leg, the same woman, heavyset but not overweight, regular exercise combating a slowing metabolism. Perez's eyes followed down the leg past the calf, down to the ankle and foot. She saw pale skin, spidery veins across the foot bones. The person was mature, the skin wrinkled more here.

Perez's breath caught.

Her eyes went wide, the photo revealing something else as well. Something that Perez had seen before—an image of something, blurred but unmistakable. Pincers, four pairs of legs, segmented tail. This particular image as unique as a fingerprint.

"You've got to be kidding me."

Perez found her breath again and smiled with uncharacteristic glee.

Letter #4

My Darling,

The hardest thing was saying goodbye to you at JFK. That moment when they called my flight and I had to let go of you, unwind your arms and hands from around me, otherwise I would have missed my plane! Maybe I should have just let it go without me. That way we could have spent more time together.

What an amazing weekend we had in New York. Walking through Central Park. Taking so many selfies of us kissing on top of the Empire State. Holding you close to me, your fragile heart beating against my chest as I cradled you, protected you, our faces turned to the wind as we stood at the rail on the Staten Island Ferry that night watching the Statue of Liberty slide past in all her beauty. Even as I write this now, I can still taste your lingering kisses from that night, the saltiness of your lips, the earthiness of the red wine on your tongue.

Then going back to our hotel room, drawing back the drapes and making love until dawn with the Manhattan skyline in the background, just us together, entangled as one, in a city of millions, the whole world watching. I don't care who was watching. I want them to watch, to stare, to be jealous of what we have because it's so special. These moments with you I will treasure for the rest of my life.

I know you were a little embarrassed when we walked into Tiffany's and you saw what I had planned for you. Don't be embarrassed. I wanted to buy it for you and I know you've always wanted to go there. When you wear the necklace, I hope it will remind you of the wonderful time we had in that great city. Who cares about the money? I'm in love and you are worth it. And in return, I have something more valuable, something that money can't buy. You!

I've always been in love with you, even before we met, I just knew it, felt it deep down inside me. You were always out there, somewhere. I just had to find you. Now that I have, I never want to breathe, to exist, to live without you.

Love you forever,
Michael xxx

Chapter 32
Amber

"Sabine, I just thought I'd mention that Hank and I haven't received our distribution check for the month. Just wondering when it will arrive?" Maggie asked.

It was a full house for the coffee catch-up and they were clustered around the table at Sabine's house.

Sabine gave a dismissive wave of her hand, "Don't worry about it, Maggie. I'll check with Mark. He did mention this month there was a glitch with the reports and his IT guy is working on it."

Maggie nodded. She wasn't too bothered; she just liked to keep on top of managing their finances each month. However this was the first time since Hank and Maggie had been clients of Mark that their distribution check was late.

"That reminds me," Sabine said as she sat across from the others, "Mark also said it was a bumper month for profits, 'right off the charts' I think were his exact words." Sabine looked directly at Paige as she said this. She was tempted to ask Paige if she had finally made a decision whether or not to invest, but she bit her tongue for now. She'd given Scott one more chance to convince his wife otherwise she was going to take a more direct approach.

Sabine then gave a deliberate wriggle in her chair, like she couldn't get comfortable.

Seeing this, Paige couldn't resist. "You seem to be squirming there Sabine. Is everything OK?"

Sabine gave a slight smile. Bait taken.

"I've got on these new panties and I'm just trying to get comfortable. I think they are one size too big," she said sweetly at Paige. "Meant for someone who's got a bigger ass than mine."

Paige returned the smile, yet behind her pursed lips she was grinding her teeth. For the life of her, Paige couldn't find the panties for the matching set of new lingerie she'd recently purchased. She wanted to wear them the other night when celebrating the good news about her pregnancy with Scott.

Then something changed her mind.

Scott still insisted that Paige not share the good news with anyone until a few more weeks had passed, despite the fact that Dr. Goodmyer had confirmed the very next day that she was indeed pregnant. However, Paige couldn't resist telling her parents. Her mother was absolutely delighted at the news. Her father, while still pleased, was slightly more reserved in his reaction. He seemed more interested during their telephone conversation in the little favor Paige had asked of him. Her father certainly had the resources and the connections to carry out his daughter's request and he promised that he would get back to her within twenty-four hours.

If politics had taught her father anything, it was the value of digging up dirt on your enemies. It was one of life's lessons that he had had passed on to her at a very early age. In the cut and thrust of Washington D.C., her father often said, "If you wish to kill your enemies, first you must bend your knee and gather up the sword they have dropped at your feet." In other words, most people leave themselves completely open and vulnerable, and tend to provide you with the mechanism for their own downfall. You needn't look far.

Paige had bent her knees, just the other day in fact, when she was sorting through the laundry hamper to do the washing.

It was a lesson she was about to put into practice.

The rest of the conversation shifted to local gossip and any recent news. However, nothing much had happened in the last few days and Becca saw this lull as an opportunity. "I just wanted to ask everyone if you happen to know a woman by the name of Amber. Maybe she used to live here or still lives close by?" Becca looked at each woman in turn.

Zoe frowned and shook head. "I know no one by that name."

Sabine just shrugged and said she didn't know anyone called Amber either, which Becca found unusual given Sabine's wide network of friends and acquaintances.

"Nope," Paige said with a shrug.

Becca's gaze then fell on Maggie and she noticed Maggie's facial expression had suddenly changed. Her smile had been replaced with a thin tense line.

"Why do you ask?" Maggie asked, her voice almost caught in her throat.

The others all noticed Maggie's sudden change as well.

"No reason, really," Becca said. "It's just that I'm getting mail sent to me at my home addressed to someone called Amber." It was an answer she had rehearsed. Becca hadn't anticipated the next question though.

Paige made a face, "Amber who?"

Becca racked her brain, "Amber Michaels." She almost said "Amber Heard", Johnny Depp's ex-wife. It was the only Amber she could think of. "I've received a couple of bills for her." Another rehearsed lie.

Maggie shifted uncomfortable, avoiding Becca's eyes.

"Do you know someone called Amber?" Becca asked Maggie directly.

Maggie looked up then said defiantly. "No. Never heard of her." Maggie held Becca's gaze for a moment then looked away.

"With a name like that, she sounds like a hooker, or porn star," Sabine laughed. "Just Google her. You might find her on Facebook."

Becca nodded, but the conversation was going nowhere. Maggie's strange reaction had Becca puzzled, though. It was like a cold chill had passed through the room and settled over Maggie at the mere mention of the name.

So maybe her son did have a girlfriend called Amber? And for whatever reason, perhaps Maggie or Hank, or both, didn't approve of her. Becca made a mental note to ask Hank when she next saw him. Maybe he would be more forthcoming than Maggie.

The name "Amber" had certainly hit a raw nerve with Maggie, and Becca wanted to know why.

Chapter 33
Revelation

Perez and Richards stood at the front door, waiting expectantly after Richards had rung the doorbell.

The lock turned and the door opened. Standing there was Maggie Vickerman, a look of utter distress on her face.

When Mac had called through to Maggie saying two police officers were at the gate from the Hagerstown Police Department wishing to speak to her, at first she thought it was a follow-up regarding the incident that had happened with Becca, that the police just wanted to corroborate hers and Hank's statements.

Then as the minutes dragged on while she waited for them to arrive at her front door, a growing dread began to seep into her stomach, burning like acid.

"Is it Adam?" she demanded, her face now wrought with fear, as any mother's would. "Has something happened to Adam overseas?"

Richards and Perez exchanged looks. "Maggie Vickerman?" Richards asked.

"Please tell me!" her voice more frantic now. "Has something happened to my son, Adam?" Maggie edged forward, and for a brief moment Perez thought the woman was going to grab her by the shoulders and shake an answer out of her.

"Mrs. Vickerman, we're not here about your son," Richards said, his voice calm.

Maggie breathed a sigh of relief. "Thank God," she said, all fear and anguish faded and her shoulders relaxed as she let them inside.

They sat in the plush living room, a montage of delicate wallpaper, rich expensive furnishings, and thick carpet. Maggie offered them coffee but both Perez and Richards said they were fine. Perez looked around. She hadn't taken much notice of how opulent the room was the other evening when she was here. So this is what wealth and prestige buys you? Mill Point Road seemed different. The manicured grounds, the huge houses, the almost theatrical display of wealth seemed more pronounced in the daylight than it was in the dark of night.

Maggie sat across from them on a large sofa, her posture rigid, while Perez and Richards sat on the edge of plush chairs, a huge slab of coffee table between them. Richards introduced himself and Maggie confirmed that she had already met Officer Perez the other evening. Richards was carrying a folder with the photos Perez had printed off inside, waiting for the right time to open it and show the woman. "Mrs. Vickerman, is your husband home today as well?" Richards asked. Given the sensitive nature of the photographs, the question wasn't an invitation for Hank Vickerman to join them, rather to make sure he wasn't present to witness the folder being opened and his wife's nakedness put on display.

Maggie gave a dismissive wave of her hand. "No, he has gone into town to run a few errands and grab some hardware I believe.

He should be back in about half an hour if you think we should wait for him."

Richards glanced at Perez then back to the folder in his hand. Thirty minutes should be enough time to ruin Maggie Vickerman's day before her husband returned.

"Mrs. Vickerman, we would like to ask you some questions about a young man named Adam Teal." Richards asked, studying Maggie's face closely.

There, right there, Perez saw it. The slight tightening of the muscles around the jaw. The subtle flutter of her eyelashes. The small shift in her posture as though she suddenly realized she was sitting on a baseball.

Richards had seen it too, in her reaction. Maggie Vickerman recognized the name.

"I honestly have no idea who you are talking about," Maggie shrugged.

Richards was hoping to have his questions answered about Adam Teal without having to resort to opening the folder. He guessed wrong.

Maggie leaned back on the sofa, shaking her head firmly. "I don't recall the name," she said. "Should I?"

Perez felt like standing up and slapping this pretentious woman across her face. "So you've never heard the name Adam Teal?" Perez said, trying to keep her anger in check.

She glanced down at Maggie's ankles. When Perez sat on the sofa talking to Rebecca Cartwright the evening she had been knocked out, she noticed the tattoo on Maggie's ankle. It was hard not to miss; Maggie was wearing shorts that evening. But now she was clad in ornate print leggings, covering completely her ankles all the way up to her waist.

Maggie noticed Perez staring down at her feet. She shifted

awkwardly, crossing her legs. "I was just on the elliptical machine before you arrived," she said, explaining her attire.

Richards placed the folder on the coffee table. "Mrs. Vickerman, Adam Teal was a young man who was found dead in a ditch near Black Rock Road, in Beaver Creek not more than four miles from here. It was in all the local newspapers the last few weeks," Richards said.

Maggie's eyes settled on the folder on the coffee table. She spoke without taking her eyes off it. "I don't read the local newspapers. Not really sure what happens around town or in the local press."

Both Perez and Richards stared at Maggie Vickerman in disbelief. The woman lived in her own little bubble, high atop a ridge, behind walls, security fences, automatic gates and CCTV cameras, oblivious to what was going on in the world outside.

The crime scene photos of Adam Teal flashed in Perez's mind. Hands and feet bound, skin pale, bleached of all life, face submerged in dirty ditch water and stinking mud. She felt her anger slowly growing listening to the woman's denials.

Richards could sense Perez tightening like a coil next to him. He gave her a quick look, their eyes met, a small imperceptible shake of his head.

Richards persisted with Maggie. Judging from her build, the shape of her legs and thighs under the skin-tight leggings, she did resemble the woman in the photos. He needed to be certain and her stubbornness left him no choice.

He leaned forward, opened the folder, and calmly spread the photos in front of Maggie.

Maggie's eyes went wide as she gazed down at the photos.

Neither Richards nor Perez said a word. There was nothing to say because the look on Maggie Vickerman's face said it all.

Richards deliberately placed the close-up shot of a left foot, the tattoo of a scorpion clearly visible just above the ankle, in the middle of the spread, right in front of Maggie.

Perez gave a smirk. *That's right, you bitch. That's you, isn't it?*

Maggie felt sick. Her shoulders slumped and she let out a long labored breath, all the fight in her gone.

"Mrs. Vickerman, are these photographs of you?" Richards asked.

For a moment Maggie said nothing, just stared at the photos, regretting allowing Adam Teal to take them. She was flattered, any woman her age would be. He had said that she was beautiful; "voluptuous" was the exact word he had used. No one had said that to Maggie in a long time, certainly not Hank.

So Maggie thought there was no harm in him taking a few photos of her on the bed after the lovemaking. Adam Teal had assured her he would not show them to anyone else, that they were just for his private pleasure and this pleased Maggie even more.

Maggie finally tore her eyes away from the photos but couldn't look Richards or Perez in the eye. Instead she just stared down at her hands in her lap. Finally in a low voice she said, "Yes... it is me in the photographs." Maggie knew they would find out anyway, no doubt the young female police officer had noticed her tattoo on her ankle the other night. Now she understood the original question Marvin Richards asked about whether or not her husband Hank was home. These were discussions to be had behind closed doors when one's husband was far out of earshot.

"Mrs. Vickerman, can you tell me how you and Adam Teal met?" Richards asked. Perez took out her note book and began writing.

Maggie Vickerman spoke in a hushed tone, as though she was either embarrassed by what had transpired between her and Adam Teal or as though she felt someone else was listening. "I first met Adam at one of the stores at the outlets, where he worked." It was a luxury brand store, the name and address was in the case file, but Perez noted it down anyway, thinking even the smallest purse from that particular store would cost her a week's wage.

"He was working behind the counter, as a store associate. He was just so helpful, so nice, attentive," Maggie recalled, a faraway look in her eyes, tears forming. "He didn't treat me like some old woman, a grandmother looking for a present for her daughter." Maggie pulled out a tissue from under her sleeve and dabbed her eyes.

Richards said nothing, preferring Maggie tell her story.

Perez continued to scribble down in her notebook, curious as to how the chance meeting escalated from a young man serving a complete stranger, a married woman, in the store, who looked three times his own age, into what was obviously a full-blown sexual relationship.

Maggie continued, "I guess one thing led to another. I know I'm married and I'm not perfect." She looked pleadingly at Richards. "Please, I implore you not to tell my husband."

"Mrs. Vickerman, that's a personal matter for you and your husband. That's not my role. What people do in their own private lives, as long as they don't break the law, is for them alone. However, I am here to find out who killed Adam Teal, and I will do everything in my power to catch that person."

Maggie nodded, slightly relieved. "I don't know anything about how he died. I had no idea. I haven't seen him for weeks or been back to the store for a while." Maggie paused, and then spoke again. "Please don't think badly of me, but I knew he needed money. So I paid him."

Perez stopped writing and looked up.

Richards jumped in before Perez said what he was thinking. "You paid Adam Teal to have sex with you? Is that correct?"

The tears increased. "No, no, it wasn't like that at all."

Perez continued writing, feeling no sympathy for the woman. It disgusted her, in fact. Maggie Vickerman was paying a young, vulnerable man to have sex with her, a man who was only trying to help his mother and provide for his other siblings. But selling sex for money? From what Perez had read in the case file, the interview notes with his family, college friends, and work associates, it seemed out of character. But then again how well does anyone really know their friends or work colleagues?

"He refused the money at first," Maggie continued. "But he was in community college he told me and could only work part-time in the store. He was very appreciative." Maggie looked at both Perez and Richards. "I'm not stupid," she said. "I knew right away that there was no love involved. It was just sex, but he was so gentle, considerate, caring. I wanted him to be compensated, help him out with college. God knows I have enough money."

"Where were these pictures taken?" Richards tapped at the photos on the coffee table.

"In our bedroom upstairs."

Both Perez and Richards glanced up at the ceiling, imagining Maggie and Adam Teal entwined.

"How did you get him here?" Perez asked. "Without someone seeing him or the both of you together?"

Maggie gave a sarcastic smile. "You mean how did I get him past the security guard, the CCTV cameras, and my nosy neighbors?"

Perez waited for an answer. She still felt like slapping the stupid woman across the face. Maybe use her fist, knock some of her perfectly straight, perfectly white teeth out of her smug, little Botoxed mouth.

"We would meet in the parking lot behind his work after his shift if it was late. There's a blind spot away from any CCTV cameras. Or we would meet at an agreed spot on the side of the road. I would text him and he would text me back. He would ride in the trunk and I would drive straight here, through the gates and into my garage. When the garage doors had lowered completely I would open the trunk and he would climb out. No one saw a thing."

In essence Maggie Vickerman had smuggled Adam Teal into her house in the trunk of her car, like an illegal immigrant crossing the border, so that no one would see him.

She went on to explain that their secret rendezvous was timed while Hank was away in town or had gone out to have a beer with his buddies.

After they had sex Maggie simply reversed the process. Adam got back in the trunk, and she drove out the gates. She usually dropped Adam off in Ravenwood or along the side of the road near the Beaver Creek Country Club. She imagined he lived around there somewhere but she had no idea where exactly.

There is no disputing the fact that Adam Teal was prostituting himself to Maggie Vickerman.

The more pressing question though was: were there any other women that Adam Teal had similar arrangements with?

Chapter 34
Hamilton

"I take it that's your son, Adam?"

Maggie looked up and followed Richards' gaze. She wiped her nose with a snivel. "Yes, that's Adam."

"Handsome young man," Perez added.

Maggie got up from the sofa and picked up the silver framed photo from a row of photos that sat on the sideboard. She paused for a moment, wiping the dust from the glass carefully with her tissue. Looking fondly at the photo, she smiled. Suddenly thinking about Adam was the only ray of happiness Maggie had enjoyed amidst the dark clouds of shame and distress she had felt in the last half hour.

She returned to the sofa, clutching the photo frame to her chest, sat down then handed it to Richards. "It was taken just a few months ago, just before he went overseas."

He was definitely a young, good-looking man. Taller than Maggie, who was standing next to him in the photo, her arm around his waist, Adam's arm protectively around his mother's shoulders, the bright lights of Broadway in the background.

Maggie explained it was taken outside a theater in New York where they had gone to see Hamilton, the musical. It had been a wonderful three days spent in New York.

Richards handed the picture to Perez.

She, like Richards, noticed that Hank Vickerman was not in the shot. Perez looked around the living room. The walls were adorned with framed family portraits, clusters of framed photos sat on the sideboard and on smaller tables. Most of the photos were of Adam and his mother. Arms around each other at a restaurant. Posing against the rail on the Staten Island Ferry, the Statue of Liberty in the background. Outside the Flatiron building. At the top of the Empire State Building. Maybe Hank Vickerman had taken the photos? But for some reason Perez doubted it. It was just a feeling she got sitting in this room that resembled a shrine to Maggie's son.

Perez handed the silver framed photo back to Maggie. No doubt Richards would have noticed this strange anomaly as well. There wasn't much he didn't notice, Perez had determined from the short time she had known him. He observed and made a mental note here and there, scribbling it away in his mind. Unlike herself, Perez had never seen Richards actually pull out a notebook and write anything down.

"And where is Adam now?" Richards asked. "You said he went overseas."

Maggie held the photo and looked down at it lovingly. A mother's love can conquer anything, well almost anything. "Traveling around Europe with friends. He was in the United Kingdom a few weeks back, and I believe now they're somewhere in northern Italy." She looked up at Richards and Perez, wondering what Adam would make of what she had done. A tearful smile lingered on her face. It was obvious she was missing her son terribly. "We talk to each other on Facebook a few times a week, when Adam can get internet access," Maggie explained. "And he posts regularly, nice photos of where he is, the sights he has seen. He's having a wonderful time."

"But he does live with you, Mrs. Vickerman?" Perez asked. "This is his home, correct?"

"He's always lived here; he's only nineteen years old. At the end of high school he didn't really know what he wanted to do with his life. He loves the arts, music, but is particularly fond of the theater. We've seen many musicals together in New York, just Adam and me." For a moment the sunshine went out of Maggie's face as a dark cloud rolled in. "Hank never comes with us. It's not usually his thing."

"And when do you expect Adam to return, Mrs. Vickerman?" Richards asked.

"It is really open-ended. I imagine he'll be home in a couple months. It came as a bit of a surprise that he went, out of the blue so to speak. But it will do him a world of good. See the world."

Both Perez and Richards never mentioned the fact that they had been trawling through Adam Vickerman's Facebook page, had seen his updates. "So Adam didn't go alone? He's with friends; he's traveling with other people?" Richards asked.

Maggie frowned. This was the second time someone had asked this of her, if Adam was traveling alone or in the company of others, like it mattered.

Likewise, Perez and Richards couldn't actually ask Maggie why was it that, in the pictures on Adam's Facebook page, there were no actual photos of Adam himself. There were plenty of pictures of monuments, landmarks, well-known tourist attractions. But not a single photo of Adam or his traveling companions.

"Yes, he has friends in England, he said. He mentioned they were meeting up and were traveling together. I don't know them personally, and he's never really mentioned before that he had friends overseas, let alone in England. But I think he met them online, through Facebook or something."

Richards smiled. "Young people these days," he said. "They can be very trusting. Meet people online and before you know it they arrange to meet up with them in person, without ever really truly knowing who the people are."

Maggie offered a conciliatory smile. "It's a very different world today, Detective Richards, compared to when you and I were teenagers."

"That it is," Richards agreed.

"But Adam is a very sensible young man," Maggie added. "He wouldn't do anything foolish."

"We won't take any more of your time," Richards said, standing up, the meeting over. He slid the photos back into the folder. "We may come back and question you again, Mrs. Vickerman."

Maggie nodded. "Anything I can do to help." She paused, her face troubled. "And my husband?"

Perez closed her notebook.

"Like I said," Richards replied. "That's for you to sort out. But it is a murder investigation, and at times it can be hard keeping it private or out of the press."

Out in the hallway at the front door, the house felt very eerily quiet, empty. Perez could sense certain heaviness, something that she couldn't quite put her finger on, something unsettling.

Outside, they paused in the street in front of the car.

Rebecca Cartwright's house was just two doors down, just past Mark and Sabine's house. "Let's pay an unexpected visit to Rebecca Cartwright," Richards said. "I haven't met her yet."

Chapter 35
The Dark Spot

The dark spot on the wall was definitely getting bigger.

At first, when Becca was in the basement two days ago, she believed it was a trick of the light, a shadow that had fallen across a section of the wall. It was the same section of wall that Josh Daniels had commented on when he came to fix the water heater, saying that it looked like part of the wall was new, had been recently replaced.

Becca looked at the wall. From where she stood, a few feet away, her head tilted, appraising the spot that was getting darker, wider, like it was spreading. It was at about head height on the wall, not really a spot at all now, maybe the size of the dinner plate, a growing blemish. Not black. More grayish, spreading from that center outward like an ink drop diffusing through paper fibers.

Christ, that's all I need, she thought. A leak somewhere in the wall. Maybe dry rot or water somehow getting into the space between the external wall and drywall. Becca looked overhead but noticed no pipes, nothing that could leak in behind the wall.

And this section of the basement wasn't dug into the earth. It was partially covered on the other side with stone.

She placed a hand hesitantly on the dark area, feeling it. It wasn't damp, and the drywall was smooth to touch. She walked along the length of the wall tapping with her knuckles. It was definitely hollow except for framing behind it.

She backed up ten or so feet and regarded it again. No, it was definitely a darker shade in that area that wasn't there a few days ago.

She was going to have to call Josh again, get him over to take a look. It was most likely a leaking pipe behind the wall or somehow moisture was getting in from the outside.

Becca knew nothing about how the house was built, about waterproofing or insulating it from the elements. She needed to get it sorted, otherwise it could get worse and cost a lot of money to fix if she just left it.

Trudging back upstairs, Becca went into the kitchen and found Josh's card again. He had been her savior. Apart from remodeling certain aspects of the house, he had also fixed things she didn't know needed fixing. "Preventative maintenance," he had called it, would save her a lot of money in the long run.

His cell phone automatically went to voicemail. She left a message, nothing urgent, but she described what had happened: a growing patch of discoloration on the section of new drywall he had pointed out to her.

She hung up.

Maybe the new section of wall wasn't done correctly, especially if it was done by the previous owner. What was it with people these days? They seem to be obsessed with home improvement shows, flipping houses here and there, taking shortcuts rather than doing a proper job. Maybe the previous owner had done a fast renovation downstairs, a quick fix job hoping no one would notice. Either way she'd get Josh in and find out.

Taking a flashlight this time, Becca went back down to the basement again. She stood in front of discolored area and panned it around, seeing if there was any sign of mold or mildew. But she could find nothing.

It was then Becca heard the front doorbell ring and she looked up at the ceiling as though she could see through the floor above.

She didn't expect any visitors today, and Mac at the gatehouse would normally buzz her first before letting anyone through.

This was odd.

Becca let out a sigh and climbed back up the stairs to see who it was.

Opening the front door, Becca saw Officer Perez and a tall man standing beside her, blank expressions on their faces.

Cops, she thought to herself as she regarded them. They always seemed to have a look of utter boredom or mild expectation that if they stared deadpan long enough at you that you would feel the urge to confess all your sins.

Perez nodded as Becca recognized her, and Richards introduced himself.

"We were in the neighborhood and I thought we would check on you given what happened to you the other night," Richards explained.

"I'm fine, detective," Becca said. She nodded at Perez. "Officer Perez was very understanding. I feel like such a fool for what happened. I just went for a walk like I said in the woods, in the dark, got disoriented, slipped, and hit my head. Nothing more."

Richards studied Becca's face for a moment as she stood there, door half open, no offer to come inside.

There's no point pursuing further, Richards thought, despite what Perez had written in her report. The woman was sticking to her story, as unconvincing as it seemed.

"We don't want to impose any further," Richards said. "We were just two doors down talking to Mrs. Vickerman about the incident, just going back over her statement."

Nice, Perez thought, giving Maggie an excuse as to why the police were seen at her house.

"Sorry again for the intrusion. We hope you have a nice day."

"No problem." Becca smiled and closed the door.

As they made their way back to the car, Richards said, "I want you to focus on Maggie and Hank Vickerman. See what you can find out about the two of them, their past, anything."

Perez nodded. "You think that she's not telling the truth?"

Richards didn't know what to think. It seemed like the women around here weren't being completely honest, completely forthright with the truth. "I think there's more to it," he said, climbing into the car. "There is something not quite right here, and now we have a direct link from her to Adam Teal. See if you can get hold of the CCTV footage from the security guard at the gatehouse. If you have any problems I'll get a subpoena."

"So what are you going to do?" Perez asked as Richards started the car. He looked clearly irritated. Richards had already interviewed some of the coworkers at the luxury goods store where Adam Teal worked. But he had an idea, a new approach. He glanced at Perez. "I feel like looking at some luxury handbags."

There was no smile on his face.

Chapter 36
The List

It took threats of a subpoena against the luxury store at the outlets, but Richards finally got what he wanted.

So when Perez arrived at work the next morning before her shift, she was greeted by a two-inch stack of computer printouts. It was a complete listing from the store, where Adam Teal had worked, of the customers who had made purchases during the last six months.

A note from Richards was stuck on the top page asking Perez to comb through the printouts and highlight the dates and times when Maggie Vickerman had visited the store. Like most retail stores, it was policy that all the register staff capture at least the email address of a customer when they rang up the sale and ask them if they wanted to join their free customer loyalty program where they would be emailed store specials and discounts. People usually didn't bat an eyelid to handing over their email addresses and personal information to store assistants for the purposes of building a database and marketing to them.

Richards was hoping that this was no different for Maggie

Vickerman. If she was a regular customer at the store, her purchases would be logged.

Richards also said in the note that he was going to follow up on the other cases and revisit Adam Teal's mother, Valerie, to see if her son mentioned at all a woman called Maggie Vickerman. He doubted it but he felt that the Adam Teal lead was the best one they had so far.

Perez had a full eight-hour patrol shift for the day and when she came off late that afternoon, she took the pile of printouts home with her to go through that evening. There were at least two thousand lines of text. It would have been so much easier if the store had just run a search for Maggie Vickerman's name but Richards wanted an entire list for the last six months of all customers. Richards was convinced that the store where Adam Teal worked was the key. Someone met him. Saw him or took an interest in him when they either went in and shopped or was with someone who had. Maggie Vickerman certainly had. But Perez and Richards didn't know what they were looking for. So in cases like this, you request all the information so you can refer back to it later when other persons of interest come to light.

Armed with a ruler, a pot of freshly brewed coffee, and a pack of Sharpie highlighters, Perez settled down at her small dining table and slowly but surely worked her way through the list.

Two hours later Perez had found dates and times when Maggie had visited the store. In the months leading up to the disappearance of Adam Teal, she had been a regular customer, visiting the store almost one or two times a month, purchasing various items, a handbag, pair of shoes, a scarf. Two hundred dollars for a scarf? She shook her head. Obviously Maggie Vickerman had too much money and too much time on her hands.

Then something odd stuck out. The frequency of the purchases didn't escalate, but the transactions did. Items were returned or exchanged on a more regular basis. Rash purchases, done on a whim. Maybe the purchases were fabricated, so that Maggie had an excuse to return to the store to see Adam Teal.

The last transaction was the day before Adam Teal disappeared. Three days later he was dead. Perez checked the dates against the case file.

Taking a break, she walked into her tiny kitchen and put on a fresh pot of coffee to brew. While the machine gurgled away, she went out onto her narrow balcony to join the dead potted plants that were out there, the remnants of good intentions.

It was dark and the sound of people laughing and eating floated up to her from the street below. A couple across the street walked hand in hand, laughing and cajoling. People sat at outdoor tables, crammed onto the sidewalk, cars slowly slid by, and a man on a bike threaded his way recklessly across the street, narrowly missing a car coming out of a side alleyway.

The coffee maker gave its final sputter and Perez went inside and settled back down at the table with a cup of coffee.

All the lines on the list were beginning to blur together. Dates, names, and purchases droned on. Perez continued past the date that Adam Teal disappeared, nearly at the end of the report. Maggie Vickerman's name didn't appear again.

Reaching the end of the report, Perez flipped back to the beginning, a neat line of Post-it notes stuck out from the side where she had tagged the pages Maggie Vickerman's name appeared. She went back and reviewed the pages again.

She was halfway through checking her tags when she stopped. Perez rubbed her eyes and squinted at the lines of text. Her heart skipped a beat.

No!

She quickly flipped open her police notebook and leafed through to the page she wanted. There was a list of names on the page, nine in total, all of them paired up except one. Perez glanced back at the print out.

She smiled. Taking a different color highlighting pen, she ran a line through the name, a different name, not Maggie Vickerman this time. Another person's name appeared a month before Adam Teal died.

Perez sat back staring at the name she had just highlighted, the cogs in her mind ticking over, berating herself. As she was scanning the pages, her eyes, her mind wasn't attuned to looking for anyone else's name, just Maggie Vickerman's. Richards was right when he had requested the entire report. Perez would have missed the other person if it was a report listing only Maggie Vickerman's trips to the store.

Perez folded the report back to the beginning, set her notebook next to it, open to the page she wanted. She wasn't just looking for one name now; she was looking for nine names, nine suspects, nine people who may have known Adam Teal as more than just a faceless young man working in a store.

Chapter 37
Raccoon

It did look strange, like nothing he'd seen before, and Josh Daniels, in ten years of running his own handyman business, thought he'd seen it all. Water leaks, mold infestations, termite damage. There was a really bad case of dry rot he was called out to take a look at last year, for an old lady who still lived in the house she was born in. The wood decay, which is caused by a certain type of fungi that actually consumes wood, was so bad the entire house had to be condemned. Her adult children shipped her into an assisted living facility and the woman died within six months, heart-broken of having to leave her home, reckoned her presence was the only thing holding the house up.

Josh turned away from the wall. "How long has this been happening? I was just here the other day and didn't see any staining."

Becca was standing behind him. She shrugged. "I came down here a few days ago, thinking it was a shadow or a trick of the light. Then it seemed to be getting bigger."

Josh nodded and turned back to the wall. He touched the

surface. It was smooth and cold. He tapped it with his knuckles. The wall still felt and sounded solid, no signs of cracking or brittleness. It definitely wasn't dry rot or any kind of fungi that he had seen. "What's this?" Josh asked without turning.

There was a vertical black line that seemed to slice through a segment of the discoloration.

"Sharpie," Becca said. "I drew it two days ago, just to make sure it wasn't my imagination. At the time the line was outside the discoloration."

Josh traced the line from top to bottom. It disappeared into the body of the dark blob, only to reemerge at the bottom, like it was slicing a third of the shape. "So in just a few days it's grown by a couple of inches." Josh said, thinking out loud.

"Can you fix it?"

"Must be something leaking behind the wall. Like a pipe or something. We haven't had any significant rain in nearly two weeks so it can't be run off. Josh glanced up at the ceiling. "I'll have to see if I can trace the pipes under the flooring above and see if they run behind this wall. Could be clean water or waste. Not sure."

He turned back to Becca. "Do you want the bad news or the really bad news?"

Becca slumped. "The bad news first."

"Well, I'm going to have to cut into this wall, see what's behind there, but it could be leaking from someplace higher up the wall or even upstairs. This spot could be just a pipe junction or elbow where it's pooling and then seeping through."

"OK," Becca said cautiously. "What's the really bad news?"

Josh gave a forced smile. "The worse news is that I can't get to it for another couple of weeks. I'm on a big renovation job in Frederick. Won't finish up there for another two weeks, full days, and weekends too. I'm behind on that job and the homeowner is busting my balls." Josh stared back at the wall. "Something like this is a full day at least; once you get started you don't really want to stop."

Becca was resigned to the fact that she would have to wait. She didn't want or trust another contractor. Josh had done so much around the house for her that they had built up a rapport. "Will it get worse?"

"Just keep an eye on it, Becca. If you start to see liquid seeping through or pooling at the base of the wall, call me right away."

Becca nodded.

"Sorry I can't give you better news. I can recommend another—"

"I just want you," Becca said firmly. "I will wait."

"OK."

Becca had an idea. "Josh do you know any one called Amber?"

Josh looked suspiciously at Becca. "Why?"

Becca just shrugged. "You're a handyman who has lived around here for a while, you know a lot of people."

Josh gave a wry smile. "So what you're saying is that I know a lot of women." He'd taken it as a compliment.

"I didn't mean it like that." Becca sighed.

Josh made a show of thinking. "I'll have to check my little black book," he said, rubbing his chin.

Becca gave him a playful nudge. "I'm serious." She liked Josh, a lot, but had decided as a friend only. "Someone who lives around here, close by."

Josh took the hint and thought seriously about it for a moment. Finally he said, "The only Amber I can recall works at the sports bar in town. I used to go there on the weekends and she was usually behind the bar. But work got so busy lately that I haven't been there for a few months now. But I'm sure she isn't the only woman named Amber around town."

"How old?"

"Maybe twenty, twenty-one," Josh said.

She was about the right age if it was Adam Vickerman's girlfriend.

"Why do you ask?"

Becca gave a nonchalant look. "No reason." Then she decided to confide in him. "I found a bracelet in the backyard; it had the name 'Amber' on one side and 'Adam' on the other. I just thought it may have belonged to Adam Vickerman, you know Maggie's son. Maybe he had a girlfriend called Amber."

Josh frowned. "I don't recall Amber saying anything about going out with Adam Vickerman. Mind you, our conversations never really got that personal." Josh had a puzzled look on his face.

"What?" Becca asked, seeing his expression, like he wanted to say something else.

He shook his head. "That Adam Vickerman. He is a bit strange. I haven't really spoken to him much. But he acted a little odd when I was over at the Vickerman's doing repairs last time."

"Odd?" Becca asked. "Like how?"

Josh furrowed his brow, thinking back. "Just the way he would stare at me. A bit creepy. Once I caught him watching me while I was working on installing a new door. I had no idea he was standing around the corner watching me. Good-looking kid but something wasn't right with him."

"Maybe he was just shy," Becca offered. "Young men mature slower than women, they don't have the social skills that young women do at the same age."

Josh didn't seem convinced. "No, it was something else. There is his mother, Maggie, as well."

Becca gave a questioning look.

"She smothers him, if you ask me," Josh went on. "They were always doing things together. Don't get me wrong, I love my mom. But their relationship seemed a bit strange. Clingy."

"Clingy?" Becca repeated.

Josh smiled. "Yeah, like how most women get after a few months into a relationship."

Becca rolled her eyes. "Pass me your hammer so I can hit you over the head with it."

Josh held up his hands defensively, "Hey, I'm leaving."

Outside Josh sat in his truck with the light on. It was nearly 8:00 p.m. and he had driven to Becca's house straight from finishing up for the day at the Frederick job site. He wrote some notes in his diary then paused for a moment and looked up at Becca's house. Come to think of it there was the job a few years back he had done at an old farm house. Same sort of staining pattern that Becca had on her basement wall Josh suddenly recalled, but it was on the ceiling, slowly spreading. Josh had climbed up into the roof crawl space and found the source of the stain that was seeping through the ceiling drywall.

Turned out to be the decomposing body of a large raccoon that had found its way up there and had died.

Chapter 38
Casanova

He felt like he'd been hit by a truck that had then backed up and run over him again just to make sure he was dead.

Scott Hamill opened his eyes, and instantly felt sharp, searing pain cut through his skull. The sun, a huge gaseous ball of blinding light was high in the sky above. He held up his hand, shielding his eyes from the blinding ball of light. Gradually he was able to open the slits of his eyelids a little farther and then fully. Blood pulsed at the corner of this temples, his mouth beyond bone dry. The ceiling was yellow and skinned with a layer of grime.

The sun was a single, low wattage bulb dangling from a thin cable overhead, the source of his self-induced cerebral agony.

Painfully he raised himself to one elbow, certain that his head would topple off if he moved any faster. He looked around the motel room. He saw cheap artificial wood paneling, faded threadbare green carpet, brown frayed drapes, and chipped laminate furniture, in a mélange of sickly hues and geometric patterns from the eighties.

The room stank as well, from a lifetime of smoke, the imprisoned odor of take-out meals, human sweat, and paid sex. On the nightstand next to the bed sat a half empty bottle of tequila. At the sight of it, vague memories of the recent past came rolling back in Scott's groggy mind.

"Christ" was the first word he muttered, as he wondered how he got here, wherever "here" was, a hovel, a room with no view, just acres of vintage laminate and polyester.

A gap in the curtains told him it was nighttime outside. *Shit!*

Scott moved with the sudden speed and finesse of a hobo racing a rat to a discarded french fry. He ripped back the bed covers, ignoring pain and the urge to vomit. If he did indeed vomit on the already discolored and stained carpet, no one would have noticed.

Scott heard a noise and suddenly froze.

Naked on the edge of the bed he recognized the sound of the toilet flushing. Moments later the bathroom door opened and Sadie from the sports bar walked out.

"Hi, sweetie," she said merrily, adjusting her impossibly short skirt, and straightening her breasts under her incredibly tight top so they didn't appear lopsided.

Scott grimaced. Every sound seemed amplified in his head. "Where am I?" he croaked.

Sadie strutted over to the bed. "You tell me, honey," she said. "*You* brought me here. Don't you remember?"

Scott buried his head in his hands and wished it was all a bad dream. He could vaguely remember driving to the sports bar around lunchtime earlier today. God, he hoped it was earlier today. Paige had gone out for a few hours so he thought he would go out himself. He never intended to go to the sports bar. He just ended up there, drawn to it like a moth. He remembered sitting at the bar having a couple of beers and talking to Sadie. After that his memory became fuzzy. "I can remember coming into the bar, having a few drinks," Scott said. The pain in his head had now spread to his jaw. If he stood up he knew for certain the room would start spinning and he would fall down.

"That's right, hon," Sadie said soothingly. "You came in, had a few drinks and then waited until I got off my shift at four. Then you took me to another bar because you wanted to buy me a drink." The sports bar where Sadie worked had strict rules for staff. They weren't allowed to drink there straight after finishing their shift. They could, on a day off, but not on the same day they worked.

Scott moaned as more memories came flooding back. "And then what happened?"

"What happened?" Sadie said. "Hell, I'll tell you what happened. You couldn't take your hands off me. You ordered tequila shots and then one thing led to another and you brought me back here in a cab."

Scott looked over his shoulder at the tangle of sheets and blankets. The bed looked like four sumo wrestlers had fought on it all at the same time. He buried his face in his hands again wishing that it would all go away.

"Let me tell you something, honey," Sadie stood over him, hips jutting to the side. "You were like a real Casanova in the sack. Despite all the tequila. We did it three, maybe four times. I lost count. You've got real stamina, Scott, let me tell you."

Sadie went to the wall mirror to check her makeup one more time. She went back to Scott, bent down and kissed him on the cheek. "Gotta go, honey." And with that, she opened the door and slipped out.

Outside, Sadie walked halfway across the parking lot to where a taxi was parked in the shadows, side lights on, motor idling. As she approached the rear door behind the driver, the side window powered down, and a dainty gloved hand extended out, palm upward, expectantly.

Sadie pulled a cell phone from her bag, and placed it on the gloved hand.

The hand withdrew and moments later it reappeared but this time it was holding Sadie's own cell phone. She took it together with an envelope that was offered to her.

Sadie opened the flap of the envelope and quickly and expertly thumbed through the bills inside. She smiled, and gave a nod to the person who sat in the back, their face partially hidden in the dark interior.

Easiest grand I've ever made, Sadie thought to herself as she pocketed the envelope and continued walking towards the street.

The person in the backseat paid the taxi driver their fare and a generous tip then climbed out.

Chapter 39
Laying Down the Law

In the bathroom mirror Scott didn't like what he saw.

It was as if he had suddenly aged ten years in the last twelve hours. His face was gaunt, eyes bloodshot, and a few more crease lines were evident under the hissing glare of the fluorescent tube.

He splashed water on his face, trying to rub off what he saw. But when he looked up again, the same disappointed face just stared back at him.

There was a knock on the door.

"Dammit," he muttered. He needed to get out of this place fast, hopefully without being seen by anyone he knew. He had no idea what part of town this was, but judging from the furniture and the decor, it was probably a part of town he had never visited before, or intended to ever return to again.

Scott walked back into the bedroom and quickly dressed back into his wrinkled clothes that smelled of beer, sweat, and sweet perfume.

Christ.

Then another knock on the door, a little harder this time.

"Who is it?"

A muffled voice came from the other side of the door. "Housekeeping."

Scott thought for a moment. This was good. The maid could quickly make up the room, remove all traces. He'd pay her twenty bucks too, to keep her mouth shut. He silently prayed he had used a false name when checking in. As if anyone was their real self in a dump like this.

Perhaps Sadie had checked in? He had no idea. He would have used cash as well. Surely? He had all the other times with Sabine.

Scott's mind was still fuzzy, but he was coming to his senses. "Just a minute," he said and quickly went around the room checking that he had everything. His wallet and cell phone he found on the nightstand. He checked his messages or missed calls.

None.

Strange. Surely Paige—

Another knock at the door, a fist not knuckles this time, more like a thump.

"Coming!" Scott yelled. He tiptoed to the front door and looked through the peep hole.

Nothing.

Probably standing to one side with her cleaning cart.

Scott opened the door and literally jumped back in fright. Stumbling and stuttering with fear, he retreated farther back inside the four walls he had so desperately wanted to escape from just a few moments ago.

Paige stood in the doorway.

She was wearing a long coat with the collar turned up and dark sunglasses, despite it being night outside.

No greeting. No smile. No look of affection and definitely no look of compassion or forgiveness.

She stepped into the room, shut the door quietly, took off her sunglasses and looked around distastefully.

Her gaze returned to Scott and she gave him a quick once-over.

"Paige, I can—"

Her gloved hand came up in a gesture that would have halted a herd of charging rhinoceros.

She didn't want him to speak. She didn't want to hear it. She didn't even want to breathe the sordid air in the little ugly room. She just wanted him to shut up and listen. "Don't say a word. Just nod if you understand."

Scott nodded. He swallowed hard.

Paige fixed a cold stare on him. "I know you are screwing Sabine. That has to end immediately together with any other women you are seeing."

"But—"

"I said shut the fuck up." Paige spoke in a calm, controlled, and relaxed voice that was somehow more frightening than if she'd went ahead and yelled at him.

Paige began laying down the law to Scott, and if he broke the law, the death penalty awaited him. His life would be over, she explained. He may as well be dead. Instead she was offering him a life sentence, with her and their unborn child. But life according to her rules, under her laws.

Scott was going to be imprisoned, without the possibility of parole. Alcatraz for the rich and undeserving she called it. She had already thought all this through, made plans, and now she was executing them.

If he was good, he would get privileges. If he wasn't, he would be placed in solitary confinement. And if he tried to escape, well then...

Paige pulled out her cellphone, the one she had given Sadie to use. She thumbed the screen and brought up a series of photos to show Scott. There was a short video as well.

Scott reluctantly took the cell phone and looked at the screen in horror. Sex selfies taken by Sadie, the mirror on the wall opposite the bed had come in handy, so had the one in the grubby little bathroom.

Scott handed back the phone and felt the noose around his balls tighten a little more.

Sadie had been given specific instructions by Paige not to have sex with her husband. Just play along, get him so drunk that he would not know the difference. Make him think he'd had an all-out fuck session in some sleazy motel room. Paige knew Scott had wanted to fuck Sadie. She had told Paige.

Paige would continue with the charade for as long as she wanted, blackmailing him.

Scott looked very sheepish, was lost for words. He had no comeback. He had nothing. Any bargaining power he once had was now crushed by what Paige held in the palm of her hand.

But just in case he didn't fully understand the predicament he was in, Paige spelled it out further. "The flow of money will continue and you will enjoy the same lifestyle, even better. But your sloppy adulterous ways are over. My father cannot afford any scandal whatsoever. He is going to run for a higher office and I can't allow you or anyone to jeopardize his plans. Now you can sit back and enjoy the ride, but you have to comply with my rules. Understood?"

Scott nodded.

"Good. You're learning." Paige began to pace back and forth.

"You will be the picture-perfect loving husband. And we will give the public the image of the perfect married couple. I don't want to lose this baby because of the undue stress you're putting me under. Is that clear?"

Scott went to say something but then thought better. He still didn't understand how, but it would just have to be his secret, a secret that would never see the light of day. Paige was throwing him a lifeline. It was either sink or swim, there was no middle ground with her. And Scott very much didn't want to sink.

He nodded again.

"Good," Paige said. "If you fall out of line whatsoever, I will destroy you and everyone around you. I have the resources to do it."

Scott nodded again. He didn't doubt for a moment that Paige with her father would carry out her threat if needed.

Paige stopped pacing and faced Scott. "Clean yourself up, and we are never to talk about this again to each other. Do you understand?"

Like Pavlov's dogs, the newly trained Scott continued to nod obediently.

Paige slid her sunglasses back on and went to the door. "Find your own way home."

But Scott had a question, and like a kid in a classroom he raised his hand.

Paige arched an eyebrow.

"What about... Sabine?" Scott asked. Only she knew his secret. Paige still hadn't told anyone in the group that she was pregnant.

Paige looked at Scott, and for the first time she smiled. "Leave her to me."

Chapter 40
Purely Business

Marvin Richards looked up from the stack of computer printouts. It was early morning; Perez was standing at his desk in his office. "Hard to believe, isn't it?" she asked.

"You've gotta be kidding me," he said incredulously.

The computer printouts now contained two different line colors: orange denoting Maggie Vickerman's dates and times she purchased items from the store where Adam worked, and yellow denoting another person.

"We would have missed them completely if we had only just requested purchase details for Maggie Vickerman," Perez said.

Richards nodded, but the new discovery made things worse, not clearer, another person of interest added to the mix.

Before showing Richards this morning the new revelation she had found last night when she was going through the store printouts, all blurry-eyed and jacked up on coffee, Perez had done some background checking on the new person of interest.

On his desk sat a brief background report Perez had cobbled together this morning. She hadn't been able to sleep all night, her mind buzzing with possibilities, the tingling feeling you get in your gut that you're onto something. A door was about to open that would move the entire investigation closer to the truth. After tossing and turning, Perez finally got out of bed all angry and impatient in the pre-dawn darkness, had a quick shower, dressed in a fresh crisp uniform and rolled into work where she spent the next few hours researching, reading, and writing her report. She knew Richards would ask her about this person when he got in at around 7:00 a.m. after he'd reviewed the store list.

"I guess we are going to also have to pay them a visit as well?" Perez didn't relishing the idea of making another trip up there again.

Just then the phone rang on Richards' desk, interrupting his train of thought. Picking it up he seemed to listen half-heartedly. Then his eyes went wide and he glared up at Perez, an expression of mild surprise on his face. He nodded and hung up.

"No need to pay them a visit," he said.

Perez gave a dumbfounded look.

Richards stood, peeled his jacket off the back of his chair, and shrugged into it. "Because they have just walked into the foyer asking for me."

The three of them sat at the small table in the assigned interview room.

Perez had her notebook out, pen poised, Richards off her shoulder.

The visitor sat opposite, and had clearly stipulated that they were here voluntarily. No lawyers, just alone. But it was not to be a formal interview nor would they be providing any written statement.

Paige Hamill sat with her hands folded neatly in her lap, a styrofoam cup filled with water in front of her.

"I thought it would be easier if I came to you," she said calmly, composed, not intimidated by the surroundings. "I didn't want you turning up at my house for no apparent reason. With Maggie Vickerman, I guess you had an excuse to see her about what had happened to Becca."

Richards studied Paige, a little curious as to why she was here of her own volition. He couldn't wait to hear what she was going to say next. "And you don't want your neighbors to know, prying eyes, rumors, innuendo and all that," he said slowly, confirming her motivation.

She nodded. "Especially my husband, Scott. He wouldn't understand."

Richards leaned forward, "So Mrs. Hamill, why don't you tell us why you are here?"

"I saw in the paper a few weeks back, the murder of Adam Teal."

"I take it you knew Adam Teal?" Richards asked.

Paige nodded.

"But you didn't come forward," Richards stated, "to provide information to the police investigation."

"That's because I have no information for the police that has anything to do with his death and..." She paused. "It's delicate."

Paige Hamill took it upon herself to save the embarrassment and rumors that would no doubt happen if her neighbors saw police officers knocking on her door. But there was more. Much more.

"How did you know, Mrs. Hamill, that we were going to pay you a visit?"

Paige gave a slight smile that Perez couldn't figure if it was genuine or condescending. She guessed the latter.

"I may be blonde and wealthy but I'm not stupid, detective. I simply pieced it together. You came and visited Maggie Vickerman. She told us, said it was just a routine follow-up to the incident with Becca Cartwright. Becca said the same thing. But I knew Maggie was sleeping with Adam Teal."

"Maggie Vickerman told you this?" Richards asked, wondering what these women on Mill Point Road discussed when they got together.

"Not in so many words," Paige said. "Maggie likes to brag about the young men she sleeps with. While she didn't tell me his name, she did go on to describe him, in detail, and where he worked. It was almost like she was proud of it, waving it in front of me and the others like a badge of honor, almost taunting me to go to the outlet stores and see him for myself."

"And you did? You went to the store where Adam Teal worked just to satisfy your curiosity?" Richards asked.

"I had other reasons as well, detective."

I'm sure you did, Perez thought finding it difficult to keep up with the note-taking with all the new information that was being brought to light.

Paige continued. "Maggie can be very descriptive with her extramarital liaisons. We, the ladies on Mill Point Road, get together on a regular basis during the week, just to talk, mainly share gossip. At times though I feel Maggie uses the forum to brag to the entire group. She mentioned this young, college student who, in her exact words, 'Could fuck all night long.'"

"Please forgive me for asking, Mrs. Hamill, but…" Richards didn't know how to quite put it. Maybe Maggie had an excuse, not that it was a valid excuse. Maggie was much older, still active and attractive, a woman who obviously had needs her husband couldn't satisfy. Whereas, Paige Hamill appeared to be completely different. What Richards saw sitting in front of him was a young, articulate, graceful, and extremely attractive woman who, according to Perez's report, had a young, equally attractive husband.

But somehow Richards had the distinct feeling that Paige Hamill was about to tell him what had caused her to fall from grace.

Paige nodded, like she knew what Richards was thinking. "I don't have affairs, detective. Like I said, I had other reasons."

Perez stopped writing and glanced up.

Richards waited for the answer.

There was a subtle shift in Paige's otherwise flawless expression, like she was wrestling whether or not she should tell the full story. She knew that if she wasn't completely honest with them, things could get ugly, and she definitely didn't want Scott, or more importantly, her family to know.

"Mrs. Hamill, a young man is dead. So are others. I need to know exactly your relationship with the deceased, Adam Teal," Richards said.

Paige gave an exasperated sigh, resigned to the fact that she had to tell them her dirty little secret. "I paid Adam Teal to have sex with me on a regular basis so that I would get pregnant."

For a few moments no one said a word, the only sound coming from the vents above as cool air trickled in.

Richards leaned back in his chair, his mind trying to comprehend the last few days, hoping his face wouldn't reveal the utter disbelief he now felt. What was it with these women? It was unfathomable how they could think money could buy them anything, the perfect lifestyle, a child, anything. And apparently it could.

"You see detective, I've been trying to become pregnant for some time now. My husband, Scott, and I desperately want to have children, to start a family. Adam Teal was simply my backup."

Backup? Perez couldn't believe what she was hearing. The woman was unemotional, clinical, as she described her relationship with Adam Teal, who was simply an unknowing sperm donor. Perez didn't condone what Adam Teal had done, after all he was dead and Perez believed he had a good heart. He just wanted the money for his mother and siblings. And yet, these cold, calculating women had taken advantage of him for their own selfish ends.

It was almost as if he was being shared around among these women. Perez wondered who else was using Adam Teal for sexual favors.

"And you paid him, Mrs. Hamill?" Richards asked.

"Correct detective. It was purely a financial relationship, the financial transaction between two consenting adults done in privacy."

You cold, selfish bitch, Perez thought. Using money to get anything you want, including a baby.

"But I broke off the arrangement about a month ago, prior to his death, and I haven't seen him since. Then I read in the papers that he was found dead."

"How did this arrangement work?" Richards asked. "Between the two of you."

Paige went on to explain how on numerous occasions, she would arrange to meet Adam Teal. They had a prearranged location not far from his work, secluded enough so no one would see him getting into her car. She never brought him back to her home. Sometimes they used the motel a few miles out of town, paid in cash by Paige. But for most of their interludes together, she would drive to an old abandoned farm on the outskirts of Ravenwood. There, hidden in the barn they would have sex on the hood of her car. Unglamorous, but functional.

As Paige Hamill gave a detailed account of her adulterous ways, she showed no remorse, no regret, didn't once say that she was sorry or apologize. She never uttered a word of how sorry she was that Adam Teal was dead. Her descriptions, story, and reasoning were black and white, clinical, stripped back to the basic fundamentals of supply and demand. Paige Hamill, in her obsession to get pregnant, had a demand that Adam Teal fulfilled.

Adam Teal was simply my backup.

"And did it work?" Perez asked, in a flat tone, tinged with anger.

Richards allowed the question. He was about to ask it himself, any good detective would have.

Paige swiveled her head slowly towards Perez, as though noticing her for the first time. It was definitely a condescending look, staring down her nose at the young female police officer. Pure arrogance wrapped up in designer clothes and expensive jewelry. "I beg your pardon?"

Under the table, Perez's leg began to jitter up and down, a new trait that she had recently and unexplainably acquired.

"Did it work?" Perez repeated with a little more conviction this time. "Did you get pregnant?"

Paige's eyes turned a shade of glacial blue. "I don't see how that is any of your business." She turned back to Richards, dismissing Perez with a flick of hair, like she was nothing, insignificant.

"Mrs. Hamill, have you ever been on Black Rock Road? Driven along there?"

"I may have a few times. Sometimes I would pick him up from a spot along there. It was his idea. And when we were done I'd drop him back to the same spot." She thought for a moment. "For the life of me, I can't imagine why he chose there. It's such a desolate, rundown part of town. And the road at night, there's no street lights. But he insisted."

"That's because his home was there, with his family."

Paige just gave a dismissive nod.

It was Paige Hamill in her car that Valerie Teal had seen on occasions driving up and down the street at dusk, picking up her son, literally. Paige Hamill, driving around, a place so far removed from her own privileged world of luxury cars and sprawling homes, safe behind security gates and high walls, surrounded by swathes of lush, pampered Kentucky bluegrass where Adam Teal would never have set foot upon.

"Your father is Senator Brooks?" Richards asked, "Is that right?"

Paige nodded.

The implications were damaging, to her family and her father's political career.

Perez could just see the headlines: "Senator's married daughter fucks college student on hood of her BMW just to get pregnant. College student later found murdered." Well maybe not the word "fuck" but "had sex with" would probably be used. It certainly took the meaning of "sheer driving pleasure" to a whole new level.

Paige Hamill knew she could get the lawyers involved, put up a wall of silence, and refuse to cooperate with the police. But that's not what she wanted. She was hoping that the relationship wouldn't be made public if she wasn't a suspect and if it wasn't relevant to the case.

If it was to become known, it would be embarrassing not just for her and Scott, but also for her father and the important people her father and mother knew as well. Paige would bring immense shame upon the family name and that was a legacy that she wanted to avoid at all costs.

Paige decided to play her main card. "Detective Richards," she said, "I am more than willing to be fully cooperative with the police. However it is only on the strictest condition that I do so anonymously."

"Unless requested to by the courts," Richards continued.

"I hope it doesn't come to that," she replied, holding Richards's gaze, her perfect white teeth behind perfectly made up lips. "Ask me what you wish but on no account is my husband, my family, or friends or anyone else to know."

It certainly was an offer Richards welcomed. If Paige Hamill was telling the truth, and being upfront and honest with him, he needed her cooperation.

Taking out a tissue, Paige dabbed her nose before she leaned forward and looked Richards directly in the eye again, then uttered, "And in return for my anonymity, I'm willing to pay you."

Richards frowned, so did Perez, unsure of what the woman just said. *What? She's offering a bribe?*

Paige saw the strange look of disbelief on their faces. Her eyes dilated and she gave a devious smile, like a predator watching its prey close up. "Pay you," she repeated, her voiced hushed now, "in a commodity that's worth more than money or gold."

Richards raised an eyebrow. Perez raised two.

"Information," she said. "About everyone else on Mill Point Road."

Chapter 41
Downfall

The first sign that something was wrong was when Mark and Sabine's house came into view, and Becca immediately saw a flatbed tow truck parked in Sabine's driveway, bed tilted back, winch cable hooked up to Sabine's Bentley, slowly hauled inch by inch onto the flatbed.

Becca slowed her car.

Two boxy SUV cruisers from the Washington County Sheriff's Office were parked out front and three deputies were mingling on the lawn watching proceedings.

Becca squeezed past then pulled into her own driveway just before Zoe Collins came bounding out of her front door, towards Becca.

"What's going on?" Becca asked as they watched the scene unfold in the front yard of Sabine's home.

"No idea," Zoe replied. "Maggie just texted me. Apparently they arrived ten minutes ago outside Mark and Sabine's house. I thought she was joking."

After the Bentley was securely tied down, the tow truck driver signed some paperwork on a clipboard handed to him from a deputy, jumped into the cab of the tow truck and drove off. Moments later a large semi-trailer truck groaned its way up the rise before finally turning into Sabine's driveway, cutting the corner, its meaty tires tearing a deep gouge into the pristine lawn.

Zoe and Becca watched as four large burly men climbed out of the cab, lowered the rear hydraulic tailgate, then quickly and efficiently removed heavy duty dolly trucks and began to wheel them inside the house.

Becca had a feeling as to what was happening, and it didn't involve the Millers relocating to a new home. As she and Zoe watched, the four burly men finally emerged, lugging a huge flat screen television, computer equipment, and furniture. "What the hell is going on?" Zoe whispered as the procession of men went back and forth between the truck and Sabine's home, wheeling out anything and everything of value and placing it inside the back of the truck.

"Their assets are being seized," Becca said. "The party's over." But before Zoe could ask Becca what she meant, Maggie came running along the sidewalk, all flustered and panicky, waving her cell phone in her hand. "Our investment account," she cried. "All the funds, our entire retirement savings are gone!"

Becca said nothing, just gave a wry smile.

Maggie caught her breath. "I went to check on the balances this morning and the monies have been cleared out," Maggie said, a look of desperation on her face.

"Where the hell are Sabine and Mark?" Zoe asked.

Just then another sheriff's cruiser rounded the bend of the rise and pulled up alongside the other two vehicles. A contingent of deputies climbed out, went inside the open front door of Sabine's house, and moments later, sandwiched between two deputies, and in handcuffs, they marched Sabine Miller outside, along the path and to the curb.

"Oh my God!" Zoe said, a hand to her mouth. "What the hell is going on?"

Maggie took off toward where they had Sabine standing, venom in her eyes. "Where's our fucking money, you bitch!" she screamed as she approached.

One of the deputies turned and cut her off, holding her back. There was a brief tussle of arms and threats before Maggie was dumped unceremoniously on the lawn and told not to move otherwise she would be cuffed as well.

Sabine looked up for a brief moment toward where Becca and Zoe stood. They caught a glimpse of her face. It was a picture of utter dejection, deep pitted eye sockets with dark circles, gaunt cheeks and pale skin, like all the Botox had been sucked out of her face leaving behind a wrinkled, shriveled, defeated person.

Then a not-so-gentle hand pushed Sabine's head down and she was placed in the back of one of the SUVs.

Maggie was allowed to return to the group. "Bitch just ignored me," she spat.

"Like I said, their assets are being seized, they owe money I imagine, a lot of money," Becca said.

"Why?" Zoe was aghast. "How?"

Becca turned to both women and explained to both about the letter that had been mistakenly placed in her mail box. "All I can imagine is that things haven't gone all that well with their investment company. No doubt a lot of people—creditors and investors—are owed money and brought an action against them."

Deep down, Maggie Vickerman knew it was true. It really had been too good to be true.

"I'm only guessing that," Becca said. "Time will tell."

They could see Sabine in the back seat of the sheriff's SUV as it pulled away from the curb, her face turned away.

The burly men worked at a steady pace, slowly emptying the house and filling up the back of the truck. And as she watched, Becca couldn't help but think about all those occasions when she had gone shopping with Sabine, how she was constantly trying to coax store assistants, restaurant owners, anyone and everyone in her network of friends and acquaintances to invest in her husband's investment firm. She had a feeling of what was going on now with Sabine and Mark Miller. Their extravagant lifestyle. The vacations in the Bahamas. The cars, the lavish jewelry, the expensive handbag collection. All of it was a charade based on the deception of being fabulously wealthy and successful, when in fact, from the little insights that Becca had observed and had worked out, the Millers were broke. The banks and creditors owned everything and were now calling in the debt.

But for Sabine to be arrested and placed in handcuffs meant that there was more to the charade, something much worse. The house of cards was slowly collapsing, and no doubt the full extent of what was happening would eventually come out.

Becca left Zoe and Maggie standing in the driveway and went back inside her own home, wondering why Paige hadn't come outside to watch the spectacle.

After all, her car was parked in her driveway.

Chapter 42
Backflips

There was an empty place at the table, a lone chair where Sabine Miller would have sat this morning had she not been sitting in a jail cell.

Zoe, Becca, and Maggie sat around the table in Paige's kitchen, pondering what had happened. Something stronger was called for than coffee this time. It was almost noon so wine glasses had now replaced coffee cups, with Paige playing hostess, circling the table, a bottle in each hand filling up everyone's glass. "This is a wonderful cabernet from the Napa Valley. You simply must try it," Paige said as she went to pour a glass for Becca, as though the news of the past week meant nothing and life went on.

Becca looked up, placing a hand over the rim of her glass. "Just white for me, Paige, thanks."

"How could you not like red wine?" Paige asked in mock astonishment.

Becca just gave a shrug. "Never tried it. It reminds me too much of blood."

"Your loss," Paige replied, pouring white wine into Becca's glass. Paige stared down, spying the gold Tiffany & Co necklace around Becca's neck. "Is that new? I haven't seen you wearing that before."

"Now you are starting to sound like Sabine," Maggie snorted. "Bitch was a thief."

Becca touched the necklace. "Yes. I bought it for myself." Becca had invested in her own jewelry after Michael's death. He had found jewelry pointless, a waste of money because you could never sell it for what you paid for it. The closest thing to jewelry Michael had ever bought for Becca was a ninety dollar Swatch watch for her last birthday.

"No wine for you, Paige?" Maggie noticed that Paige just had a tall glass of mineral water in front of her.

Paige rolled her eyes, chastising herself. "Drank too much last night. Still feeling it."

"Celebrating were we?" Zoe asked Paige.

Paige sat down and gave an innocent smile. "No, not really." Behind her contrived expression, Paige was doing backflips. She hadn't stopped celebrating since she saw the dejected form of Sabine Miller being placed in the back of the sheriff's SUV and driven away at high speed.

The women sat in silence, drank, and contemplated the events of the past week. Enough facts had filtered through the town and the media as to what had happened. On the table in front of them sat a pile of local and national newspapers, outlining in disgraceful detail the demise of Sabine and Mark Miller's investment empire, revealing for the first time the true scam it was.

The women hadn't met formally together in over a week. Reporters and television crews had picketed the front gate, and a drone had even flown overhead trying to capture pictures of the home where the Millers lived. Mac had tried to keep the reporters out and had threatened to shoot down the drone if he saw it again.

Eventually the interest faded and the reporters finally packed up and left.

"My attorney said we've most likely lost everything," Maggie finally said, reaching for the bottle of red, topping up her glass none too carefully. Her eyes were ringed red, crying tears of frustration more than of sorrow. They might have to sell and move to a smaller place. Hank wouldn't like that. They had argued almost every day since the news. If their marriage was bad before, it was much worse now.

Paige reached over and squeezed Maggie's hand, offering a few words of comfort along with her trademark look of concern.

"It was a plain and simple Ponzi scheme apparently," Becca said. She had trawled the online news sites that were still buzzing with the story. The fallout was going to be huge. With her journalistic prowess, she had formulated a detailed story of the facts and speculation so far. "The whole thing relied on a continuous stream of new investors coming into the structure that Mark and Sabine had created. That's why I guess Sabine, ever the salesperson, was always approaching potential clients, trying to convince them to invest."

"What happened to all our money?" Maggie asked with a sniffle. "We were getting regular income checks from Mark. I would go online into our account and see our portfolio balance, all our investments, it was all there."

Paige remained silent, even though she knew more about what had happened than all the women around the table.

Becca shook her head. "Maggie, you and Hank weren't

actually earning income from your investments. There were no actual investments. You were getting checks, but they were funded by the capital invested by new investors not from any profits. There were no profits. And as far as your online account was concerned, it probably was an elaborate hoax, a fake website with fake figures fed into it just to give you the appearance that it was real, to make you feel and believe that your money was safe and your investments were earning the incredible returns. So what you and Hank believed was profit, was just someone else's money who had invested after you. It all went around in a circle."

"So the bigger it got, the more people Sabine and Mark needed to keep the charade going?" Paige asked, acting naïve.

Becca nodded. "That's correct. They had to keep paying returns out to all the existing investors so everything looked normal. They were just shuffling other people's money."

Maggie knocked back the glass and muttered a word under her breath that started with "c" and ended in "ts."

"How do you know all about this?" Zoe asked.

Becca turned to her. "I did a story a few years back about a similar Ponzi scheme. An accountant in Florida had set one up, and had basically ripped off all his clients, family, friends, and other investors. He managed to convince them to invest in a fictitious hedge fund. Millions of dollars were lost. People's lives were destroyed, young and old, retirees, newly married couples, wealthy individuals, lost everything. He simply took their money and shifted it into an offshore account and spent it all. He falsified bank statements, earning reports, everything. By the time authorities caught up with him, he'd spent it all on a lavish lifestyle."

Maggie spilled more red wine as she topped up her own glass. "That bitch Sabine wore, drove, lived, and vacationed with our money, that is what Becca is trying to say."

"What I can't understand," Zoe said, "was in the newspapers it said Sabine was in custody but they still can't find where Mark is."

"Probably dead, I hope," Maggie said bitterly before gulping down her wine. "Maybe he took money from less than dubious people who found out about the scam and decided to take the law into their own hands."

Upon hearing this, Paige attempted a triple backflip inside her head, and landed gracefully on her two feet.

Hank waited until Maggie was gone. Waited for her footsteps to fade through the ceiling above and the front door to close. She was scuttling off to Paige Hamill's house to seek sympathy when ultimately *she* was the cause of their demise.

Christ, that annoyed him, and Maggie had certainly surrounded herself with her own kind.

And now this! Their money all gone. *His* money. *His* retirement. *His* comfortable future stolen all because his stupid whore of a wife trusted another dumb whore with their money. Hank never liked nor trusted Sabine Miller, had told Maggie countless times. And what did she do? She went ahead anyway and invested their retirement savings with them.

After the Navy, Hank had worked hard, started a small local freight company with just one truck. Then applied what he had learned from being in the military: supply chain management, logistics, planning, and anticipation. All the things that were essential in running a successful freight business. Soon he had a fleet of trucks. Then he sold the business and made a fortune. Now that fortune was gone.

Christ, what a dumb bitch I married.

Hank had a new truck lined up, the latest Dodge Ram, with all the bells and whistles. He even put a down payment on it at the dealership in town. Now that was gone too. Probably lose the down payment as well. No matter which way Hank looked at it, he could see his destitute future stretch away before his very eyes.

No more eating out. No more twenty-two ounce porterhouse steaks at fancy restaurants. No more rounds of twelve-year-old single malt Scotch for his buddies. No more trips down to Los Cabos where Maggie lay around the pool sipping margaritas, while he slipped away into Cabo San Lucas to visit those special clubs he liked so well. Instead, it would be dining at Denny's, drinking at home alone, and watching porn on the internet, which he did anyway.

Hank led a frugal life. It was Maggie who was the problem, the big spender. He didn't envisage his retirement years being spent in a mobile home, in some shitty sun-faded trailer park on the side of a gritty dusty highway, cutting out discount coupons, and searching the back of the sofa for nickels and dimes. The more he thought about it, the more Hank raged. The last time he was this angry he had killed someone. Now all he could see was red, with Maggie's mocking face in the crosshairs. This was all her doing. She'd ruined his life, his marriage, his dignity, and any prospect of a comfortable retirement.

But if the Navy had taught Hank anything, it was to always have redundancies in the battlefield. If one critical component failed, always have a backup you could switch to. And Hank's backup was the few million he had squirreled away in an offshore bank account that Maggie knew nothing about. It was his contingency plan, to move on without her grubby and greedy little hands getting to his stash of cash. First, he needed to take care of her, and not in the spousal sense either.

Hank went to his desk and pulled out his hunting knife again. He'd spent the last hour sharpening it, using Maggie's pathetic voice on the phone upstairs as she ranted at length to some lawyer as impetus for honing the blade so that it was razor-sharp. Maybe it was too messy, too violent, too obvious. He tested the blade on his thumb, drawing a ribbon of blood.

Obvious? The cogs inside his devious little head started turning, scheming, planning.

Stabbing her with the knife wouldn't do. He needed to strangle her, stare her right in the face as he wrung the life out of her. Watch her panic-stricken eyes bulge in horror before he extinguished them for good.

He opened his scrapbook. The pages were crammed with press clippings, carefully trimmed, then glued in place. He thumbed through the pages thoughtfully. Yes, this will certainly do. Obvious without being blatant.

On a shelf he found some cable ties, and he had plenty of rope hanging from hooks around the basement. As he gathered his tools and tasted more bitterness, a plan started to formulate in his head that was after all... obvious.

Chapter 43
The Smell

Whatever the reason was, Perez still had her suspicions about Becca Cartwright. There was just something behind those cool eyes, her somewhat deliberate blank expression, and that delicate smugness she so easily displayed.

Even though Richards had not asked Perez to look into Becca's background, rather concentrate on Maggie and Hank Vickerman, and now Paige Hamill, Perez took it upon herself.

She sat at a workstation, the din of police officers buzzing around her, phones ringing and the occasional curse of frustration. Perhaps it was her detective's instinct starting to form, that small seed that begins to sprout in your gut that continues to grow into something more than just a feeling, more than just instinct. Perez commenced an initial background check that quickly developed when something caught her attention.

Rebecca Cartwright was a journalist by trade, who worked for a small local newspaper in Connecticut. She had no criminal record just a few traffic violations for speeding.

How can a journalist afford such a luxury mansion on Mill Point Road?

Digging a little deeper, she discovered that Michael Cartwright, her husband, had passed away.

The initial search on Michael Cartwright turned up nothing. Apart from his place of employment there were no details about him.

She then ran his name through the police databases, and what she discovered piqued her curiosity.

Now she understood why she could find so little about Michael Cartwright.

There was an unwritten code of conduct in the media as a sign of respect for the family and friends of the departed not to specifically report on certain things or just to provide scant details to the public. There wasn't much that the media didn't report on these days, with an obvious disregard for respecting privacy. However, in cases like these, the media always seemed to follow this rule.

Law enforcement was another matter. They had to report on the cold hard facts, no matter how brutal or insensitive they were. Perez's search revealed a reference to a police report from the Hartford Police Department twelve months back that Perez slowly read—twice. The two officers first on the scene had taken detailed notes and this pleased Perez to no end.

The subsequent follow-up by the senior officer in particular was with the insurance company that held the life insurance policy for Michael Cartwright. The insurance company had requested the full police report, autopsy report and then conducted a phone conference with both police officers and a senior detective as a matter of company protocol in instances like this.

After months of deliberation and subsequent information requests from the Connecticut PD, the insurance company closed the file, accepting the police version of events regarding the death of Michael Cartwright.

Perez made detailed notes and printed off everything Connecticut PD had on the case and made her way to see Marvin Richards.

Richards was hunkered down at his desk, behind a pile of paperwork, the ringing phone on his desk going ignored. He looked up when Perez walked in with another stack of paperwork to add to his already hectic day.

"I know you didn't ask me to, but I did some background checking on Rebecca Cartwright." Perez sat down without being asked and began thumbing through the paperwork.

Richards leaned back in his chair, pushed his glasses forward and regarded her for a moment. He didn't know where Perez was going with this new line of inquiry but what he had seen of her so far was that she was direct, thorough, and didn't waste her time on senseless tasks. "So what do you have?" She must have found something, otherwise she wouldn't have bothered printing off reports.

Over the next ten minutes, Perez laid out in detail what she found about the background of Michael and Rebecca Cartwright while Richards listened patiently. When she was done she waited for Richards to digest the information.

"So he died and his wife got a huge insurance payout. Now we know how she could afford such a place," Richards said. "From what you have said, it seemed like an open and shut case. The insurance company agreed to pay her out, eventually. I guess they just didn't want to pay out such a large amount unless they were absolutely certain."

"It was the manner of his death that intrigues me the most," Perez said.

She passed Richards a copy of the police report she had printed off and the word she had circled red on the third page under "Cause of Death."

Richards slid his glasses back on and read the single word that was inserted in the space.

Perez continued. "I know when someone close to you dies, like your spouse, a close family member or friend, it can be extremely traumatic and distressing," Perez said. "Death is death, I know but when—" Perez couldn't formulate the words she was trying to say to Richards. "I just thought she would act differently, perhaps more distressed, perhaps more introverted, given how her husband had died. Taken longer to grieve. Just my opinion."

Richards placed the police report down and stared at the ceiling for a moment. He had only met Rebecca Cartwright briefly while standing on her front porch. "Maybe she is on medication, antidepressants, happy pills," he said, turning his attention back to the police report, and the single word that Perez had circled multiple times in red.

Suicide.

Squatting down at the base of the wall, Becca shone her flashlight along the seam where the wall met the floor. She could see a thin line of murky brownish-red liquid of some sort.

Great. That's all she needed.

She didn't want to touch it, but it definitely wasn't there the last time she had checked the progress of the stain on the basement wall. The stain seemed to have stopped spreading, but now something was leaking out from the base of the wall. She slipped the flashlight between her teeth, and while aiming the beam of light at the glistening line of liquid, she snapped a photo with her cell phone. Standing she thumbed a quick message to Josh telling him of this new development. She didn't want to call him, take him off the job he was busily working on. She asked if he could call her tonight when he got home. Becca attached the photo and was about to send the email when she cocked her head. There was a faint smell, something earthy, just a slight tinge she was certain. She took a step closer toward the wall.

It was coming from the wall. Maybe there was a dead animal behind it. Somehow it had burrowed into the wall, gotten trapped then died. She added this new revelation to the email to Josh then pressed send.

Becca sighed as she trudged back up the basement stairs, more than a little relieved that it wasn't anything serious.

Chapter 44
The Whiteboard

By 10:00 a.m. Richards had issued orders for impounding both the vehicles of Maggie Vickerman and Paige Hamill for forensic testing to see if they could matching DNA to the DNA they had of Adam Teal and of the other victims.

At 10:30 a.m. Richards with Perez gathered again in his office in front of the whiteboard where they laid out everything they knew so far, the victims, key persons of interest, evidence. Maggie Vickerman and Paige Hamill had been added to the whiteboard and now Rebecca Cartwright. While there was no direct link between Cartwright and the other victims, especially Adam Teal, both Richards and Perez felt there was something about the woman that didn't feel right. Like she was hiding something. Maybe the connection would reveal itself, like it had for the other two women who happened to live on Mill Point Road as well. It was all too much of a coincidence.

The police phone tip line set up two weeks ago to garner any public information had provided little.

Perez stood leaning against the desk while Richards went

through and summarized what they knew so far.

With the other three victims—Adam Bailey, Adam Thurston, and Adam Drake—all family, friends and work associates had been interviewed multiple times, and still no one had seen or heard anything regarding the abduction of the three young men. There was also nothing in their history that would suggest anyone had a suitable motive to want to abduct, detain, then murder them.

However, Richards was convinced that Adam Teal was their best prospect for leading them to the Eden Killer. He had led them to two women who lived in the same exclusive gated community in Ravenwood. There had to be a connection, somehow.

Both Maggie Vickerman and Paige Hamill admitted to being in a sexual relationship with Adam Teal. Both women shopped on a regular basis at the luxury goods store where Adam Teal had worked. The sales reports for the last six months proved this and supported the link between Maggie Vickerman, Paige Hamill, and Adam Teal. However both Richards and Perez didn't believe either of these two women were capable of such heinous and brutal crimes.

Richards had marked out on a large wall map the area around Black Rock Road and the red pin where Adam Teal's body was found. There were three other red pins denoting where the bodies of the other three victims had been discovered. They were all in close proximity to Mill Point Road.

"Valerie Teal had said on several occasions that, at dusk before her son's disappearance, she remembered seeing a vehicle driving up and down Black Rock Road, where they lived," Richards tapped the location on the wall map.

Perez nodded thoughtfully as Richards listed off the facts.

"Paige Hamill admitted to dropping off Adam Teal after their sexual rendezvous on Black Rock Road."

The forensics team had advised Richards that their analysis and DNA testing would be concluded within twenty-four hours once both vehicles belonging to Maggie Vickerman and Paige Hamill had been seized.

"These women are still not being completely truthful and honest about their relationship with Adam Teal," Perez said.

"That's because they are hiding something," Richards said. "What we also know is that there is a definite biblical connection between the victims and the killer, hence the name he has been given. Young males, all under the age of twenty-five, all named Adam."

"Female retribution?" Perez offered.

"So you believe the killer is a woman?" Richards asked.

Perez nodded. "I don't think she's named Eve though. But I think the motive is driven by an extreme dislike of men."

Richards hadn't ruled that out. "A vendetta against men, believing that men or mankind is the root of all evil and sin. So you believe the motive is purely religious?" It was a theory he had considered because of the obvious names and gender of all the victims. However, Richards didn't believe there was a religious nut out there stalking and killing young men on some holy crusade to punish for the sins of Adam from the book of Genesis. There had to be another motive.

"We're all sinners in one form or another," Perez said. "However, sin doesn't discriminate between male and female. If you're asking me, 'Do men commit the majority of crimes, including some of the most evil and abhorrent against women and children?' my answer is yes."

"I agree as well," Richards said. "But I also don't think the motive is entirely religious either. I think the person is taking a stand, the fact that the victims are young men all named Adam is symbolic for them. I think the person is extremely righteous, devout in what they believe in, faith or otherwise."

"And ironically," Perez countered, "this crusade they are undertaking taints them as one of the worse sinners as well."

"An eye for an eye," Richards quoted. "Matthew, the New Testament." He stood back, looking at the whiteboard, wondering where Rebecca Cartwright fit into all of this. She was new to the community on Mill Point Road. Single, no children, a journalist by trade, whose husband had committed suicide, thereby she received a large insurance payout.

Perez pushed off the desk and stood next to Richards, and they both stared together at drawn arrows, photos, scrawls of notes, harsh underlines, and the ghost of words not completely erased from the whiteboard. "Maybe we are not dealing with one killer?" Perez finally said. "Maybe it's a group of attractive women, who live together, share the same ideals, the same beliefs."

"And are all neighbors?" It sounded too unbelievable to Richards. "All living in one street?"

From experience, Richards knew killers worked alone. However there were rare cases of serial killer pairs that had been well documented over the years: Fred and Rosemary West, David and Katherine Birnie, Delphine and Maria Gonzales, just to name a few. But a group of unrelated women, banding together to fulfill some sort of male hatred fueled killing spree? It was too left field to comprehend. But right now, they didn't have much to go on.

"And where does Rebecca Cartwright fit into this?" Richards asked, his eyes now on her photo on the whiteboard that had been pulled from the DMV. Like Perez, Richards believed there was a link, although tenuous, to Rebecca Cartwright if only for the fact that they were all neighbors.

"She's hiding something too," Perez said. "There is something about her I don't trust. It may just be baggage from the past, but the woman is hiding something. I'm sure of it."

"Gut feeling?" Richards asked.

"I prefer to call it a woman's intuition of another woman," Perez replied.

"But there's no connection between her and Adam Teal that we know of."

"Not yet, anyway."

"What about the husbands, where do they fit in?" Richards asked.

"You just asked me to focus on Maggie Vickerman and Paige Hamill."

Richards sat down at his desk and pondered everything on the whiteboard. It felt like the answer was somewhere right in front of them, in plain sight. He could feel it too, niggling behind a door in the dark recesses of his mind that had yet to be opened.

Everything pointed toward Mill Point Road.

Just then his phone rang. He picked it up and listened, his expression instantly dire.

"What's up?" Perez asked as Richards ended the call.

He looked at Perez. "There's been some kind of domestic incident up at Mill Point Road. EMS is on their way."

Chapter 45
Found Out

It was a single sheet of paper, one of eight pieces that had been stapled together.

Detective Marvin Richards swiveled it around then slid it across the table toward Hank Vickerman. He then sat back and watched Hank carefully.

Hank's left eye was black, swollen almost completely shut. His forehead sported a bandage. Underneath was a neat little row of nine stitches courtesy of a heavy Waterford crystal vase.

The corners of Hank's mouth twitched as his eyes ran down the lines of text on the page in front of him, his mind not comprehending how they were able to download this information from his computer. He had used a Windows washer and the cache scrubber thereby erasing every trace of his browsing history. However, in front of him, in painfully exquisite detail, were the names of every website he had visited in the past six months, their IP addresses, his IP address, and the duration of the videos he had watched.

Richards sat silently across the table from Hank. Slowly he

could see beads of sweat breaking out across the man's brow, the trembling of his lips more pronounced the further his eyes went down the page.

Finally Richards spoke. "Our IT guys say these are some of the most depraved sites and video footage they have ever seen."

Hank placed the page down, refusing to look Richards in the eye.

"We also dusted your keyboard and mouse. We only found your fingerprints, no one else's."

The implication was obvious. Hank couldn't use anyone else as an excuse for accessing his own computer. It was him and him alone.

Richards stared at the single sheet of paper, a vile digital roadmap that contained descriptions such as *child torture, child rape, sodomize my daughter, sharing my children, Polly's bath time pics.* Marvin Richards by nature wasn't a violent man. Not prone to bouts of anger or fits of rage. But after he had viewed just a small portion of what they had found on Hank's hard drive, he could've easily choked Hank Vickerman, or reached out across the table and cracked the man's skull against the table top.

While he hadn't perpetrated any of the heinous acts on the videos, the sheer quantity of downloaded content and footage viewed online placed him, in the mind of Richards, within spitting distance of those who had committed such atrocities. Back in New York City, Richards was friends with the detectives in the child exploitation or cybercrime units. He had certainly heard some of their stories. But their words didn't prepare Richards for the glimpse of hell he had seen this afternoon on Hanks computer.

Pulling out a large sealed evidence bag from a cardboard storage box at his feet, Richards slid it across the table, directly under Hank's nose. "We also found this."

Hank looked down at his scrapbook and said nothing. The mounting weight of evidence against him seemed to be sucking all the air from his lungs making him incapable of saying anything at all.

Richards continued. "It's quite a collection of press clippings you have there. Do you enjoy the notoriety of what you've done? The men you have murdered. How you abducted them, and then imprisoned them in that steel room we found in your basement." They had found the modular steel storm shelter that Hank had installed in his basement. With power providing ventilation and light, it was perfect for holding his victims alive until Hank strangled them before dumping their bodies.

Hank looked up, his mouth jittery, his breath short. "What I've done?" he cried in anguish, his hands flustering about on the table. "I've done nothing!"

Hank was slowly breaking. Richards could see this now.

Richards ignored the obvious distress in Hank's face. The man was simply in denial. They all were when confronted with their sins, pronouncing their innocence, saying it was a setup, that it was someone else. Richards had heard and seen it all before, and quite frankly his patience was wearing a little thin right now.

Richards flipped through the open file in front of him, selected another page and slid it across the table. It was a copy of Hank's criminal record that Perez had found after she had done some digging on him.

Richards had enough evidence to charge Hank Vickerman. He was the Eden Killer and the state attorney had given her approval, after reviewing the case file that Richards had presented to her.

"You beat a homosexual man to death outside a bar in Washington, just after you returned from your second tour of duty in Vietnam in 1970."

"It was self-defense," Hank grizzled, twisting his head side to side like his shirt collar was slowly tightening around his throat. "He attacked me!"

Richards gave a doubtful smile. *Defiant to the end.* "Judge didn't seem to think so. You did time in prison." The charges had been reduced from murder to manslaughter. Thanks to an exemplary service record and good behavior, Hank was released early from his sentence. But Hank was no war hero, no service man who deserved his country's respect, that was for sure. Some of Hank's Army buddies, who gave evidence in court, testified that Hank hated gays, black people, and Asians. He took immense and sometimes cruel pleasure with some of the innocent villagers in Nam during field operations.

Hank balled his fists, his face turning red.

It all seemed to fit together for Richards and the SA. The fact that Hank was homophobic. The fact that he had killed a gay man back in 1970. The fact that they had found a scrapbook in his basement that contained a detailed history of press clippings and stories of the exploits of the Eden Killer. And the steel storm shelter that Hank had installed in the corner of his basement. Right at this very moment the steel room was being scoured by the forensic team as they searched for any possible trace evidence or DNA matching the past victims. It was only a matter of time before they found something to link Hank directly to the murders.

Hank looked at Richards, anguish in his eyes. "But—I didn't kill anyone. I never killed those men," he said, his voice stuttering.

Richards gave Hank a blank stare, not believing anything that came out of the man's mouth. The SA was pushing for life without parole, premeditated, intentional, first-degree murder.

"You've gotta believe me!" Hank sobbed. "It's not me."

Richards packed his gear and placed it back inside the storage box. He stood up, and left the room without a second glance, leaving Hank alone to contemplate his own fate.

Haley Perez didn't look up from the one-way glass as Richards walked into the observation room and stood beside her. She remained focused, staring through the glass watching Hank Vickerman.

"What do you think?" Richards asked, placing the storage box on the desk next to her.

"He looks guilty," Perez replied as Hank stared around the room, then looked straight at her before his gazed moved on.

He was displaying the classic symptoms of someone who had done something wrong. However, as she watched him, Perez had the distinct feeling that something was not quite right. While she hadn't conducted any criminal interviews herself, and had only watched a few in the observation room, there seemed a disconnect between how Hank presented himself and behaved compared to what she imagined the Eden Killer would be like.

She was disappointed. She had read all the victims' case files in-depth. Whoever had stalked, abducted, then killed these young men was highly organized, meticulous, and had planned everything thoroughly. They weren't prone to being careless or simply impulsive. They were very intelligent, and extremely cunning. They had to be, given the fact that they hadn't been caught yet... until now.

Motive and method. The two words Richards had drilled into her, she kept turning over in her head.

"What do you think?" Perez turned to Richards.

Richards watched Hank through the glass like he was a specimen at the zoo. He certainly was an interesting animal, not unlike many of the other perps and pedophiles Richards had arrested before. "Maybe he's a good actor," Richards said. "Maybe he thinks if he pleads guilty to the attempted murder of his wife, possessing child exploitation material, and visiting child abuse websites, he'll be out in a few years. Better than admitting to the charge of multiple homicides."

Motive and method. Motive and method.

"Do you think it's him?" Richards asked. "Do you think he's the Eden Killer?"

"He's guilty of something," Perez said. "I feel we need more, though."

It was exactly how Richards felt. They needed more than a scrapbook of news articles to link him as the Eden Killer. Hank's past criminal conviction would be inadmissible anyway in a court of law. "I'm going to apply more pressure to him," Richards said. "See if he confesses, see if I can get him to admit to the murders. I'm going to keep him here for twenty-four hours. That should be more than enough time for forensics to find something more compelling in his basement."

"So are we just going to let him go after that?" Perez asked. She disliked Hank immensely, given the sheer volume of material they found on his computer hard drive and what he had done to his wife, Maggie. Yet no matter how hard she tried, she couldn't picture him as the Eden Killer. He was guilty of attempted murder of his wife and that charge would stick. Maggie Vickerman was recovering in the hospital, her trachea partially crushed. That was a clear-cut case, given that they also found the video library of his wife having sex with more than sixty different men, including Adam Teal.

From hours spent in his basement watching the videos of his wife, Hank had finally snapped. Maggie Vickerman had done what any self-respecting woman would have done when a man, in a jealous rage, tried to strangle them. She punched him in the face then clobbered him with the closest thing she could find.

Richards headed for the door again. "He ain't going anywhere. He tried to kill his wife, don't forget. I want to work on him some more before his lawyer turns up."

"What do you want me to do?" Perez asked.

Richards paused in the doorway. "Go back up to Mill Point Road and see if you can get anything more out of Paige Hamill."

Chapter 46
An Unexpected Visitor

If the knock on the front door wasn't unexpected, the face of the person standing on the porch when Becca opened her door definitely was.

Despite the hastily thrown together disguise, Becca knew who it was. "Jesus, Sabine what are you doing here?"

"Becca, please. I need your help. Can I come inside?"

Becca hesitated for a moment. It was dark outside, the sun had gone down two hours ago.

"Becca, I'm begging you," Sabine pleaded.

Against her better judgment, Becca opened the door wider and stood aside as Sabine swept inside. Becca closed and locked the door, then turned around.

Sabine took off the dark sunglasses and an ill-fitting hat. She was dressed in an old T-shirt and what looked like tracksuit pants and a pair of sneakers. Sabine caught Becca's gaze. "I know how I look. I'm sorry. They took everything and just left me these clothes."

Becca didn't know what to say. Sabine looked gaunt, her

features drawn. She had no makeup on, and she looked like she had lost weight. But her eyes still burned bright and fierce, a cornered animal that was going to fight to the very end.

"They've allowed me back into my own house, until it gets sold, that is." Sabine's eyes welled-up with tears. Genuine or put-on, Becca was unsure.

"They confiscated my passport, and I can't leave town. I'm scared, Becca, really scared. I don't know where Mark is, where he's gone and they're asking me all these questions I have no clue about. No lawyer wants to touch me so I've had to rely on a court-appointed lawyer, who is a complete idiot."

Then came the outpouring that Becca didn't really want to hear but she couldn't get Sabine to shut up. It was all Mark's fault; she knew nothing about the Ponzi scheme or what he was doing with the money. He even threatened her with divorce if she didn't bring to him a steady flow of new clients. Over the next few minutes Sabine painted a portrait of how *she* was the victim in all this. How, while on the surface, they appeared to be happily married, behind-the-scenes, it was a marriage of convenience.

Becca didn't know whether Sabine was telling the truth or not. The woman was a compulsive liar. There was no fine line between the truth and the lies that sprouted from her mouth.

Finally Becca held up her hand. Enough. She didn't believe a word of it. "What do you want from me, Sabine?"

Ignoring the question, Sabine continued with her rant. "You know Mark used to hit me. Gave me a black eye once. I couldn't be seen in public for two weeks, I had to hide. That was all before you arrived here, of course."

"Then why didn't you just tell the police, Sabine?"

"Because I was frightened for my life. Mark said he would kill me if I ever told anyone."

Becca sighed. "What do you want, Sabine?" she repeated.

"I just need some clothes, that's all. Just something decent to wear and some shoes. I have a court appearance tomorrow and I've got nothing to wear. Please, Becca."

Maybe if she gave the woman what she wanted she would leave, be out of her hair. Becca finally conceded, and she and Sabine went upstairs into Becca's walk-in closet where she kept most of her clothes and shoes. Becca waved her hand. "Take what you'd like, Sabine."

Sabine looked around for a moment, and then began to shuffle through the hanging dresses and clothes.

"Did you hear what happened to Maggie?" Becca asked, surprised that Sabine hadn't mentioned it first.

"Yes, terrible, isn't it?" Sabine spoke with obvious disinterest as she continued rifling through Becca's clothes, pulling things out, turning up her nose before moving on to the next garment. "Like I said, I'm as much a victim in this as Maggie and Hank."

Becca couldn't believe what she was hearing. Instead of Sabine being racked with guilt or remorse, she had deflected the blame away from herself.

Despite Becca's act of kindness, her show of charity and sympathy, Sabine couldn't resist slipping in a final barb. "I thought you had more of a selection, Becca." She pushed hangers back and forth impatiently, not hiding the obvious distaste she felt in Becca's choice in clothes.

Becca could feel her anger rising. Who the hell did she think she was, this woman? Becca bit her tongue, holding back that she kept all her eveningwear and her more recent and more expensive purchases, in the closet in a guest bedroom down the hallway. In this closet Becca kept her everyday clothes, what she would wear around the house, casual and comfortable garments. However, what she also kept here were all her shoes, because there was no shelf space in the guest bedroom and this closet had wraparound deep shelving above.

Sabine picked out a linen shirt and some stylish trousers. "These will have to do." Sabine looked up and saw rows of neatly stacked shoe boxes above. "I'll need a pair of shoes too." She glanced at Becca. "I promise I'll return these when I'm back on my feet again."

Becca just smiled, resigned to the fact that whatever Sabine took, like other people's money, it was gone for good.

"Why don't you do something?" Sabine asked over her shoulder.

"What do you mean?" Becca answered, puzzled.

Sabine turned to her. "You know, about Zoe."

"Zoe?"

"Jason abuses her. It's so obvious. You see it. I see it. We all see it."

Becca had to agree.

"All men are bastards," Sabine concluded as she went back to rummaging through Becca's clothes despite already having chosen something to wear. A few dresses had fallen off their hangers, but Sabine didn't bother picking them up and rehanging them again.

Becca had noticed what had been going on between Zoe and Jason. The bruises. The awkwardness of how she sat at times during the regular coffee catch-ups. The abrupt way Jason had spoken to Becca, brushed her off when she tried to talk to him in their driveway. It had made Becca angry. She disliked women who gave into men, women who continued to stay in a relationship despite the abuse, hoping that things will get better.

Sabine paused, like she was thinking. She turned to Becca. "Where's that cute tote bag you bought when we went shopping?"

Becca frowned.

"You know, the navy one that I bargained fifty-percent off for you in that boutique," Sabine said.

Becca then remembered. Not because of the bag itself, but because of how Sabine had haggled with the poor female sales assistant to the point of almost making a scene right in the store. Becca had never felt so embarrassed. The sales assistant's face slowly sank, her commission evaporating before her very eyes as she finally conceded to Sabine just to get the painful women out of the store. Becca hadn't even used the bag yet, had been put off by the whole episode. She actually felt like returning it. But she did the next best thing.

"I lent it to Zoe," Becca replied.

Sabine looked at Becca like she was insane. "You lent it to Zoe?"

Becca nodded. "She was going out to dinner last week. A special occasion."

Sabine scoffed. "Jason's form of an apology for hurting her again, I guess." Sabine just stood there, prompting Becca.

"She hasn't returned it yet," Becca said, seeing where this was going.

"She's home now, I think," Sabine remarked, pushing the point. "It would look fabulous with this outfit of yours."

Becca said nothing, hoping Sabine would change her mind.

Sabine put on her best, sad puppy dog face. "Please..."

Becca teetered.

"I swear to God, I'll return everything Becca. I promise."

To Becca, Sabine's promises, past and future were now worthless. Like the woman herself.

"She's just right next door, Becca. I'll be a few minutes trying on shoes. Then I'll be gone, out of your hair."

Becca finally relented. "OK, I'll go and fetch the bag for you." If it meant getting Sabine out of her house any faster, Becca would have walked across the Mojave Desert and back.

"Thanks, Becca. You're the only friend I really have around here now."

Becca watched as Sabine turned her back on her and began pulling down more shoe boxes than she could possibly try on in just a few minutes. Maybe she just didn't want to go back to her own empty house. It would be depressing.

"How long will you be, Sabine?"

"Not too long," Sabine replied, her back still turned. "I'll be done by the time you're back with the handbag."

Becca didn't want to stay and watch as Sabine rifled through her shoes. She would tidy up later after the woman had gone. And it wouldn't hurt if Becca quickly went next door, to fetch the bag and check on Zoe as well. She really liked Zoe. She should do the neighborly thing and make sure she was all right. She would certainly want someone to show concern and check in on her if there was something wrong. That's what friends are for, right? And Becca needed more friends. Sabine certainly wasn't one of them. "I'll just be five minutes," Becca said as she turned and walked out of the closet.

Sabine gave another distasteful look, as she opened a shoebox and peered inside. "Don't mind me."

Chapter 47
Inverted Reality

Following the lit up pathway, Becca arrived at Zoe and Jason's front door.

She hesitated on the porch, her fingers resting lightly on the door. Then she noticed the door was slightly ajar, and a faint draft coming through the gap. She glanced sideways back toward her own house, wondering if she should just turn around and go, tell Sabine that Zoe wasn't home despite the lights being on.

Should she ring the doorbell? There was no need though; the door was unlocked, open in fact.

Becca pushed the door inward and crossed the threshold. She stood in the atrium, a vaulted ceiling of high windows and polished floors. An ornate cluster of cut-glass light tubes dangling high above her, bathing everything bright white.

Becca called out Zoe's name.

Silence.

The sweep of the staircase was on her left and Becca called out again, this time her voice slightly louder.

Still silence.

This could wait. She was about to turn and leave when she heard a sound. Becca paused, straining to listen. Was it the wind? Or had she really heard something? She shrugged and headed for the door.

Then she heard the sound again. Someone crying out, a high-pitched wail. It came from upstairs. Becca's eyes narrowed, her brow furrowed and she gritted her teeth.

Fucking Jason! She took the stairs, two at a time.

At the top landing she glanced both ways, unsure of which direction to head. A passageway peeled off to the left, another one to the right, closed doors along both.

She held her breath, straining again to listen.

Nothing.

She took a deep breath, resigned to the fact that perhaps it was the wind or their cat.

Then the sound again, this time louder, definitely a cry of pain or anguish, coming from the right.

Becca slowly walked down the passageway. There were beautiful paintings on the walls, calm and serene seascapes, colorful swirls, soft textures. She stopped at a closed door and pressed her ear to the surface.

Whimpering. Someone sobbing. She could hear it through the door. Someone trapped inside the room. Becca steadied herself, memories flooding back. She slid out her cell phone, and dialed up 911 on the screen, her thumb hovering. She needed to record this, get proof, evidence. It would be important later, when charges were pressed. Jason would lie, they all did. He would say that it was consensual. Or that he was just angry and it was an accident that he'd hit Zoe. Or worse still, Zoe had fallen, that she had had an accident and injured herself.

Men were full of such horseshit when it came to beating

273

women. Becca needed proof, irrefutable so the little bullying bastard couldn't worm his way out of it, like Michael had done. Becca wasn't going to make the same mistake twice.

She heard voices now from the other side of the door. Arguing. Yelling. A woman's voice, loud, the words unclear, just snippets that sounded like threats. Then begging and pleading. Jason was in the room, with Zoe, threatening her, standing over her, trouser belt in one hand. The door suddenly became transparent, like glass. Becca saw herself in the room, on the other side, cowering on the floor, face turned away, hands held high, begging, pleading Michael to stop.

Quickly Becca activated the camera, brought the cell phone up to eye level, and gently pushed down on the door handle with her other hand. The handle levered downward, silently, effortlessly, all the way.

The door latch clicked.

The pressure released.

The door swung silently inward, all the way until it rested against the door stop.

Becca pressed record as she stood there in the open doorway, one eye taking in the scene through the cell phone screen. The red dot recording light started to blink at the bottom of the screen; the counter began to count upward at the top of the screen.

1 second.

2 seconds.

3 seconds.

The phone's small white focusing rectangle bobbed and weaved, searching the room for movement, a face to latch onto, adjusting for depth of field. All the while Becca's other eye gazed around and past the smooth beveled edge of the cell phone, focusing into the room, on the two shapes in the distance.

Becca's brain came into focus as well, her brain processing two points of view of the same thing. Foreground and background. One eye saw a moving image through the cell phone aperture, in high resolution, clear, sharp, precise, the best color accuracy, true blacks and remarkable contrast, the highest pixel density as promised by the manufacturer of the cell phone.

The same image, a natural image came through to her other eye. Unhindered, raw, right there.

4 seconds.

5 seconds.

6 seconds.

Becca's throat went dry. She felt her gut tighten at the sight before her two eyes. Two distinctly separate views of the same disturbing scene converged into one inverted reality.

She brought her other hand up to her mouth in shock.

"Jesus Christ..."

Chapter 48
Real Love

Becca fled the bedroom, tore back down the passageway, furious at herself for being so stupid.

How could she have been so wrong?

She had to get out of the house, get out of this demented place.

Images flashed in her mind, disgusting, perverted images she knew would never leave her no matter how hard she would try to scrub them from her memory.

She could hear footsteps behind her, coming on fast.

"Becca!"

It was Zoe, screaming after her, chasing her, pleading, begging. Wanting to make her understand. Becca didn't want to understand. It was too disturbing.

"Becca. Please stop!" Not the same voice Becca had heard through the bedroom door just moments before she opened the door and was confronted by something horrific she would never forget. Those cries of help, pleas for mercy and begging for it to stop came from Jason Collins, not Zoe, his wife.

Sick bitch! Becca reached the top of the stairs, turned and looked back.

Zoe was running toward her, her nakedness now covered by a short satin kimono. But she still wore the black leather studded dog collar around her neck and the shiny stretch thigh-high lace up dominatrix boots. Thankfully the kimono covered the nipple clamps and chain that she wore underneath. Zoe had dropped the leather riding crop on the floor when she turned in shock to see Becca standing wide-eyed in the bedroom doorway, cell phone in her hand, recording what was transpiring.

"Please, Becca."

Becca rounded on Zoe at the top of the stairs, venom in her eyes. "How could you?" Becca hissed.

Zoe grabbed Becca by the wrist but Becca tore her arm away. "Get your hands off me, you sick bitch!"

Zoe had a pleading look in her eyes. "But I love him. And he loves me."

"Love!" Becca rolled her eyes. "Spare me. How can you call that love!" she screamed, pointing back down the passageway, toward the bedroom, to where Jason Collins lay cowering on the floor, fetal position, a lattice of angry red welts across his back.

"You don't understand," Zoe pleaded.

Becca shook her head vigorously. "I don't want to understand." It felt like utter betrayal to Becca.

Becca stepped toward Zoe, glared at her face, stuck a finger in Zoe's chest. "Here I was thinking that it was you who was the victim, the one being abused, beaten, and even tortured. Turns out I got it all so wrong."

"Look, I can explain." Zoe's face was streaked with heavy black mascara either from tears of frustration with Jason or from the exertion of whipping him for the last two minutes because he wouldn't hit her hard enough.

"I saw enough," Becca replied, her anger boiling. "You're forcing him to beat you, is that it? Is that what you like? To be beaten? What kind of woman are you?" Becca demanded.

Zoe couldn't meet her eyes. She stared at the floor, not ashamed by her own cravings. She knew others wouldn't understand, that's why she had kept it a secret. No one could understand.

"We love each other," Zoe murmured. "We really do."

Becca stared at Zoe like she was insane. Maybe she was insane. "Love?" Becca's face scrunched in utter disbelief at the sad pathetic sight standing right in front of her. "So you have some sick perverted fetish to be beaten, physically abused by your husband?"

Zoe said nothing, just stared at the ground.

"And you force him to do it! And when he refuses, you whip him? Discipline him? Force him? Is that it? Do I have it right? Is that how you see true love?" The accusations came thick and fast.

"I knew you wouldn't understand," Zoe said, her voice like a child's.

"No one would understand!" Becca yelled. "There are real women out there Zoe, women who are getting abused every day and I thought—" Becca threw her head back in frustration. "Where's your self-respect? Women are dying every day and you're encouraging violence against women?"

Zoe looked up straight into Becca's eyes.

"I thought you were one of them!" Becca spat. "Those victims. I thought it was you who was getting abused. The bruises I saw. How uncomfortable at times you looked when sitting. The pain I saw in your eyes. I believed Jason was beating the shit out of you! Turns out you made him do it for your own sick enjoyment." Nothing was what it seemed.

"He is my brother," Zoe said, her voice feeble.

Becca did a double take. The earth stopped rotating. Becca's brain stopped thinking. The air went perfectly still and silent throughout the entire house.

"You are brother and sister?" Becca's eyes went wide. As if things couldn't get any worse. "You're married to each other? You're fucking each other as well as you forcing him to brutalize you?"

Zoe just nodded.

"Shit, you are *both* sick!"

"Like I said," Zoe said defiantly, her courage returning. "We love each other. We aren't married. We just pretend we are. It's better that way."

Becca tilted her head. "So as to look like a normal couple? But it's a sham? All an act so you can hide your sick relationship?"

"To us it is a normal relationship," Zoe said, jutting out her jaw.

Becca stepped back, away from Zoe, like she was some kind of repulsive creature. Then she whispered, her own eyes blurred with tears. "You have any idea what it's like to be beaten by a man when you have done nothing wrong, do you? You stupid woman."

Zoe stared at Becca, then a look of disbelief slowly crept across her face. Zoe brought her hand to her mouth.

Becca slowly nodded. "Yeah, you have no idea what it is like to be beaten, to be kicked like a dog when you haven't asked for it."

Zoe gestured toward Becca, her hand outstretched, a heartfelt sorrow in her eyes now. "I'm sorry. I had—"

Becca cut her off. "Get away from me." Becca went back

down the staircase, out the front door, and into the night without looking back.

Becca stormed up her front path. She didn't want to talk to anyone. She just wanted to go inside her house and calm down. Coffee would be good. A stiff drink would be better. Once inside she slammed the front door shut behind her, then leaned back against it, as if trying to keep the demons out who were now hot on her heels, demons from her past she had so vigilantly tried to keep at bay.

Until now.

She closed her eyes, willing her memory to scrub the scenes she had just witnessed. She was more enraged than shocked. Her blood boiled, not with hatred or contempt for Zoe. Nor pity. Becca felt enraged at the stupidity of the woman, forcing her brother to abuse her. My god! It was a choice for Zoe, a desire, whereas Becca never had a choice toward the end of her relationship with Michael.

Becca opened her eyes and blinked hard once. She needed to regain focus, composure. She shook her head, trying to get rid of the images of handcuffs, whips, and leather masks from her mind before glancing up the sweeping staircase, almost forgetting about Sabine.

Would she tell Sabine? Christ no! The woman would tell everyone, use any scrap of information to her advantage.

Shit! Becca had a horrible thought. She pushed off the front door and tore up the stairs, taking them two at a time, a sick feeling growing in her stomach.

Letter #5

My Darling,

I think she knows, or at least suspects. I'm pretty sure she's monitoring my phone calls, checking my texts, emails too. I don't know how she is doing this but I'm certain of it.

She hasn't said anything yet, but she's been acting strange lately, watching me, studying my every move. It's quite creepy in fact. At dinner, or just standing by the sink brushing my teeth, I can tell she's watching me out of the corner of her eye. I can see her mind ticking over, thinking, almost like she wants to ask me something but she doesn't have the courage. She always was a weak woman. Not like you. I'm actually looking forward to telling her, seeing her face, watch her panic. I'm taking everything. She'll be destitute. I don't care.

Some days she is really warm and friendly toward me, while on other days she can be cold and distant. We haven't made love for months now. I know I said I had to keep up the charade with her until I tell her I'm leaving, but no matter how hard I try, I just cannot bring myself to touch, to place my hands on her. It seems like such a betrayal, like I'm betraying you not her if I did. I don't want any other woman except you.

At times when I leave the house and go to work, I'm sure she's gone through my things, my drawers, the closet, the desk in my study. I don't know what she's looking for. Maybe evidence, maybe the proof she needs. I don't know. As a precaution I've hidden everything. There is nothing that she can possibly find about us. I'm thinking of purchasing a new cellphone, just so I can call you, secretly, without her knowing. When I'm on the subway and even walking the busy streets, I feel eyes on me, like someone's watching me. Maybe it's her. Maybe she's stalking me, wondering if in fact I am really going to work and not meeting another woman.

My love, we have to be very careful now. We're in the final stages of being together, forever. It will be done soon enough, I promise. Then we can move on with the future, our future, and our new family. I don't know how she's going to handle it, when I tell her, that is. But she will never find us even if she hires a lawyer, even a private detective. It makes me think, maybe she has? I honestly don't know. I can't imagine she would be that devious. But then again if she has her suspicions, who knows what she's capable of.

Maybe someone is following me after all? I'll take more care, see if I can catch her. I want you to be more cautious as well. She doesn't know where you live, the place I have rented for us.

I don't think we should meet any more until it is done. Just let me do what I have to and tell her, and before you know it we will be in each other's arms forever.

I'll try calling you from a public phone if I can. But until then it's pen and paper. No phone calls, no texts, and don't email me for Christ's sake, especially not at work.

Everything is in place. I'm not going to have her spoil it for us now.

Like this letter, I'll keep writing, letting you know what's happening. I'll keep walking past our apartment, dropping the letters into your mailbox. Please check it daily. I'm sorry but it's the only way we can communicate until it's done. I'm telling her this weekend. I'm counting the days, my darling.

Soon we will be together, my darling Rachel, I promise.

This is what we are going to do—

Chapter 49
The Devil Returns

He made good time up the hillside through the woods in the dark, black on black, so no one would see him.

But this time it would be different. No chloroform soaked pad in a sealed plastic bag. No pocket-sized stun gun as a backup. No "bag of tricks" in which he usually carried his ropes, cable ties, and other paraphernalia required to restrain a strong, fully-grown young man were required this time. His purpose this time was not to restrain, to immobilize, to capture then transport back to his Garden of Eden that awaited in the basement of his house. His purpose this time was to kill, to destroy, to make an example of the woman. It would also be an exercise in misdirection, deflection, and of pointing the finger of blame at someone else.

Reaching the top of the ridge, he paused for a moment under the shadow of the tree line to gather his thoughts and go over again what he planned to do. He regarded the house in front of him. Muted light shone from a few first floor windows and more of the second floor windows were lit up. But the kitchen was in darkness. It didn't matter, the external lights weren't on and the backyard was still in relative darkness. He couldn't wait until she went to sleep. He needed to act now, decisively.

The last email he had intercepted had spurred him into action. But he didn't mind. It was only a minor inconvenience. He had contingencies in place, and like everything else in his carefully constructed world of plans and countermeasures, he had anticipated that exact moment right then. And his plan involved Hank Vickerman. What better way than to blame someone else?

There was going to be no improvisation or rash decisions made on the fly. He had been grooming Hank for some time now to assume the role, to be the subject of blame, to have accusations made when the moment came as it had. Of course stupid Hank was clueless as to these machinations. That's what made it all the more perfect.

Looking left he noticed the only house that showed no signs of life, had no lights on, was Maggie and Hank's.

Good. This was perfect. It played right into his hands and made executing the first stage of his plan easier. Maggie was probably out screwing one of her many young acquaintances and Hank was probably in the basement doing what he usually did when he was home alone. Hank had already told him of his wife's indiscretions, had confided in him at the same time when he had told him about their son, Adam. And like any dutiful neighbor he had listened patiently, a look of pious concern on his face with just the right amount of empathy in his soothing voice while Hank had divulged such tantalizing dirty family secrets, oblivious to the fact that the person sitting on the other side of the confessional screen was in fact the devil himself. Hank was just a pathetic sniveling wretch who had no balls, spent his life stewing in his basement, watching kiddie porn and brooding over what to do about his adulterous whore of a wife.

He moved out from under the cover of the woods and blended into the darkness of the backyard, his soft sole shoes silent across the damp grass. And as the devil moved stealthily and silently, he couldn't help think to himself: *Congratulations, Hank. I'm about to make you the Eden Killer.*

Using a small strip of steel designed especially for such a job, he easily popped the latch on the sliding glass patio door. He had done this many times before, been inside the houses of others, in the darkness, while they slept.

Gently closing the door behind him, he moved into the kitchen. He didn't need to pause to orient himself in the semi-darkness. He knew every cabinet, every countertop edge, every boxy shape that loomed in the background. The hall light was on in front of him and it threw dulled light into the otherwise darkened kitchen. Silently he crept across the tiled floor, past the island bench then stopped. Looking at the ceiling, he heard noises coming from the second story, footsteps, a person moving about.

Good. It would be better to do what he had planned upstairs, with just his bare hands.

His eyes fell on a block of knives sitting on the countertop next to a coffee machine, not where he had preferred to keep his own knives, though.

It gave him pause, to reconsider, to be flexible.

He pulled one of the blades, the biggest, and regarded the smooth razor edge for a moment. Apparently, like him, she appreciated quality knives as well.

He wanted something different this time, make it bloody and messy, take things in a new direction for the sake of Hank, make it look like the man was enraged, had decided to break in to his neighbor's home and deal with her himself. Take his frustrations out on her instead of his wife. Hank had told him about the hunting knife he kept, how he would like to stab his wife.

Then the police would find incriminating evidence in Hank's basement, a few carefully chosen mementos of past victims. He certainly had enough in his "collection" to choose from.

In time he would find another cause to vent his displeasure at mankind. There were plenty of sinners out there to bolster his flock. The Eden Killer would be captured, people would once again feel safe in their little suburban homes, and once again the smug veil of contentment would settle over the town again.

A little improvisation would be good, he finally decided. More grist for the mill to be used to make Hank his scapegoat. Taking the knife he moved toward the hallway.

Bloody and messy it was.

Chapter 50
Betrayal

As Becca entered her bedroom she thought it was unusually quiet.

She saw Sabine standing in her closet, barefoot, her back to her, boxes and lids scattered on the floor around her. One box in particular caught Becca's attention. It sat next to a pair of black gloss high heels. The red ribbon that secured the box had been undone, the lid sitting beside it on the floor.

Becca tensed.

Sabine glanced over her shoulder and froze, a sudden look of guilt on her face. She slowly turned to face Becca.

It was then Becca saw something clutched in Sabine's hand.

A letter.

One of the letters from inside the box.

A box that was always secured tightly with a red ribbon.

A box that was never to be opened and the contents of which were certainly never to be read by anyone else other than Becca.

Becca could see the letter clearly now, could distinguish which one it was. She knew each of the letters intimately. The dates. The tone. The words of undying love and affection.

The letter Sabine held in her hand and was reading had particular significance for Becca. Crisp sheets of pale yellow weave, 100gsm, linen texture. It was the last letter Michael, her husband, had written before he tragically died.

Sabine just pursed her lips. There was nothing to say.

Becca stepped forward, blocking the only way out of the walk-in closet.

"Becca, these are the most beautiful letters I have ever read," Sabine said.

So you have read them all? Becca drummed her fingers against her thigh. One of her eyes began to twitch.

"My god, your husband simply adored you." She held up the pages. "It's so romantic, how he expresses himself, his devotion to you." Sabine for once was almost lost for words. The letters, all of them were truly beautifully written. Personal love letters penned by Michael's own hand, his deepest thoughts and dedications of love embellished in ink on luxurious paper.

Sabine clutched the pages to her chest. "My God, Becca you poor thing. He was so in love with you. The things he said about you."

Becca just stood there. No words.

Sabine caught Becca's expression then felt guilty. "Good Lord! Just listen to me," Sabine gasped, trying to make light of a situation that was becoming increasingly more uncomfortable by the second. "I shouldn't have looked inside the box. It's just that it fell down from the shelf above"—Sabine gestured behind her—"when I was bringing down another box of shoes. I thought there were shoes inside. I never imagined it was letters. I'm sorry, Becca. It was rude of me, I know. I shouldn't have read them, any of them."

Becca began to grind her teeth, her jaw muscles bunched and tight. Bright white light flared behind her eyes, blocking out the image of Sabine in front of her. In her mind she was standing on a deserted beach, her gaze set far out to sea, the growing discomfort of the stones under the bare soles of her feet.

Water lapped at her toes, gently at first. She squinted into the distance. There was something there, far out beyond the flatness, a line of white, end to end, across the horizon, building, growing taller.

The tide was rising, sloshing up to her ankles now, then her shins, cold salty water rising fast. It touched her knees, then her thighs. Within seconds the water surged around her waist, still rising. A restless boiling tide of confusion, then anger, then betrayal. It all came flooding back, brought on by this meddling, nosy, arrogant, judgmental bitch.

Sabine felt a little awkward now, wondering why Becca just stood there, motionless, no expression, just dead eyes staring not at her but through her like she wasn't there. It was a little creepy, disturbing.

Fuck, you can keep your shitty love letters for all I care. "I'm so sorry," Sabine said again. She knelt down, and began folding the letter and placing it back into the box. "I'll put it back. It's none of my business."

The letters were in disarray inside the box, not in their usual neatly tied bundles that Becca had them organized in.

A few strands of discarded string lay on the floor. Sabine hastily tried to bundle up the letters again, too preoccupied to notice that Becca had stepped closer toward her.

"The only thing I don't understand," Sabine said, not looking up, "the woman's name, who the letters are addressed to..."

Sabine glanced up at Becca, then asked, "Who is Rachel?

They are all addressed to her in each envelope. I just assumed that "Rachel" is your middle name? You know, how some women prefer using their middle name."

Becca finally spoke, her voice cold and even. "Rachel was his lover," she said. "The woman he had been in love with and who he was fucking for the last three years of our marriage while he was also fucking me."

The air inside the closet grew suddenly still and quiet.

Horror seeped across Sabine's face, her brain processing what Becca had just said. She glanced down at the box of love letters, a strewn mess inside where Sabine's greedy fingers had rummaged and invaded in salacious delight.

Information, a tangible commodity. Silver coins had suddenly become ingots of gold to Sabine. No, better than gold.

Sabine started, "You mean—"

Becca cut her off. "These were written by my husband. But not to me. He wrote them to *her*. He was going to leave me for her." Becca's fingers bunched into tight fists, then relaxed, then bunched again. "They were love letters my husband wrote to her, not me."

"But what happened?" Sabine was aghast. She stood up. "You said he died in a motorcycle accident."

Becca gave a slight smile. That wasn't exactly true. Michael had committed suicide as soon as Becca had discovered his final letter. He had committed "marital suicide" in Becca's mind.

When you don't want to be discovered, you choose old-fashioned pen and paper to hide your indiscretions. Not text messages. Not emails. Not voicemail. All of which leave a trace, a trail of your guilt and of your infidelity.

At the funeral for Michael, his lover Rachel had the hide, the balls, to turn up to pay her respects to the dead body lying flat in the casket, not the living body standing upright next to the gaping hole in the ground that was his wife.

Becca saw her immediately, pathetic, huddled, sobbing on the fringe of the crowd at the cemetery.

God! How young was she? Twenty-two? Twenty-three?

Afterward Becca walked right up to her and wasn't conned when Rachel had said that she was a past work colleague of Michael.

Calmly, casually and out of earshot of everyone else, Becca leaned in and under the guise of a cordial kiss of appreciation whispered in the young woman's ear, "Deliver to me all the letters Michael wrote to you in the next twenty-four hours or I will go to your place of work and tell everyone exactly the kind of whoring slut you are."

Needless to say, a neatly wrapped bundle was delivered by courier the very next day to Becca's house.

Becca had only first discovered one letter before Michael had the chance to deliver it. The one written on pale yellow paper, the one Sabine now held in her hand when Becca had walked in and caught her. It was Michael's final letter. Had Sabine not been interrupted by Becca, she would have finished reading. In it, Michael described how he had finally made the decision to leave Becca, and had outlined in great detail the plans he had for their joint betrayals. The apartment he had recently leased under a false name in a pretty, faraway town while they looked for a new house, a new home for them. How they were going to finally make new lives for themselves, lives they had spoken about thousands of times before. How there would finally be no need to hide their treachery and could openly display their love for each other without fear of discovery.

And, lastly and perhaps the most, hurtful and soul-destroying revelation of them all; Michael's suggestions for baby names if the child Rachel was now carrying was a boy or a girl. *His* child, fathered from *his* seed. A child spawned through deceit and betrayal.

And yet Becca had argued so vehemently with him for years that she wanted to have children, she wanted to start a family of her own. With him! Plans that were so adamantly crushed by Michael's constant refusals.

Becca had kept the letters and re-read them over and over again, for her own moral support, to bolster her. Not to reminisce. But to reaffirm her actions, that what she had done to Michael was the right thing to do, the only thing she could have done, else suffer endless regret and indignation for the rest of her life.

The killing of a loved one then staging it so perfectly to convince the police, the court, and the insurance company that it was suicide was never going to be an easy task for Becca. But she did her research, made a plan, and carried it through.

It is a common myth that life insurance policies won't payout on suicide. But Michael's policy did. Becca had checked.

And in a final twist of irony, Becca had discovered, unbeknown to her, that Michael had increased his life coverage to five million dollars, ten times what it had previously been. He wanted to provide for Rachel and his new family should anything happen to him. Yet, in what could only be described as a "love-struck" oversight, Michael hadn't changed Becca as the sole beneficiary of his policy in the event of his death. So blinded was he by this new, young lust he didn't read the finer details of the life insurance policy.

The money was all Becca's.

Becca had to move quickly, and she did. Killing him then

playing the grieving widow just long enough to get the insurance money.

Suddenly Becca felt the hairs on the back of her neck quiver.

Sabine's gaze shifted, her eyes looking past Becca, behind her. She craned her neck. "Garrett?" Sabine frowned. "What are you doing here?"

Becca turned.

Standing there behind the two women was Garrett Mason.

He was holding a large chef's knife in one hand.

Chapter 51
Eve

Perez pulled up at the gatehouse and dialed Paige Hamill's house on the illuminated keypad. It was just after 9:00 p.m. The call was answered on the third ring and Paige's voice came through the speaker box. "Hello?"

"Mrs. Hamill, it's Officer Perez. I was wondering if I could come in and ask you a few questions about Hank and Maggie Vickerman?"

There was a pause and Perez could visualize Paige Hamill ensconced behind wrought iron, stone, and granite, thinking she was untouchable. Just like everyone else up there.

"Now is not a good time," a defiant response crackled out of speaker box, the voice empty and hollow.

Undeterred, Perez powered down her window farther, leaned out and glared up at the CCTV camera that was pointed down at her, knowing full well Paige Hamill was doing the same back at her. "Please, it will only take a few minutes and I thought it would be more convenient than having you come down to the station." Perez left the veiled threat hang.

More silence. Suddenly there was a mechanical click and whir of the electric motor and the barrier began to lift.

Putting the police cruiser into gear, Perez followed the curve of streetlights up the hilltop, the sprawling line of mansions slowly revealing themselves, outlined in warm pools of light.

Perez pulled to the curb in front of Paige Hamill's driveway. Getting out, she stood in the middle of the road and looked at all the houses. The street was quiet, the night air still and cool. Maggie and Hank's house was in darkness. Forensics had called it a day. No doubt they would be back tomorrow bright and early.

Pools of light spilled from windows of all the other houses. Perez glanced at the front door of Paige's house then started to walk toward it. Then for some reason, she stopped and looked down the road toward Becca's house. She glanced back at Paige's front door, hesitating, caught in a rare moment of indecision. She really wanted to talk to Becca, try again, and see if she could get the truth out of her about the other evening. It didn't seem critical to the case, but Perez felt there was more to it. No matter how hard she tried, she couldn't wipe from her mind that the woman was hiding something.

It would only take a moment.

With her mind made up, Perez changed direction and headed down the sidewalk toward Becca's home.

As Becca had blocked Sabine's escape out of the closet, Garrett Mason now blocked both of the women's escape. Mason's intent was clear.

Becca panned her eyes up slowly. On any other day, she would have seen a man in his mid-forties, brown soft leather loafers, navy chinos, creaseless white button-down shirt, slim build, long neck, kind brown eyes behind classic tortoise shell glasses, and a scatter of unruly sandy-colored hair. Everything said academic, timeless, and spoke of a careful deliberateness about the man. But now all she saw was the same man but dressed head to toe in black, an intruder, a killer dressed for purpose with cold, cruel eyes and a lipless, nasty little smile.

Becca saw the knife a moment before Sabine did. Her brain lagged a tad to register what it meant. There would be minimal or no conversation at all, just brutal, up close and violent death within the confined space in the next sixty seconds.

Becca took a step back, deeper into the closet, reducing her already limited options. It was natural, to gravitate away from danger.

The entrance to the closet was narrow, the door standard width. There was no way the women were going to escape without succumbing to the blade.

Oddly Becca said nothing, seemed calm. She moved slightly to her right, searching for one red shoe box among an inventory of white, careful where she tread, not looking down, her eyes fixed on Garrett Mason, her feet pushing aside scattered Jimmy Choos and Alexander McQueens.

Sabine was another story altogether. She was riddled with fear. "What the fuck are you doing, Garrett?" she demanded. "Why are you holding a knife?" As stupid as it sounded, for some desperate reason Sabine clung to the thought that maybe, just maybe Garrett Mason had mistaken the upstairs closet in Becca's bedroom to the downstairs pantry in the kitchen and was looking for a side of beef to carve up.

Mason gave a tight smile. He had never killed a woman before, and now he had two of them right in front of him, close proximity, like shooting fish in a barrel. It didn't bother him. Further adaptation was required as the story ebbed and flowed in his head. Same outcome. Better motive. Hank had broken in to kill Rebecca Cartwright. Then to his surprise he discovered Sabine Miller was inside her house too, the wife and co-conspirator of the now notorious con man Mark Miller. Garrett Mason had read the newspapers too. Seen the headlines. Now as he watched both women, tomorrow's headline started to form inside his demented head, based on what was going to transpire in the next sixty seconds in the closet. Seeing Sabine Miller only further fueled Hank's apparent rage. Losing all his life savings, what was a man to do? Hank had also confided in Mason about their investments in Mark Miller's company. Sabine had tried to convince Garrett Mason to invest as well when he lived in this exact house. But he was too clever, felt the returns were too good to be true, preferring the safety and security of the university pension plan.

Perfect. Tomorrow's headline was complete. Improvisation wasn't so bad after all.

Mason ignored Sabine. Instead his cold malevolent gaze settled on Becca. In his mind, she was the more dangerous of the two.

Maybe he'd do what he had done with Adam Vickerman, make both women a permanent fixture of the house, a hidden museum of the dead. There was still plenty of room in the basement walls, and he was sure Adam Vickerman could use the company.

No! The voice of reason hissed in Mason's head. *Stick to the plan.*

The blood on the carpet would be a nice touch. Front page photos to accompany the headlines. In a tight space such as this, among the confines of dresses, shoes, shelving, and hanging rods in the closet, it was going to get messy, brutal, animalistic. Fingers, teeth, knees, hands, elbows, tuffs of hair and torn skin. It would be carnage. But Hank had been very angry.

More ideas flooded Mason's head as he stood there, knife in hand. Too many choices now.

Perhaps the knife could act as a deterrent or incentive, get them to comply, so they were more malleable. Get one to bind the other. But his bag was in the trunk of his car, parked all the way back in the parking lot of the picnic grounds. He just needed to restrain both women temporarily so he could retrieve his tools, truss them for ease of transport, throw them in the trunk. Then he would take his sweet time with them. Two Eves instead of one Adam.

But Sabine, God bless her, made a subtle movement that threw those plans out the window in a split second.

It started as a slight kink of her right elbow, up and back, a movement normally reserved for someone drawing a handgun from a holster on the hip. But in this case it was to draw a completely different type of weapon. A weapon that in Sabine's hands, wrecked marriages, revealed the indiscretions of cheating spouses, composed and sent hateful messages, instigated breakups, spread salacious rumors, threatened reprisals, and a whole plethora of other harmful and hurtful things.

However in this instance, she just wanted to dial 911.

Statistics show that seventy-three percent of women keep their cell phone in their back pocket, protruding just enough to draw out quickly.

Sabine Miller went for her phone and Garrett Mason went for them both.

Perez detested doorbells. They had a clanging, almost game show connotation to the sound they made.

Also, it was a cop thing, not wanting to announce your presence to the entire world in a garish ding-dong manner, giving fair warning to the other side. Banging on the door with your fist had a more authoritative feel to it as well, a not-so-subtle threat that said "open up or my foot's coming through the door next." So she gave the front door a gentle but firm rap with her knuckles, stood to the side when she did it too, habitual training and all that.

Unfortunately the sound of her knocking didn't carry all the way up the flight of stairs to the first story of Becca's home, along the corridor or through walls and eventually into the main bedroom and into Becca's closet. It petered out somewhere in the expanse of tile and vaulted ceiling of the entrance and only made it halfway up the sweeping stairs. If by some miraculous feat of acoustic engineering it had carried all the way up to the closet in the master bedroom, the sound waves would've been lost among the mayhem, and carnage that was unfolding inside.

Sabine's cell phone cleared her back pocket, but never made it past her right hip before Becca barreled backward into her, pushing them both into a tangle of garments, swinging coat hangers, and shoe boxes.

The blade came on fast, a blur of forged steel as Mason pressed forward aiming the point of the knife squarely at Becca's gut. He had visions of plunging it all the way in to her, to the hilt, almost past his grip, a burst of bright red warm stickiness surrounding his fist, before wrenching it left and right, effectively gutting the bitch like a fish.

Women's high heels are a dangerous thing however. Just ask any man who has told his wife he's having an affair. The floor of the closet was strewn with such high-heeled obstacles, the veritable minefield of stilettos, ankle strap heels, kitten heels, sling back heels, and a myriad of other shapes and wedges, all discarded by Sabine in her messy efforts to find the perfect pair.

It was a good thing, however.

Mason stumbled sideways, his ankle jarred as his foot came down on a lonesome Alexander McQueen. A tragic waste enshrined forever in an exquisite black suede sandal with a three-inch heel that lay on its side.

It wasn't much but it was enough. The blade faulted, some of the initial inertia of the thrust lost.

Becca grabbed at a handful of garments not caring what they were, balled them into a tight fist and battered the blade aside, pulling Mason's shoulder forward, across and down with her other hand.

Mason stumbled forward drunkenly, tilted, and then lost his balance completely. They tumbled backward as one, a sexual threesome never intended. Sabine on the bottom. Becca in the middle. Mason thrashing about on top. The sound of a crack was Sabine's head hitting the edge of the built-in drawers along the back wall. She went instantly limp, rendered unconscious as Becca and Mason slithered over her body among a sea of garments, shirts, jeans, dresses, shoes, and shoe boxes tumbling over and around them.

The knife had come loose in the mayhem. Mason groped for

it somewhere under the mess of clothing with a spare hand, his other hand around Becca's throat.

Mason's twisted face filled her vision, all teeth and snarls, frothy with spittle, inches from her own face, his body pressing down on her, crushing the air from her lungs. His eyes were the devils, the depths of darkness they had witnessed were now overflowing with hatred.

He growled in rage and frustration. His hand stopped searching through the mayhem for the blade of the knife. No need now. Two hands would do, always had. He was going to take great joy in squeezing the life out of her, watch as all warmth left her eyes, until all that remained were two cold orbs frozen wide in death.

Cast-iron hands wrapped around Becca's throat and she went for his eyes, not because of logic, but because they were the evilest things she had ever seen.

Her fingernails slashed and gouged. Fingers tore and ripped at nostrils, ears, wrenched cheeks, tufts of his hair came away in bloody handfuls.

Mason thrashed in pain.

Becca's feral onslaught intensified, a caged animal fighting for its life with a monster in its cage. A hardened cuticle found the soft gelatinous orb of his eye and Becca thrust home, inward, deep into the socket. Tissue and membrane burst, warm liquid gushed out.

Mason screamed, reeled back clutching his eye socket, the eyeball now just a mushy dribble of blood and vitreous fluid that ran down one cheek.

There was a flash of red on the floor partially covered by a sweater and Becca swiveled her hips under Mason, and reached for it. She fumbled with the cardboard lid. Fingers hungry and desperate closed around the cold stippled grip, the feel familiar in her hand.

Mason's remaining eye swiveled toward Becca. He wanted to kill her so badly, this vicious animal of a woman who was ruining his plans. This Eve, this vile creature in his Garden of Eden, trampling on the beauty he had so painstakingly created.

And it was in this exact moment of pure hatred that Garrett Mason, the Eden Killer, realized that all humans were sinners, not just men. Women too.

Both Adam *and* Eve.

Perhaps Eve was the worst of the two species, because he was fighting a wretched Eve now, and she was proving more difficult than any Adam he had ever encountered.

Mason leaned forward and slithered his hands once again around Eve's throat. What a vile creature she was. "Die you—"

Becca swung her arm up and tight across her chest, elbow tucked close to her ribs and shoved the barrel of her handgun into the gapping mouth of Garrett Mason, choking off his voice.

He gagged, gurgled, his one eye went wide.

She pulled the trigger and sprayed the ceiling above his head with his brains and skull.

Chapter 52
The Aftermath

In the days that followed, Perez would replay over and over again in her mind those final few moments, wondering *if only?*

If only she had gone straight to Becca's house first, not been so indecisive and stood on the footpath sidewalk wasting precious seconds. *If only* she hadn't paused on Becca's porch, more precious seconds wasted wondering if it was a woman's scream she had heard on the other side of the door. *If only* she had kicked in the front door on her first attempt and not on her third. *If only* time had stood still with everything frozen all around her except for her own movement and hindsight had become foresight, and that she had X-ray vision, so that the walls and the stairs and ceiling didn't impede her sight. Then perhaps things would have turned out differently. Perez could've saved one of the women.

But it didn't, and couldn't, and she hadn't.

A million variables hadn't quite synchronized on that fateful evening to carry Officer Haley Perez to the doorway of the closet in the master bedroom in time.

She remembered standing there, gun drawn, taking in the scene before her, not sure what she was looking at or whom she was aiming at. The body of a man twisted, buckled and motionless lay at her feet, most of the top half of this head blown completely away.

Further back, Rebecca Cartwright, chest heaving and with blood-streaked hands that resembled claws, stood over the body of woman who was on the floor, a kitchen knife buried deep in her chest. So much blood in such a small space that was filled with a deafening silence.

The woman would later be identified as Sabine Miller.

Perez would remember feeling something drip onto the crown of her head from above and reaching up to touch her hair, her fingertips coming away with a gray mushy residue. Then looking up at the ceiling and seeing the weeping blemish of gray and red, remembering a glob hitting the cheek of her upturned face, now knowing where the top of the man's head had ended up.

In the aftermath, she couldn't remember trying desperately to resuscitate the woman, not pulling the knife from her chest, fearful that it would start an outpouring she could not stop.

However, she vaguely remembered paramedics pushing past, not so gentle hands pulling her up and away, police officers manhandling her out of the closet and dumping her onto the bed.

She remembered Marvin Richards crouching down in front of her, careful not to touch her, her hands red and sticky. Sadness and pride in his eyes as he whispered silent words.

But most of all she remembered Rebecca Cartwright standing in the bedroom, talking to police, all the while her eyes were on Perez. No look of concern or pity or sorrow. Just a glint of fear in her eyes.

In the aftermath Perez would be interviewed multiple times by various detectives, but not by Marvin Richards. He would wait until Perez was ready to tell her side of the story to him when they were alone and certainly not in the cold confines of an interview room under interrogation conditions.

He would have to wait almost twenty-four hours for that privilege. And when the time arrived, everything would be revealed.

Chapter 53
Faces

Like trophy heads mounted on the wall, the faces stared back at Perez as she sat in the office, the doors closed, strangers in dark suits milling around outside. The FBI had taken over the case of Sabine and Mark Miller. Their agents were crawling all over Ravenwood right now, had descended on the town two days ago like an invading army.

Richards stood next to the whiteboard, adding more flesh to the carcass of lies, deceit, and murder that they had both been building. He had just gotten off the phone this morning with the Miami Beach Police, new information had come to light that Richards wanted to get Perez up to speed on. They also wanted to do another review of the facts, get their strategy clear before they stepped into the room down the corridor.

Richards tapped the first photo on the board with his dry erase marker. "Maggie Vickerman is still in the hospital. When she regains consciousness, I'll tell her the news." The doctors had put Maggie into an induced coma last night when a CT scan showed she had bleeding on the brain.

"She will recover?" Perez asked. She felt sorry for the woman given what they had just found out.

"The doctors say she should make a full recovery. Her condition has improved over the last couple of days," Richards said.

He moved to the next photo. "Sabine Miller is an entirely different story, and according to her surgeon, it's still touch and go." It had been two days since what had unfolded at Rebecca Cartwright's home. Perez had insisted on coming back to work the very next day to talk to Richards, tell him her version of events. But he had spent nearly every waking hour either up at Mill Point Road or at a modest house in the quiet leafy street in Ravenwood that belonged to Garrett Mason, coordinating forensic teams, liaising with the sheriff's department and trying to piece everything together. When Perez had finished her interviews with other detectives and even with the FBI, she finally had her chance to sit down with Richards, across the street at the diner and talk.

"The surgeon gave me an update this morning," Richards continued. "Given that it was a fairly nasty knife wound, sliced through a few arteries and the fact that she had lost a lot of blood, she did expect further complications. Sabine Miller started hemorrhaging again during the early hours. She's just come out of surgery for the second time this morning and has stabilized, but she's still listed as critical. We will have to see in the coming days, but the surgeon said Sabine seems to have plenty of fight in her. Fingers crossed."

"She must have," Perez said, still wishing she had gotten there faster before Garrett Mason had the chance to stab Sabine Miller.

Richards moved onto the next photo on the whiteboard, the face he'd just been updating the details for.

"What did the Miami Beach Police say about Mark Miller?" Perez asked.

"They're not happy. But I guess it's nothing that they haven't seen before, especially in Miami." In a gesture of irony that wasn't lost on Perez, Richards tapped the forehead of Mark Miller's photo with his pen. "Two taps to the head, execution style. Miami Beach Police are still processing the motel where they found him this morning. Inside they found three cellphones, and two packed suitcases. Looks like the motel room had been ransacked. Anything of value would have been taken. They also discovered two airline tickets for a man and woman, and matching passports in false names with pictures of himself and Sabine. They intended to fly out to Doha, in the state of Qatar, on the Arabian Peninsula. One-way."

"Qatar?" Perez asked.

Richards gave a slight smile. "Qatar is a huge financial hub for the Middle East. Plenty of millionaires and billionaires. No extradition treaty with the United States either. Very appealing if you're on the run from the FBI." Richards glanced out the glass wall of his office at the men in suits.

Perez took the cue and reached for the swivel to tilt the blinds slightly. "So with new identities, they were going to set themselves up again. Fleece the wealthy on the other side of the world this time," Perez said.

"Looks that way," Richards replied, turning back to the whiteboard. "Looks like Mark Miller was hiding out, waiting for Sabine to rendezvous with him. One suitcase was packed with women's clothes. Except he didn't count on the fact that things would escalate so quickly and the Feds would get involved."

"Sounds like someone else found him first. A pissed off investor." Perez thought for a moment. "So why didn't they flee together?" Perez asked.

"From what we know so far, looks like Mark Miller may have been spooked, someone else got the jump first, was already on to his trail before the Feds got the call. They're going through his phone records and emails now but it looks like he used burner phones, no trace. He already had plans in place that maybe Sabine knew nothing about."

"An escape hatch," Perez added.

Richards agreed. "Looks like he had every intention of telling his wife, once he found a safe house to hide out. I believe Sabine Miller was in contact with him pretty soon after he disappeared. She was going to run as well but then everything went to hell in a handbasket."

"So it looks like Mark Miller didn't discriminate with whose money he took. Clean and dirty money were all the same to him."

Richards had been talking extensively with the agent in charge of the FBI investigation. It was still in the early stages, however, initial reports indicated that Mark Miller's investment firm had a book of very dubious clients as well, including several crime bosses from Chicago and Boston and front companies that invested surplus funds for several low-level domestic drug gangs.

"That's what ultimately got him killed," Richards said.

"So someone caught him first before we did," Perez said.

Richards nodded, "And I have an idea of how that happened."

Richards skipped two faces along the line and arrived at the photo of Paige Hamill. Of all the photos on the whiteboard, only two of them had a slight smile, almost a subtle smirk. One of them was Paige Hamill.

Richards turned back to Perez. "Got a phone call last night from someone very high up in the FBI in D.C. about the investigation into the Millers. The person wanted me to reaffirm our cooperation with them, with the federal investigation. Make of it what you wish."

"Senator Brooks, Paige's father?" Perez asked.

"I imagine she whispered in her father's ear and that started the ball rolling."

"The information that she gave us," Perez said. "You think that it was provided by her father?"

"It was of a high quality that I don't believe a married woman with no occupation living in a small town in Maryland could have gotten hold of," Richards replied. "Her father certainly has the means and the resources to dig up that kind of information. I expect her father read the research first before passing it on to his daughter."

"And she knew he would," Perez added.

Richards nodded.

A thick, sealed envelope was miraculously left at the counter addressed to Detective Marvin Richards a few days ago. Inside were detailed reports, statements, and research supporting the fact that Mark Miller's investment company was money-laundering as well as running a complex Ponzi scheme.

"I imagine the Senator couldn't resist passing it on to the Feds, take some of the credit for himself as well. It would stand him in good stead with the rest of the Washington royalty, people of influence and power like himself," Richards continued.

"Not to mention the voters too." Perez smiled. Senator Brooks had already been on CNN this morning talking to Anderson Cooper, preaching that the current administration needed to get tougher on white-collar crime.

"And Zoe and Jason Collins?" Perez asked.

Richards rubbed his jaw. "I don't believe they're involved."

The young couple was more of an anomaly who mainly kept to themselves. And when Richards had interviewed them on his own, they said they really didn't know much about what had happened. And yet, as Richards looked at them during the interview, something seemed strange, out of place with the young married couple. Their mannerisms, how they looked together, sitting side-by-side, certain similarities.

"I've noticed they have listed their house for sale," Perez said. "Getting out of Dodge, so to speak."

"The feds aren't allowing anyone to leave Mill Point Road until they, too, have spoken to everyone," Richards said. "Except Rebecca Cartwright."

"I don't blame her moving into a motel after what was found in her basement and being attacked," Perez said. Becca's home was a crime scene, would be for some time, Perez imagined.

Richards had already shown Perez the grisly crime scene photos taken from her basement. Forensics had been there for two days now, working around the clock.

It was like an investigation within an investigation. The FBI was only interested in the Miller's case and if the other residents were involved too. But Richards still had his own investigation to conclude in relation to Garrett Mason, the Eden Killer. Perez and Richards still had to tie up a few loose ends.

Finally Richards got to the second photo with the subtle smirk: Rebecca Cartwright. "Interviewed her again this morning. I'm not sure what to make of her." Richards remembered the glacial coolness of the woman, her face not revealing anything. "I still think she's not telling us the whole truth."

"The woman is probably still traumatized by what had happened. A simple case of self-defense." Perez stared at the photo of Rebecca Cartwright. The subtle smile of indifference stared right back at her. Perez wasn't present at the interview this morning with Rebecca Cartwright. Perez felt it would be inappropriate, and Richards agreed. He wanted to talk to Becca alone. Perez had already given Richards her detailed report of what happened, and they had discussed it at length, numerous times.

Perez glanced up at the remaining two faces on the whiteboard they hadn't covered. One was dead, the other was very much alive. All they had to do was confirm a link between the two.

"Ready?" Richards asked, slipping on his jacket.

Perez stood. "Ready as I'll ever be."

Chapter 54
Adam & Amber

Marvin Richards had a theory as to how the final pieces would fit together. But he wanted to test that theory by not giving away too much information. He wanted someone else to confirm that his theory was correct, and that someone else sat in interrogation room number three.

Hank Vickerman's stay had been extended, courtesy of the state attorney. He was brought up from what was affectionately known as "the Tombs," the holding cells in the basement of the police station and placed in the interrogation room where Marvin Richards and Haley Perez were waiting for him.

Richards opened proceedings. "How long have you known Garrett Mason?"

Perez started taking notes, but was observing Hank very closely.

Hank's eyes narrowed, the question taking him by surprise. Being arrested and placed in a holding cell meant that he had no information about what was happening in the outside world. Especially the recent developments. "He was a neighbor of ours for about five years. We talked, I knew him. Not personally. We weren't friends or anything. He is a respected university professor. He was just different. Why?"

Richards ignored the question, and thumbed through the pages in his file in front of him. "You have a storm shelter, a safe room in your basement. We found an almost identical one in the basement of Mason's new home." The forensics team had found a lot more than just that in Mason's house.

Richards was holding back information about Garrett Mason and what they had found in his house. He wanted to feed enough details to Hank to get him to talk, to tell them what he knew, to confirm the connection. Perhaps Garrett Mason never knew Hank had been taken into custody.

Richards didn't want to be heavy-handed, and try and force Hank to admit his involvement. He wanted Hank to understand the predicament he was in, and help his own case by cooperating with the police. Now was not the time to hide secrets. Richards explained all this to Hank, hoping the man would come to his senses.

Hank gestured with his hands. "The shelter was his idea. I saw it one day in the basement of his house when he used to live in Mill Point Road. He said it was a good idea to have one installed in case of a home invasion or a tornado. I thought about it then decided to get one for Maggie and me."

Richards referred to his notes, "So he had one installed in the basement of Number 8 Mill Point Road, where Rebecca Cartwright now lives?"

Hank nodded. "Maybe he moved it, took it with him to wherever he went. I have no idea. But yes, he had one installed in his house."

"Have you stayed in contact with Garrett Mason since he moved?"

"No. Where is this going?"

Richards pulled out a photo and slid it across the table toward Hank.

"Did you install this in Rebecca Cartwright's basement?"

"Never seen it before," Hank replied. "What is it?"

Forensics had found the small device hidden in Becca's basement. They passed it on to the tech guys who told Richards what it was.

Perez spoke up, this was her area. "It's a long range wireless network adaptor. I don't understand the technical side fully, but I'm told it's used to hack into someone's internet Wi-Fi. It sends out a signal that blocks their internet so they then have to enter their password again into a fake Wi-Fi router login page, telling them they need to do a fake update. Most people don't know what their router login page looks like, so out of frustration to get their internet back online they re-enter all their passwords. And when they do, the hacker has access to everything. Their email, browsing history, everything as though they are sitting at their computer themselves. It's much easier and faster than trying to hack in with a brute force attack and guess their passwords." Perez tapped the photo. "Eighty bucks online and a few lines of code and you're good to go."

"Were you spying on Rebecca?" Richards asked Hank. "Maybe installed this little device so you could see what she was doing on the Internet? What she was searching? Maybe reading her emails too? Did you get into her basement while the house was empty? Maybe during a showing you snuck downstairs and planted this?"

Hank shook his head. "I don't know what you're talking about. I've never seen that before in my life."

Richards paused, and then decided to change tack. "Tell me about your son, Adam."

Hank became agitated, bristling. Not the typical response a father would have when asked about his son. Hank appeared almost antagonistic.

Then after a few moments of fidgety contemplation, Hank began to talk. "He is different, not normal."

"How do you mean, not normal?" Richards asked.

Hank bristled some more, like he was getting irritated. He said nothing for a moment, twisting his fingers. Finally he spoke, resigned to the fact that he needed to be upfront and honest. "It was disgusting, filthy. It all began after he finished high school. He told Maggie and me what he wanted to become."

Perez stopped writing and looked up. She then wrote the word "become" in her notebook, underlined it several times, and added three question marks.

Hank went on to explain that Adam came out of his bedroom one day dressed as a woman, makeup on and everything, including pumps. He told his shocked parents he'd known for a while that he wanted to be a woman. Adam explained that's how he felt deep inside, always had. It was a strong and powerful emotion he couldn't ignore any longer. It just felt right to him; he was more comfortable as a woman.

"He told us he wanted to undergo transformation surgery, whatever that is," Hank said bitterly, thinking back to that day when everything changed, that day when his own son, their only child, told them he wanted to be a woman and not a man.

"And how did that make you feel?" Richards asked.

"How do you think it made me feel!" Hank replied angrily. "To be told my only son is some kind of freak, some kind of weirdo."

Perez's leg started jittering up and down under the table. Without looking at her, Richards reached across under the table and placed his hand gently on her knee.

The jittering stopped.

Hank continued. "He said from now on he wanted to be called Amber, not Adam. Can you believe that? My son, a transvestite or whatever the hell he is."

Perez tried to keep her emotions in check. So Adam was Amber and Amber was Adam. Two names, two personas, one trapped inside the other trying to break free and craving acceptance.

"I was ashamed of him," Hank said. "Embarrassed. I can't have a son who is like that."

"Is that why there are no pictures of you and your son in your house?" Richards asked.

Hank looked at Richards defiantly. "He brought shame on us, Maggie and me."

Perez felt anger not sorrow for Hank Vickerman. His son was just being honest with how he felt, how he identified himself, as a woman not as a man. And for his sins, Adam or Amber Vickerman was condemned. One day Perez knew she would get married, have children. And when she did she would love them no matter what.

"At first Maggie was shocked, but then she accepted it," Hank continued. "But I could never accept it. I had a son not a daughter." The bitterness and contempt was clear in Hank's voice as he spoke. His face became contorted, his eyes searching, a man struggling but failing to comprehend.

"Then what happened?" Richards asked.

"Maggie and I couldn't see eye-to-eye on the matter. Adam became reclusive, spent more time in his bedroom and Maggie and I drifted apart."

Maggie found solace in the arms of younger men, while

Hank's anger continued to fester as he recorded his wife's indiscretions.

Hank just stared at his hands. "I guess a mother's love is unconditional. But I couldn't accept it. Not under my roof. I confronted Adam one day, told him to leave."

So while Maggie wanted her son to stay, had accepted who her son was, Hank disowned him, made him an outcast.

"It was a good thing he decided to go overseas, to leave," Hank said, reflecting back on what had transpired. "To tell you the truth, I couldn't stand the sight of him once he told us," Hank admitted. "It was best for everyone that Adam was gone. I'm hoping he will change his mind while he's away, rethink his position, return as a son and not as a daughter I don't want."

The next question Richards and Perez knew the answer to. But Richards needed to know if Hank was telling the truth.

"Where is your son now?" Richards asked.

Hank gave a puzzled look. "He's overseas. You know that. You came and spoke to my wife. I just told you that as well."

As planned, Perez looked up from her notes. "You're very conversant with Facebook, aren't you, Mr. Vickerman?"

He gave Perez a dismissive wave. "Maggie looks after all that. She's been following Adam on Facebook, all the places he goes. I just use Facebook to keep in touch with some of my old Navy friends. We've got a closed Facebook group where we share stuff."

Perez continued with her line of questioning. "It would be easy for you to take over someone else's Facebook account, like your son's, assume his identity, post stock images of tourist attractions, make it look like he is overseas."

Hank glared at Perez. "I don't know what you're talking about. Like I said, Maggie does all that. She's obsessed with

Facebook and seeing what Adam is up to."

Richards had asked Perez to check U.S. Customs. There was no record of Adam Vickerman leaving the country in the past twelve months.

That's because he hadn't.

Adam Vickerman had never left Mill Point Road.

Chapter 55
The Wronged and the Dead

Richards resumed the questioning. "Did you tell Garrett Mason about your son? Did you confide in him, ask his advice? After all he was living in the same street as you. You were friends."

"I never said we were friends," Hank cut in.

Richards persisted. "But you had spoken to him many times. He was a respected university professor as you say." Richards deliberately chose the word "was" rather than "is" when describing Garrett Mason. It was a subtle but important distinction that Hank did not pick up on.

Richards paused, waiting for Hank to answer. Richards was way in front of Hank, further along the path he wanted the man to follow. In the end Hank would eventually get there, be led there, Richards was certain.

"What about the trail down the ridge, through the woods, the one that leads from the backyard of Rebecca Cartwright's property down to the road?" Richards asked, "You knew about it, didn't you?"

Hank fidgeted for a moment.

This time it was Perez's turn. "Was it you in the woods that night? Did you hit Rebecca Cartwright on the back of the head, knock her out, then pretend to have discovered her and carried her back into your house?"

Hank shook his head vigorously, "That wasn't me. I found her as she was, unconscious. I've nothing to do with attacking her."

"Then who did, Hank?" Richards asked. "Who else knew about the trail through the woods?"

Hank said nothing, just clenched his fists and twisted his neck like he was trying to shake out a pinched nerve, jutting out his jaw at the same time.

Richards leaned forward this time, more direct, less cordial. "Did you tell Garrett Mason that your son was using the trail through the woods? That's how Adam was coming and going undetected, wasn't it, Hank? There are CCTV cameras at the gatehouse entrance that would have recorded someone. But there's another way out of the community, a way where no one can see you come and go."

Hank glared at Richards, hatred burning in his eyes.

"I think Adam used the trail in the woods, maybe he was meeting someone perhaps, as Amber not as Adam. Your son dressed as a woman."

The pinched nerve in Hank's neck tightened a little more. He could feel the blood pulsating at his temples, his face turning darker.

Richards kept on going. "You followed your son into the woods one night, didn't you? And when you got to the bottom of the hill you hung back in the darkness, in the trees. Perhaps there was a car there waiting on the shoulder of the road on the other side of the fence. Perhaps that's how they met in secret, Amber and her lover."

"Adam!" Hank screamed, "My son's name is Adam!"

It was a missing piece of the puzzle that Richards needed. Both he and Perez didn't know that Adam Vickerman wanted to be a transgender woman until moments ago when Hank had told them. It was irrelevant. But Richards had a theory that Adam was using the trail through the woods to leave and return to the gated community undetected. It made sense after what Hank had just said and what Perez had discovered.

Hank regained his composure, but was still steaming with anger. "I saw them kiss," he finally said. "In a car, my son and another man."

Adam would transform into Amber in his bedroom late at night after his parents had gone to bed. Then she would slip out of the house under the cover of darkness, cut across the backyard, and enter the woods. Once there, she found the trail and followed it down to the road. But another person was watching too. A person who had taken a keen interest in Adam Vickerman. That person was Garrett Mason.

Perez had returned to the locked double gate at the bottom of the hill. Farther along, where the fence was partially concealed by tall bushes, she had discovered a flap had been cleverly cut into the wire. It was big enough for someone to pass through then carefully push back into place so that the cut wire lined up perfectly again.

Police officers had also found Garrett Mason's car in the parking lot of a picnic spot just a short distance from the gate at the bottom of the hill. On his body they had found a copy of the key to the padlock on the double gate. Mason could come and go as he pleased into the gated community without anyone seeing him.

Perez had guessed that the concealed flap in the fence had been made by Adam. Only now did they learn the real reason why: so that Amber could meet her lover and then return before dawn without anyone knowing.

No one spoke for a few minutes.

Richards finally broke the silence. "Did you tell Garrett Mason about your son? About how your son was using the trail at the back of his house?"

Hank said nothing.

"You told Garrett Mason how disgusted you were that your son was dressing up as a woman and sneaking out of the house at night to meet his lover at the bottom of the hill in the dark, didn't you?"

It was all true. Hank had confided in Garrett Mason about his son. He didn't have anyone else to turn to who may have shared his concerns. He certainly wasn't going to discuss his son's "condition" with his Navy buddies. He was already feeling so ashamed without having to make matters worse.

Richards wondered if Hank knew about Garrett Mason, that he was a killer. Perhaps Mason had also confided in Hank, told him a few things that Hank kept to himself. Perhaps Hank's own secret, his hatred of gay men, his homophobic behavior, he had shared with Mason. Was it too much to conceive that Hank saw Mason as a tool he could use to do his own bidding, to kill his own son, indirectly?

Richards had to know, he had to see his reaction. This was the last missing piece of the puzzle.

It was time.

Richards took a deep breath and played his last card. "Your son is dead, Hank. Garrett Mason killed him."

There was a delay, a slight pause for the words to register and for Hank's mind to process what Richards had just said.

Hank's face morphed from anger to disbelief. He shook his head vehemently. "No. You're wrong. Adam is overseas, in Europe, traveling." He looked at Richards, searching the veteran cop's eyes, then looked at Perez for confirmation that it wasn't true, that they were wrong, that his son was alive and well.

Then, when he saw the truth in their eyes, his own features slowly started to melt and sag and everything inside him began to collapse. Hank buried his face in his hands and wept.

Richards and Perez exchanged looks.

Hank hadn't killed Adam. Yet maybe, accidentally or indirectly, without even knowing, he may have played a part in the murder of his own son.

"Hank, your son never went overseas," Richards said. "We believe he was abducted by Garrett Mason, maybe somewhere in the woods at the back of his house just before he moved out. Mason waited for Adam one night in the woods either when he was leaving the community or when he returned. Garrett Mason was the Eden Killer. On his computer we found that he had hacked into Adam's Facebook account, assumed your son's identity and was publishing fake posts to make it look like your son was overseas on vacation whereas in fact your son never went anywhere."

Hank looked up, his face a crumpled mess of anguish and tears. "My son, where is he?"

Richards looked at Perez. They had discussed about whether or not to tell Hank the exact details. Maybe it was too early into the investigation. But Hank was his father, and he had a right to know.

Richards and Perez wondered how Maggie Vickerman would take the fateful news. It was better to give Hank the full details. It was a decision made not out of spite by Richards, he wanted the man to realize what he had lost, and that time was precious with your loved ones, irrespective of their inclination.

"We found your son's body embedded in the wall of Rebecca Cartwright's basement. It seems that when Mason abducted your son, it was just a few weeks before he moved out of the house. We believe he held him for a few days in the storm shelter he had in his basement and then strangled him to death. The storm shelter was then dismantled and reassembled again in his new house. We found traces of your son's DNA at Garrett Mason's new place." Richards didn't elaborate where they had found Adam's DNA.

"My son was in the wall? In his basement? All this time?" Hank questioned in disbelief.

After they had cut open the drywall in the basement, they discovered the decomposing body of Adam Vickerman wrapped in plastic and secured upright between the internal wall studs. However, as the body slowly decomposed, liquid from within the plastic leaked out and started to seep through the drywall. Richards relayed all this information in excruciating detail to Hank Vickerman.

Neither Richards nor Perez could understand the reason for this when Adam Vickerman's body was extracted from the wall. Other than the fact that perhaps it was a cruel and twisted parting gift to the Vickermans or a bizarre housewarming gift for the new owner of the home, Rebecca Cartwright. With Garrett Mason now dead, they had speculated that it was the former. In some demented, twisted irony, Garrett Mason decided to leave Adam Vickerman's body close to home, a mere two hundred yards or so away from his parents' house where he had lived.

"How did you know it was Mason who killed him? Could have been that new woman who moved in, Cartwright," Hank said. "Does anyone really know who she is?"

Richards nodded at Perez who got up and left the room for a moment. She returned carrying a plastic sealed evidence bag and placed it in front of Hank. Inside were a pair of women's burgundy suede ankle strap heels.

"We found these at Mason's house. We pulled Adam's DNA from them."

Slowly Hank reached out and touched the plastic bag.

Richards gave Perez a nod and they left the room together, leaving Hank alone to contemplate what he had done. In sharing his frustrations and disappointment about Adam with Garrett Mason, Hank had inadvertently signed his own son's death warrant.

They stood in the corridor outside.

"I had no idea," Perez said, "about Adam Vickerman." Both Perez and Richards were puzzled at first as to why Adam Vickerman's DNA had been found on the heels. Now they knew why.

Richards let out a slow breath, feeling now an intense sadness. He felt sick in that room, needed fresh air. "No one did, except Hank and Maggie and Garrett Mason."

"It still doesn't explain what happened to Rebecca Cartwright in the woods."

Richards gave a thin smile. "I don't believe Hank when he said he hadn't been in contact with Garrett Mason. I think Rebecca Cartwright found something out about Adam Vickerman and maybe mentioned it to Hank or Maggie. Maybe she found something in the house, or in the woods, something

Mason had left behind. Hank found out then told Mason."

Richards had taken some liberties, had made some assumptions during the interrogation after the revelation that Adam Vickerman wanted to be a transgender woman.

"We were wrong," Perez said. "Adam Teal was Mason's fifth victim, not his fourth."

"No one knew," Richards said. "Somewhere between the third victim, Adam Drake, and who we believed was the fourth victim, Adam Teal, Garrett Mason abducted and murdered Adam Vickerman. We have no idea how long he was held for in that steel box, or how long his body was entombed in that basement wall. Forensics and the coroner will let us know in a few days."

Perez handed Richards a business card.

"What's this?" he asked.

"The desk sergeant gave that to me before, when I went to get the shoes out of the evidence room. There's some guy out front who wants to talk to us about Rebecca Cartwright. He says he's an insurance fraud investigator out of Connecticut. Been tailing her for a few months. I briefly spoke to him while I was out of the room. He said there is something suspicious about her husband's death and wants to talk to us."

Richards pocketed the card. It wasn't a priority right now. He would speak to him when he was done with Hank. "Tell him to sit tight, get some coffee and com e back in an hour."

Perez nodded. "So what happens now?"

"Hank Vickerman's charge sheet just suddenly got longer," Richards smiled. "As well as the attempted murder of his wife, I want to charge him with being an accessory to the murder of his son."

Perez gave a faint smile. Even though the direct evidence was lacking at the moment, Perez, like Richards, had a distinct feeling that Hank Vickerman was a long way off from telling them everything. The man admitted to being so ashamed, so disgusted about his son's gender decision, that he disowned the poor young man. Maybe Hank confided in Mason, knowing who he was, just to get him to do what he couldn't: kill his own son, Adam. It was a long shot, but it was still early in the investigation.

Richards looked at Perez. She somehow seemed different. The events of the last week had changed her, for the better. And as he looked at her, he saw past her patrol uniform, past her somewhat detached, unemotional and often misunderstood demeanor. She was going to make a fine detective. Perhaps even better than him, someday.

"We work for the wronged and the dead, Perez," Richards reminded her. "And Amber Vickerman is relying on us to bring justice to those who were responsible for her death—all of them."

Chapter 56
The Chosen Path

The flowers were almost dead, wilting under the bright morning sun, the petals papery thin and brittle. The ground was heavy and damp; the air filled with the smell of freshly cut lawn and approaching summer.

The grounds people had kept the grass neatly trimmed, the area around the burial plaque tidy.

Bending down she swept away with her hand a few leaves and fallen debris from the brass plaque. She hated coming to places like this, but on this occasion she had wanted to. Needed to. She had already visited Adam Teal, stared down at him under a layer of bladed green and tilled earth and imagined about the young man, how he had suffered, what had been done to him at the hands of others and how those left behind were coping.

Coping.

That's all it was. Never managing or overcoming or recovering. There was no recovering from something like this for the loved ones, just a gaping hole of emptiness where the departed had once breathed and smiled and laughed.

Only coping, hour by hour, one day at a time.

She took a moment to contemplate, with just the sound of the birds and the breeze in the trees around her.

The initial mayhem and commotion had settled down to a steady but manageable flow of questions, press conferences, handshakes, and thankful nods from her colleagues and peers. She didn't want the attention. Never had. She just wanted to do something that made a difference, to those left behind, those who she worked for as Richards had put it.

Richards had given her only a week to decide what she wanted to do. The permanent job was hers, an apprenticeship where she could forge and shape her future off the sadness and suffering of others, but with the promise of a career as a detective.

It would be never ending. Because we were never ending in our evilness.

The story hadn't run its course. The newspapers, local and national still featured pictures of Garrett Mason. He was the story, not his victims. They barely rated a mention again. It was human nature, a macabre obsession with the unpleasant, with how someone who appeared so normal could do such a thing.

And during these subsequent weeks she had time to think. She didn't know if she could do this new job, a job where most times she would meet people for the first time and they would already be dead or dying or broken in some way. Not the best way to start a relationship, no matter how detached you tried to be.

She touched the brass plaque, ran her fingers over the raised lettering, the metal cold and inert, like everything else. She wished she had known him, known them all even for just a fleeting moment while they were alive.

Maggie was doing well; she'd been out of hospital for more

than a week now. Recovering but not fully. Her house was now empty, just her. Her husband, Hank, she would never see again. She had told Perez this, not even as a visitor at the prison where he was being held.

The branches and leaves overhead swayed in a sudden breeze, and a wave of fallen leaves swirled around her as she knelt. Something glinted, caught her eye, dragging her attention away from the brass plaque. Something was draped over one of the wilting bunches of flowers that had been placed on the ground, farther back, almost hidden.

Reaching out she took the ribbon of gold in her fingertips, careful not to dislodge it from where someone had deliberately placed it. She looked at the nametag on the bracelet: Adam, then turned it over: Amber, with a symbol engraved next to the name.

Another gust of wind came up, ruffled her hair, the sun ducked behind a passing cloud.

She glanced up and around her, wondering who had placed it there, but saw no one, just neatly lined rows of memories, flowers, and a scatter of tiny stars and stripes.

She left the bracelet where it hung, stood up and regarded the brass plaque one more time.

And while she couldn't have saved them, she had played a small part in saving those who would have fallen victim in the future. And knowing that was enough.

With her mind made up, she turned and chose the path of helping the dead by catching those still living, and saving the others who had no idea that the devil was watching them.

THE END.

If You Enjoyed This Book

Thank you for investing your time and money in me. I hope you enjoyed my book and it allowed you to escape from your world for a few minutes, for a few hours or even for a few days.

I would really appreciate it if you could post an honest review on any of the publishing platforms that you use. It would mean a lot to me personally, as I read every review that I get and you would be helping me become a better author. By posting a review, it will also allow other readers to discover me, and the worlds that I build. Hopefully they too can escape from their reality for just a few moments each day.

For news about me, new books and exclusive material then please:

- Follow me on Facebook
- Follow me on Instagram
- Subscribe to my Youtube Channel
- Follow me on Goodreads
- Visit my Website: www.jkellem.com

Also Available By JK Ellem

Stand Alone Novels
A Winter's Kill
Mill Point Road
All Other Sins

No Justice Series
Book 1 No Justice
Book 2 Cold Justice
Book 3 American Justice
Book 4 Hidden Justice
Book 5 Raw Justice

Deadly Touch Series
Fast Read Deadly Touch

Octagon Trilogy (DystopianThriller Series)
Prequel Soldiers Field
Book 1 Octagon
Book 2 Infernum
Book 3 Sky of Thorns

About The Author

JK Ellem was born in London and spent his formative years preferring to read books and comics rather than doing his homework.

He is the innovative author of cutting-edge popular adult thriller fiction. He likes writing thrillers that are unpredictable, have multiple layers and sub-plots that tend to lead his readers down the wrong path with twists and turns that they cannot see coming. He writes in the genres of crime, mystery, suspense and psychological thrillers.

JK is obsessed with improving his craft and loves honest feedback from his fans. His idea of success is to be stopped in the street by a supermodel in a remote European village where no one speaks English and asked to autograph one of his books and to take a quick selfie.

He has a fantastic dry sense of humor that tends to get him into trouble a lot with his wife and three children.

He splits his time between the US, the UK and Australia.